The Ark of Osiris

B. L. Freeman

From an idea by Tyler Freeman

*To my nephew,
Mark Freeman,
who reminded me that at one time
I had been a storyteller.*

This book is a work of fiction. Names, characters, places and incidents are a product of the author's imagination. Any resemblance to actual events, locales, or persons, living or dead, is coincidental.

Copyright © 2015 by B. L. Freeman

All rights reserved. No part of this book may be reproduced in any form or by any electronic or mechanical means including information storage and retrieval systems without permission in writing from the author, except by a reviewer who may quote brief passage in a review.

Photo of Amenhotep IV/Akhenaten by Paul Mannix, 2001, is licensed under CC BY 4.0 license.

CHAPTER 1

He had to move quickly.

He had wiped all the data from his laptop thirty minutes earlier but as a further precaution removed the hard drive.

Pulling his briefcase from under the desk he stuffed it inside along with a small box and a small crowbar. Stepping to the open window of the kitchen, he glanced down at the street through the rusting metal of the fire escape. He had never tried to stand on the little iron balcony before and wasn't sure it would hold his weight. But it was the only option he could exercise at the moment. Without further hesitation, he climbed out of the window and stood on the metal grating. It groaned and moved under him as he pushed the ladder down and, turning, climbed onto the first rung.

At that moment he heard pounding on his apartment door and a muffled, threatening voice demanding that it be opened. Had he removed everything, every bit of evidence? He didn't know if anything could be gleaned from his papers but he knew they would get no information from his computer. The rest he carried, literally, in his mind. He had to make it to the museum and find a way to transfer his research to the one man he could trust, the one man who could solve the riddle: a man who was halfway around the world. But first he had to shake his pursuers, whatever it took, so the thing he was carrying would not fall into their hands.

The pounding became louder, and more insistent, as he reached the last rung of the ladder and jumped to the ground. He heard the door being kicked in and footsteps running into the apartment. He didn't have to see them to know they had fanned out, quickly casing every room of the small space. He glanced up as a man's face appeared in the window he had just exited. He didn't hesitate but dashed down the street and around the corner of the closest building, the man's curse floating after him on the air.

The street was mostly deserted. The few pedestrians on the sidewalks paid no attention to him. He ran two blocks, darted down a side street, and followed that until he felt he had to stop or his lungs would burst. A deserted doorway allowed him to pause and catch his breath. His heart was pounding in his ears as he peeked around the doorframe. He was too old for this.

He sat the briefcase down and flipped open the lid. He knew he had stuffed the box inside just moments before but, obsessively, wanted to hold it and make sure it was actually with him and not in the hands of the enemy. He opened the lid of the little box and picked up the piece of metal inside. It seemed so inconsequential sitting in the palm of his hand. But it held the key to everything – one piece of something that, he believed, could change the world.

He slipped it back into its place and snapped the box lid shut, stuffed the box back into the briefcase and closed that as well. He glanced nervously down the street once more. Everything seemed normal. He took a deep breath, got up, and moved on.

While the path he was following seemed random it actually had a purpose and a destination. He knew the subway was out of the question, as the men who were following him would be watching it, likewise any bus or taxi. There was only one way to get to the museum and that was underground.

He had plotted this itinerary for months, knew all the entry and exit points, and the exact tunnel under the city that would take him where he needed to go.

Five more minutes brought him to the place he was seeking. He stopped over a manhole embedded in the street and removed the small crowbar from the briefcase. Kneeling down, he inserted it into the lip of the metal cover and pried it up until he could get a grip and lift it off. He climbed down into the darkness and tried to pull the cover back over the hole. Its weight made it almost impossible to pull into place and in the end, he could only get it partially back into position. He prayed as he climbed down into the sewer that it would be enough and that they would not notice it and follow him.

The little flashlight he had brought made a dim light but it was enough to show him where he was going. He could not afford to run here. The ground was slick with mud and moisture. If he fell or hurt himself, and could not go on, all would be lost. So he forced himself to walk at a rapid but steady pace. Thirty minutes later he came to another ladder and, looking up in the darkness, saw the small shafts of light seeping through another manhole cover.

His foot had barely touched the bottom rung when he heard them. The running footsteps were soft and distant but headed his way. They had discovered the road he had taken and would shortly catch up to him.

He rapidly ascended the ladder and when he reached the top, pushed upward on the cover. It would not budge. He pushed harder. Still no movement. God! Would it end here?

The footsteps were mixed now with voices. He glanced down and saw the first man appear in the tunnel below. Pushing with all his might the rim of the manhole cover made a scrapping sound as a bright beam of light pierced the darkness. He blinked and pushed harder.

A man below shouted for him to stop but he paid no heed and with a strength that surprised him heaved the cover out of its resting place and to the side. He could barely make it through the sliver of space but quickly climbed up and out as a bullet whizzed through the air next to his body.

There was a loud blaring of horns as cars swerved to miss him. He darted across two lanes of traffic and up the steps of the museum. His enemies had been watching the museum since dawn but had not anticipated he would appear from the sewers under the streets. In an instant, they had recovered from their surprise and began as one to converge on the entrance. He made it to the top of the marble steps and between the columns that soared up to the portico. His breath labored, he pushed through the doors and began to make his way toward the staircase that would take him up to the exhibit area on the second floor.

"Whoa there," called one of the guards, stopping him in his tracks. Every instinct told him to keep going but there were people in the museum, old and young alike. His enemies were dangerous and would stop at nothing. He couldn't afford to get anyone hurt. He turned to face the man in the uniform.

"Where are you going in such . . . oh, sorry Professor," he said, "I didn't recognize you from behind like that." He was just a guard, nothing more.

"It's alright, Robert," Professor Stevens said. "I'm just in a little bit of a hurry today."

"No problem, sir. Carry on." The Professor quickly ran up the steps to the second floor. He knew by now he was probably not going to make it and instinctively tried to avoid the Egyptian galleries. But as he ran past them two men suddenly stepped into the hall and pushed him into the gallery.

This gallery was deserted. They physically forced him to the back of the room and turned him to face them. Momentarily another man walked inside, leaving another at the door.

The man who had peered at him from his kitchen window forty-five minutes before calmly walked up to him and stared into his eyes. He was middle-eastern with heavy features, pocked marked skin, and black eyes.

"Professor," he said. "I believe you have something that belongs to us."

Professor Stevens laughed, a surprising sound, considering the situation he was in. "It does not belong to you. You're insane to even think it could."

"Your opinion, which means nothing. Please . . ." and he extended his hand.

The Professor clutched the briefcase against his chest.

The man smiled and looked back toward the door where another man was watching for anyone who might be walking by. He cocked his head to one side and another man of the group approached the Professor. He grabbed the briefcase out of the Professor's hands and shoved him hard against the wall.

The man in charge took the briefcase and snapped open the lid. He removed the hard drive and handed it to one of his men.

Lastly, he picked up the small box and popped open the lid. "Have you downloaded the data, Professor?" he asked glancing up at his captive.

Professor Stevens huddled against the wall.

"Well have you?" the man said and he smiled. "I can see you have."

He reached inside the box and picked up the small piece of metal, one-third of a circle, its surface covered with strange, circuit-like markings, a round hole cut off center. One side of the metal was jagged with serrations. He held it up to the light.

One of his men stepped close, his eyes wide with anticipation. "No!" the man said sharply, "Don't look into the eye!"

His boss sneered. "It has already given up its secrets," he said as he looked through the hole. Nothing happened and he placed it back inside the box. "Shall we go?" he said to the Professor.

"I'm going nowhere with you," he said.

"Yes, you are my friend or this will be the last visit to a museum some of the visitors will ever have."

Professor Stevens slumped down against the wall as his looked away with a pained expression on his face. Two of the men came to his side and, lifting him up, escorted him down the back stairs and out of the museum into the bright New York morning.

CHAPTER 2

James Iron Adams stepped to the door of the plane and blinked into the bright sunlight of Egypt. He paused momentarily, allowing his eyes to grow accustomed to the glare as a wave of hot air blew into his face. He could feel the people behind him in the aisle also pause, but with impatience, at his seeming inability to move and let them get off the plane.

He clutched the handrail as he began to descend the steps to the tarmac. When he had reached the ground he stepped to one side and stopped again, looking down the airport runway where heat shimmered in the air. "What am I doing here?" he whispered under his breath. But he knew exactly what he was doing there.

His parents had divorced two years earlier and he had to spend at least two weeks of every summer with his father. Dr. Eric Adams was an archeologist and an expert in ancient Egyptian hieroglyphics. At present, he was involved in a very important dig on the Nile River south of Karnak. The area had always been viewed as unpromising as far as archeological research went. Unpromising until the government had given permission for the construction of a new solar array that would increase electric output to Cairo. That had been two months ago.

Almost on the first day of construction one of the bulldozers, which had begun to level the sand of the new site had, without warning, broken through the ceiling of a hidden, subterranean chamber. It had crashed sideways into the gaping hole taking the driver with it. He had been pulled to safety without harm but it was immediately obvious that this was not just a sinkhole. A stone cornice, exposed during the collapse of the ceiling, showed elaborate carvings and hieroglyphics.

All work immediately stopped and the authorities were called from Cairo. Upon their arrival, the area was blocked off and guards were posted 24 hours a day while the Ministry of Antiquities began the first tentative exploration of the area. Once the bulldozer had been carefully hoisted out and removed, a team of archeologists had descended into what turned out to be a long passageway with other passages and rooms branching off of it. The main corridor led due west away from the Nile and under the desert itself.

The discovery was different than any of the other ancient sites that had been unearthed. While a typical tomb's walls were covered almost completely in paintings and carvings, here it was the exact opposite. The ornate cornice that had been uncovered when the workman had broken through the roof proved to be the only decoration in the majority of the complex. But this was quickly forgotten when the team of scientists had come to the very end of the main hallway and stepped into a chamber that made everyone stop and stare in disbelief and amazement.

The ceiling was rather low but that did not take away the impact. The room seemed to be perfectly square. Three of the walls were unadorned but the fourth wall was faced with gleaming white limestone on which was carved some of the most beautiful bas-reliefs anyone had ever seen. And there were hieroglyphics, divided into sections. Mixed in with those symbols were other pictographs no one could decipher – strange geometric shapes.

The team, after several weeks and much discussion, made the decision to ask for assistance in decoding the symbols. They had contacted the Egyptian Department at the Metropolitan Museum of Art in New York, which had, in turn, contacted James' father, at the Smithsonian Institute in Washington, DC where he worked.

James had not seen his father since that day and had spoken to him only twice on the phone. The conversations had been short: Dr. Adams had seemed occupied with his work, which was fine with James. He still blamed his father for the breakup of his parents' marriage. How could anyone be expected to stay in a marriage, as his mother had done, when her husband was constantly away on some dig in every inaccessible, dangerous place on Earth?

James wiped the sweat off his face with his sleeve and, slinging his backpack over his shoulder, headed for the terminal. The doors opened with a swish and he walked inside.

The cool air enveloped him and he opened his mouth drinking it in with a sigh. He closed his eyes enjoying the sensation and then started searching for his father in the faces of the people milling about the concourse. His father had told him he would be waiting at the gate. But James could not find him anywhere in the crowd made up of people from many different parts of the world: businessmen in casual business attire, Arabs with their long flowing robes and, of course, the tourists with their Nikes and t- shirts and cameras strung proudly across their chests. So typical of his father: always promising to be on time and always late.

He walked to the information kiosk in the middle of the concourse and inquired if a Mr. Adams had been there or if any messages had been left for him. The man's eyebrows went up as he bent over several notes on the small shelf that passed as his desk.

"No, no Mr. Adams. I am so sorry."

"Okay, thanks," replied James as he turned away. He went to find a restroom and a water cooler. Then he made his way back to the waiting area by the gate.

He knew it was useless but he picked his cell phone out of his backpack and surprise, surprise, no bars here. I could go all over the entire continent of Africa and not find any bars, he thought to himself. And even if there had been, his father probably would not answer the call. He was always too busy.

He sat and waited for two hours, playing games on his phone until the battery went dead.

Finally, he was aware that his father had arrived. He didn't really need to look to see if Dr. Adams had arrived. There was always a certain kind of energy that heralded his approach. He simply filled up the room, or in this case, the terminal. Six feet three inches and 220 pounds, he was big and fit with a deep tan and a booming voice. The people in the terminal parted like the Red Sea as he came rushing up to James.

"James! Man, I'm sorry, son. Time got away. I didn't even realize your plane had landed. Get over here," he bellowed, "and give me a hug."

He didn't wait for James to answer but simply pulled him up in one swift movement and crushed him into his chest. He smelled of sweat and dirt (lots of dirt) and as he beat James on the back a rush of questions came out of his mouth.

"How was the flight?"

"Your Mom alright?"

"You hungry?"

"Want a Coke? They got Cokes here you know."

By this point, his father had picked up James' backpack and began shepherding him toward the back of the terminal.

"No. I'm fine."

"You sure?"

"Yeah."

"Well, I'm starving. Let's get out of here and go somewhere where we can talk. I'll bet you'll be hungry by then."

James *was* hungry. He had only had a small lunch on the plane and some peanuts. But he didn't want to hang around the terminal anymore. He just wanted to get away. "That sounds good," he admitted.

They stepped out of the terminal and walked to a Jeep that was sitting in the lot. "Egyptian Ministry of Antiquities" was written on the side of the door. Dr. Adams stowed the backpack into the back of the Jeep and they both climbed in. The Jeep cranked up and they sped out of the parking space and onto the main road leading into Cairo.

By this time the sun was setting and the lights of the city were beginning to glow in the distance. The sky to the west was bathed in a purple and orange glow and James could see the man-made mountains that were the Great Pyramids of Giza.

"So seriously, James, how are you doing?" asked his father, breaking the uncomfortable silence. "The flight over was okay, right?"

"Yeah, it was fine," he replied as he stared ahead, refusing to look at his father.

"And everything's okay at home with your mom?"

"It's fine, okay. What do you care how things are at home?"

"I do care!" His voice suddenly had an edge. James knew what that inflection meant. For all his appearing to be relaxed and happy to see him, his father was tense and on edge. After a moment, he continued. "I know you're still upset about the divorce and everything. But your mom and I felt it was the best thing."

"Yeah *you* felt it was the best thing. You never bothered to ask me what I thought did you?"

Dr. Adams looked away for a moment at the passing traffic. The air was beginning to cool as night came on and they drove several miles in silence. They entered the city and came to a two-story building with a restaurant on the ground floor. It did not look like a place James wanted to eat. "God," he said under his breath. His father pretended not to hear, turned off the motor and they got out. Dr. Adams lifted the backpack up from the rear of the jeep. "Better take this along," he said and they made their way inside.

Ornate multi-faceted lamps hung from the ceiling, casting sparkling diamonds of colored light onto the yellow walls. The floor was covered in thickly woven oriental carpets where low tables had been placed for the customers. But there were no chairs, only richly embroidered cushions on which to sit. James couldn't believe the transformation from the outside. The aroma of oil and spices and roasting meat filled the air and his mouth began to water.

A young woman with dark hair and almond-shaped eyes lead them to a table by the far wall and they sat down, cross-legged. In Arabic, she inquired what they would like to drink and Dr. Adams asked for a beer for himself and lemonade for James. She left them but returned quickly with their glasses.

"Shall I order for us? How about roasted lamb and vegetables," Dr. Adams asked James.

"That would be good," James replied.

His father gave the order and the girl disappeared into the kitchen.

Dr. Adams looked at his son and said, "I understand how you feel. I know it has not been easy for you. I wish it were different myself but your mom and I came to the point where it just wasn't working anymore. It was unfair to both of us but especially to her and to you. Remember all the fights?"

James did remember. "But you could have worked it out," he said. "You could have stayed at home for a few days of the year. That's all she wanted."

"We tried. We tried a lot. Your mother wanted me there most of the time, not just a few days. And I can understand why she wanted me there. But I couldn't do it. I love my work and my work sends me all over the place, as you well know." He paused. "I don't love it as much as I love you guys but it's really important to me, just like your mother's work is important to her. That's why, in the end, we made the decision to break up and let everybody have some peace."

"You could've worked something out," James said again. "You could have tried harder."

"How? How would you have done it if you had been in our place."

"You could have compromised. Found a way to stay home more."

"How would I do that? You know what the work entails."

"I don't know. Is the work that important to you just to walk away from us?"

"It is when you love it. Let me put it this way. You love to play video games, right. You not only love it, it is one of your passions, right?"

James paused. He knew his father was laying a trap. Dr. Adams was the most logical man he knew and he could make any argument from any position and make it sound so reasonable that no one could argue it and win.

"You love your video games, right?" Dr. Adams repeated.

"Yes."

"What if I came to you and said, "You can never play your games again. That's it. How would you feel?"

"A video game is not a family."

Dr. Adams looked down at the table and then glanced back at his son. "No. You're right. It's not. A family is much more important than that. What does your mother say?"

"Everything you just said. But I know she's unhappy."

Dr. Adams looked away at the other diners. "Does she ever talk about me?"

"Yes."

"What does she say?"

"Why don't you ask her?"

Dr. Adams leaned back and smiled, "I can see you're growing up fast. Maybe someday I will," he said, the smile fading from his face.

At that moment, the food arrived. James could not remember a more delicious meal in his life. The lamb had been marinated and then cooked in spices. It came to the table in a large bowl with gravy and vegetables. He ate and ate and drank glass after glass of lemonade. Finally, he was full and sat back.

His father had been watching him, smiling. "Feel better?"

James tried not to but couldn't help smiling back. He felt a lot better. "Just a little. That was really good. Thanks."

"You're welcome. I come here about twice a week. Would you like some baklava to top it off?"

"Well, okay. Just a bite."

The waitress soon brought the sticky dessert to their table along with two cups of strong Egyptian coffee. James picked up the honey laden sweet and bit into its warm interior. Like the lamb, it was perfect and delicious. They sat silently while James finished it off and Dr. Adams finished his coffee.

"Well, listen, I want us to have some fun this week. The excavation work will go on forever but I've told them I need some time off this week to show you around. I'll have to go to the site tomorrow morning to check on a few things but after that, we can go off and explore anything you like."

"Okay." For all his anger at this father, the thought of spending time alone with him, just the two of them, made James very happy.

"I know you're not interested in archeology that much but you won't believe this discovery. It's like nothing I've ever seen. And the artwork is beyond amazing."

"Is it bigger than King Tut?" James asked. His father surprised him when he answered.

"It could be."

James was suddenly paying attention. "You mean it's full of gold masks and jewels?"

"No. That's the funny thing. There is nothing in the corridors or most of the rooms at all. I don't think there ever was. It's in the last chamber. It's like nothing I've ever seen."

"But if there is no treasure how could that be more important than King Tut?"

"It's the symbols. Some of them are completely new and unique. And they go on and on. It looks . . . well like nothing I've ever seen."

"Is it a tomb?"

"No. I know that for sure."

"Then what is it?"

"Well, that's the funny thing, and I've never told this to anyone besides you. I think it's some kind of instruction manual or some kind of diary. I just don't know what, it's trying to tell us."

"The ancient Egyptians carved an instruction manual under the desert?"

"Maybe. I just don't know."

CHAPTER 3

James turned around in his seat watching the ancient temples moving past him in the clear Egyptian light. They seemed to go on forever, the golden color of their stones silhouetted against a bright blue sky. He had never seen anything like them. And they were huge. One of the columns holding up the roof would make a man look like a little boy.

"Pretty amazing, huh?" said his father sitting beside him in the Jeep.

"They're incredible!" said James. "They're so *big*!"

"That's one of the things I love about them," his father replied. "They were built that way to make people feel overpowered and small in the presence of the gods. Imagine living back then and watching the people go into worship. The temples were painted with bright colors and all of the royal court would have been dressed in pure white. The soldiers would have been carrying flags, also in bright colors, and when you entered the temple complex you would have walked between two rows of enormous sphinxes. Once you finally got into the temple itself, under the roof and between the columns, you would have felt like you were walking through a forest where the trees had turned to stone. And all in shadows, with the smoke from incense floating through the air."

"Can we go see them?"

"You bet."

They were heading up the river to the excavation. James had slept in late, his body still trying to recover from jet lag. After they had gotten back to the hotel the night before, he had not even taken the time for a shower but had slipped out of his clothes and crawled into bed, falling asleep as soon as his head hit the pillow.

His father had not disturbed him in the morning, letting him sleep until he was ready to get up. Then after his shower, they had gone down for breakfast after which they had climbed into the Jeep for the trip south. Now they were approaching their destination.

The temples were disappearing behind them but the Nile continued to flow on their left, its waters creating a wide belt of vegetation that cut through the desert like a green ribbon.

"How much further," James asked.

"We're just about there," Dr. Adams said as he turned to his right and headed due west into the desert. They drove a few minutes before they came upon what looked like a construction site. There were many vehicles parked on either side of a kind of scaffolding that rose up from the desert floor. Beyond the scaffolding, there were small outcroppings of rock but beyond this there was only the desert. The Jeep slowed down and Dr. Adams swung it in next to a car with the same Department of Antiquities decal on its door.

They both got out and began to walk toward the site.

"Let me introduce you to everyone and then I'll take you down into the dig."

"Okay," said James.

They walked until they came even with the metal bars of the scaffolding itself. There were guards everywhere but they made no move; they just cut their eyes around to silently look at them as they approached. The scaffolding was a cover for the opening in the desert floor that lead down into the rooms below. Temporary steps had been built to allow people to descend until reaching the bottom. As his father had said, the walls were bare but a beautiful band of carvings ran along the top of the walls disappearing into the tunnel beyond.

Two men were ascending the steps as they arrived and when they saw James' father one of them raised his hand in greeting. When they had reached the top, they stopped.

"Dr. Adams!" said the elder of the two and reached out and took Eric's hand. The man looked around sixty-five years old with a deeply lined face and white hair. He was dressed in a white linen suit but had removed his jacket. His shirt showed stains from sweating in the heat but when he smiled, as he did now, he seemed younger than his years.

"Dr. Muhammad," Eric said, "I'd like you to meet my son. James, this is the Supreme Director of the Egyptian Department of Antiquities and the man considered to be the utmost authority in the world on early Egyptian history and the cult of the pharaohs."

After a title like that, James felt like bowing but he extended his hand instead which the director took in both of his. "It's very nice to meet you, sir," he said.

"So courteous. But I would expect nothing less from your son, Eric. I am so happy to finally meet the son of our renowned Dr. Adams," he continued. "Your father's assistance has been invaluable to our work. In fact, we would be lost without him. I know it is difficult for a man to leave his family for so long but we are very grateful for his help. Please allow me to introduce my assistant," and he indicated the man standing just behind him.

James turned. "This is Dr. Raza Tahan. He has been my personal assistant for many years and like your father is indispensable to our work."

James extended his hand, which Raza took after a slight hesitation. The long, tapered fingers were clammy, the handshake weak and brief. Dressed in khakis with a white cotton shirt he was taller than Dr. Muhammad but unlike the other man who was slightly overweight, look slim and athletic. His eyes were dark, almost black, under hooded brows and across one cheek was the line of a scar that stood out pale against the deep tan of his skin. It gave him a sinister appearance. He did not smile but as James looked at him his lips parted and without seeming to move at all, said, "It's nice to meet you," in a thick accent. James felt like Raza was observing him, like someone looking at an insect in a garden or a laboratory.

Eric acknowledged Raza and then turning to Dr. Muhammad said, " I would like James to see the carvings, if that's alright with you, Dr. Muhammad."

"Of course, of course. He must see these wonders," the doctor replied. "Please James, go down and look. You are the first person to see these amazing artifacts besides your father and the other archeologists who are working here."

"Thank you, Dr. Mohammad," he said and the doctor smiled as James moved away. Raza followed the director but his eyes cut to James for a second before following the director. James thought he saw disdain in the assistant's glance.

His father led James to the steps and as they were going down James said, "Raza – do you know him well?"

"No! Raza is a strange duck," his father replied softly and under his breath. "It amazes me that Dr. Muhammad keeps him around."

"I don't like him."

"Well, join the crowd. There's something about him. I avoid him as much as I can. Let's see. We need to get you a headlamp. It's dark as Hades down here."

They stepped out of the glare of the sun and just inside the tunnel. There was a table sitting to their right surrounded by an array of equipment. On top of the table were numerous helmets with lamps like a miner would wear. Eric picked several up, trying them on James' head until he found one that fit. Then he picked up the one that said *Dr. Adams* scrawled on a piece of tape on its front and slipped it on. He turned to James. "Ready?"

James nodded.

They moved into the darkness. At first, it seemed like a narrow cave maybe ten feet wide and eight feet tall. As James turned his head from side to side the light on his helmet showed him his surroundings: sand under his feet and bare walls on both sides. They came to a doorway on their left side and a hallway on their right, roughly the same size as the hall they were walking in, with yellow tape strung back and forth across its front.

"What's in there?" James asked.

"We've blocked that off until we can catalog the main chamber where the important carvings are. We went into those briefly in the beginning but they're all just small, empty rooms. Nothing to see."

They moved on. It was stifling hot. Ahead of them, James could see a glow and shortly they came into a chamber that was illuminated with powerful lights on tall stands powered by large battery-operated generators. There were also electric fans that kept the air circulating so the men could work. The chamber was roughly square, three of its walls were covered with panels of plain stone like the walls of the tunnel they had walked through. But the fourth wall made James stop and stare, spellbound, at what he saw. He had seen pictures of ancient Egyptian wall carvings in his father's books but these were nothing like anything he had ever seen before.

The main panel in the center of the wall contained two large figures standing toe-to-toe and facing each other. One had the body of a man but its head looked like a cheetah or some other kind of cat. The creature had wings standing out behind it that were enormous. The other figure was a man who seemed to be taking something from the winged creature in front of him. But what he was offering to the man was unique.

It was a disk split into three parts by jagged lines like thunderbolts. There were markings on each section of the disk but again indiscernible as to what they represented. To James' eye, they look like some kind of circuitry. Each section carried a circle carved off center. Numerous curving rays, like daggers, radiated from the disk interspersed with straight lines, each ending in a little hand.

James hardly noticed the four or five workers who were spread out across the expanse of wall, intensely focused on their work. They did not notice when James and his father walked silently into the space until Dr. Adams spoke.

"Amazing, isn't it? We hardly know what to think. Some of these symbols are completely new. We're finding it hard to figure out what they mean."

At the sound of Eric's voice the workers turned to them, and one after briefly glancing at James called to Dr. Adams. "I'll be back in a minute," Eric said and he walked to where the man was standing.

James turned his attention once more to the wall. On either side of the two central figures were many other carvings. These were blocked off into sections, each showing bands of hieroglyphic symbols with corresponding bands of symbols below them that James had never seen before. The symbols were geometric and looked out of place with the other hieroglyphics.

All the human figures on the wall were engaged in various kinds of work. James must have picked up the ability to read some of the ancient symbols from living with his father because he could translate a few of the pictures. But his gaze kept coming back to the central figures and the disc in the winged creature's hand.

When his father returned, James said, "I would swear that's part of a computer."

Eric looked puzzled. "Why do you say that?"

James glanced back toward the central figures. "It just reminds me of something you would see on a computer's circuit board. Don't you think? Not anything like our computers you know. It just reminds me of it."

Dr. Adams glanced back at the wall. At that moment, another worker called to him abruptly. "Dr. Adams? So sorry to interrupt again," he said a little too fast. "But could I ask a question here?"

"Yes . . . yes of course," Eric said, distracted. His father turned to James. "Stay here and I want you to look at the carvings and tell me if you see anything else."

"Ok."

As his father walked away James glanced past him to the other men. They appeared to be working intently but on closer observation were doing nothing at all. They stood motionless, listening, and watching him out of the corner of their eyes. One of them slowly moved closer to him but James instinctively pulled away.

He walked closer to the wall until he was only inches away from the surface of the carvings. They were truly magnificent, finely executed and apparently without damage of any kind that he could see. Then he stepped back so he could see the whole surface again. It was overpowering, like a giant jigsaw puzzle that made no sense. There was so much to take in he found himself overwhelmed and walked to the corner on his left. Part of the upper left corner was damaged with pieces of the limestone surface broken away. But he could read a few words of the hieroglyphic.

"From . . . the . . . stars . . . we . . . come . . ."

"What did you say?" his father asked at his back. Eric had come up quietly behind him as James had stood looking at the wall.

"From the stars we come . . ." James said. "Isn't that right? Up there in the corner? Isn't that right?"

Eric looked up, holding his breath while he read and re-read the passage.   The wall was so complex. He had not even looked at that section, his focus had always been on the figures and the symbols around them.

He took a step back and his eyes quickly ran over the entire wall, and like a key fitted into a lock and turned, the pieces of the puzzle fell roughly into place. How could he have missed it? But his mind refused to accept it. It was too fantastic: too fantastic to be real.

His glance came to rest on the other men silently standing to his side. They made no pretense of working now but stood rigid, staring at Eric's face.

Eric tried in that instant to understand what he saw in their eyes?

Confusion and questions?

Or menace and hatred.

Eric suddenly understood.

They knew.

They knew what he had just found out. They had known all along. It was a sham, a play. He was an actor in a play they were directing. But why? For what purpose?

"*Dad?*" James said. "What's wrong?"

Eric swallowed and tried to speak in a normal voice. "Nothing. I . . . I think your translation is a little off, that's all." He looked back to his son. You know, it's pretty hot in here. Why don't you wait outside? I should only be a few more minutes. I'll come and find you and we can go back to Cairo and see the pyramids."

"But can't I just look a little . . ."

"James! Please!"

James pursed his lips. "Fine! God, it's impossible with you!"

He headed back toward the entrance and out into the darkened tunnel. As he walked past the section where the yellow tape had been hung, he paused and looked around. If he couldn't see the wall anymore he could certainly see what was down this hallway. He knew his father would probably be upset but that was fine too. In fact, that's what he wanted.

He ducked under the tape and walked down the long corridor, looking to his left and right. The walls here, like the main passageway, were plain and unadorned, the layout random. In fact, it looked like a construction site that had been abandoned abruptly. Off of the hallway smaller rooms had been constructed at odd distances. He peered inside some of them but did not enter as they were, as his father had said, completely empty. He continued down the main passage until he came to the end.

The corridor must have been curving slightly. He thought he was walking in a straight line but when he turned and shown his light behind him, expecting to see a faint light in the main corridor, he saw only darkness instead. The heat was making it hard to breathe and he was about to turn around and head back when he saw a small doorway on his right. He stepped inside. Like the others, the room appeared empty. He wondered how many thousands of years had passed since humans had been in this space. As his helmet washed the walls with light, he noticed an imperfection in the wall directly in front of him.

Walking forward, he saw it was a small patch of what appeared to be plaster. It was expertly done and but for the bright light on his helmet, would have been easily overlooked. The bottom right corner had flaked away and reaching up he took his finger and poked it inside. The entire plaster patch broke away and peering inside the rectangular opening, he saw a little shelf carved into the stone of the wall. But that wasn't all. There was what appeared to be a small scroll and something wrapped in dirty linen: something small.

He was suddenly aware of the black void of the door behind him. Someone was approaching the door. He thought he could hear movement or footsteps. How could you hear footsteps in sand, he thought?

"Who's there," he said, the hairs standing up on his neck.

No one answered and he turned back to the wall. His imagination was getting the best of him.

The heat was beginning to overwhelm him but no matter what happened he had to look. He had to know what the objects were. Taking down the scroll first, he carefully unrolled it. It started to crack and crumble but it held together long enough for him to decipher a few of the words it contained.

"Blessed . . . is he . . . who looks . . . into the eye . . . of . . . the . . . He couldn't make out the next several symbols. "Beware . . . the . . . power . . . of"

That was as far as he got. The papyrus crumbled to dust in his hand.

With sweat pouring down his face, he picked up the linen and carefully unwrapped it.

Inside he found a triangular piece of metal like a piece of pie. The straight sides had serrated edges. The circular side was smooth and there was a hole cut in the center to one side. He turned it over and over in the light of his helmet. It carried the same odd-looking circuit shapes on its surface as the carving in the room. He suddenly realized it matched one-third of the symbol in the hands of the strange god in the main panel of the wall.

What was this?

He held it up in front of him. As he studied it, it seemed to shimmer in the light and then . . . the edges began to glow and the circuits carved on its surface began to pulse. To James it seemed to be rebooting, running through a kind of sequence until suddenly the hole cut in the middle began to glow bright red. It flashed a laser-like beam of light into James' face and he felt his body go rigid and he was unable to move. He was awake and aware but could not pull his gaze away from the beam. He stood transfixed, hypnotized by the light.

The light abruptly turned off and the talisman went dark turning back into an old piece of metal.

He staggered back, the light of the helmet dancing around the shadowy corners of the room. There were tracings there – faint symbols – appearing and disappearing in the darkness, dancing before his eyes, pulsing and moving across his vision. But they were not on the walls. They were in his head!

CHAPTER 4

Eric had lingered after James had left but now he knew he had to get away from the room, the carvings and the men who were watching his every move. "Just carry on here," he said, indicating a lower section of the wall. "I'll check back with you when you are done."

"Of course, Dr. Adams," said the man closest to him.

"I'm going to head off and take James to see the pyramids today. But I'll be back tomorrow."

"Thank you, doctor," the man said.

"You're welcome," said Eric as he turned around and quickly headed toward the front of the excavation. When he emerged back into the sunlight he expected to find James standing there but he was nowhere to be seen. He climbed the steps back to ground level and went to the Jeep but he wasn't there, either. Eric felt a stab of anxiety. He stopped and looked around. There were more guards now. You needed men to protect an important find like this but how many did you need? There were soldiers everywhere, more than when he went in. What was going on? He suddenly felt afraid.

Returning to the entrance, he asked one of the soldiers if he had seen his son. He was answered in the negative. The man said James must still be below because he had not come out.

Still inside, in the heat! James had just come from America. It took time to get used to the heat of Egypt and you had to take precautions to avoid heat stroke. He could be in trouble. Dr. Adams raced back inside. Knowing his son as he did, he could guess where he had gone.

Back inside the little room, James tried to steady himself as he swayed on his feet. He clamped his eyes shut, his head spinning, and staggered backward. Forcing himself to regain his balance, he opened his eyes once more. The streaming symbols were still there but as he watched, his heart racing, they started to fade leaving only the blank wall in front of him. Slowly the dizziness left him. He was breathing hard, panting, as the sweat poured down his face and inside of his shirt.

The medallion was still clutched in his hand. He jammed it into his pocket and quickly, without knowing why, switched off the light on his helmet. He moved into a corner, standing flat against the wall, holding his breath, and waiting.

The darkness was total and complete and yet he knew when someone walked into the chamber where he stood. He stayed perfectly still, waiting for the man to make the next move. For it had to be a man: there were no women on the team.

At that moment he heard his father call his name from a distance away, muffled but distinct. That was all it took. The intruder slipped back through the doorway and his presence left the room. James breathed again but continued to wait without making any sound. He felt disoriented and sick to his stomach. When the light of Dr. Adams' helmet finally appeared James stepped into the reflected light of the beam and called weakly to his father, "Dad, I'm in here," he said.

Eric rushed into the space.

"James – god – are you okay? What happened? How did you get all the way down here? I told you this part of the excavation was closed!" His voice was angry but filled with concern.

"I'm sorry, Dad, I just stepped inside on my way out and I, somehow, got turned around and lost."

If Eric suspected the lie he didn't let on. "Your eyes! The pupils are completely dilated!"

"I'm okay. The heat . . ." and he collapsed against his father.

"We've got to get you outside!"

Then out of the shadows, Raza suddenly stepped into the small pool of light where they stood.

"So you found him, Dr. Adams?" he said calmly, his eyes locked onto James.

"Yes. We need to get him out of here. Please, if you could help me."

Eric suddenly noticed the hole in the wall as the light of his helmet caught it and the little pieces of debris lying on the sand below. No time to investigate now. They lifted James up turning back toward the exit. They soon regained the main corridor and moments later stepped out into the light.

James had been in the tunnels without any kind of fresh air or water for almost an hour. They laid him down under the shade of the scaffolding and got him something to drink. After a few moments, he seemed to revive enough to sit up.

"A close call," said Raza, without emotion.

Dr. Adams looked up into the man's face. "Yes." Eric couldn't keep the suspicion out of his voice. "But how did you know he was lost, Raza?" he asked. "How did you know where to find us?"

"A guard told me," Raza replied, his eyes unblinking and cold.

"A guard wouldn't know we were that deep into those abandoned rooms, the last room in the complex in fact."

"Then call it intuition," Raza said.

Dr. Adams glanced at the soldiers standing around them. "I see," he said as he turned back to James.

Whatever was going on around them would have to wait. He knew the heat wasn't the only thing that had happened to James while he was in the room below. But what? He had to get him away from the dig as soon as possible.

"I think we need to return to the hotel, get you something to eat, and let you get some rest," Dr. Adams said abruptly. He helped James to his feet and they started for the car.

"May I assist you?" Raza asked.

"No!" came Dr. Adams sharp reply.

Once they were headed back to Cairo James turned to his father. "Raza is lying," he said.

His father turned to look at him. "What do you mean, lying?"

"About being in the rooms. He was in there, without a light. He came into the room where I was standing after I had extinguished my helmet."

"It's as dark as the grave in there," said his father. "How do you know it was him?"

"I know," said James. "I just know. He was looking for something."

"Yeah, you!"

"No, something else."

"Again, how do you know?"

"I just know. He's bad."

"I'll grant you he's not someone to mess with but I can't believe he was in there snooping around. He's a trained archeologist. He knows better than to try something out of normal procedures. He'd be fired on the spot." As Eric spoke the words he realized he didn't believe them. Raza *was* up to something.

"Why?" asked James. "You said yourself this discovery is like nothing anyone has ever seen. What if there is something in there Raza wants more than even his job. More than anything. Where did he come from anyway?"

"Dr. Mohammad hired him last year to be his personal assistant. I admit I thought it was odd that Dr. Mohammed would hire someone like him. There were many other men on the staff that could have been promoted to that position, men who had worked for many years in the department."

"Wait and see. He's not what he seems. There was something in there." As soon as the words were out of his mouth, James knew he was in trouble.

Dr. Adams pulled the Jeep off onto the side of the road and stopped. He turned to look at his son. "There was something in there?" he asked in an even voice. "Did you find something in that room, James?"

James knew if his father found out what he had done he would be in a lot of trouble. His father was a stickler for strict protocol. If he found out he had destroyed the scroll and then walked off with a priceless artifact he would be furious. He dared not look at his father's face so he glanced his way without looking into his eyes.

"I meant Raza. Raza was in there. I wasn't talking about finding anything." It was a lie and a weak one at that.

Dr. Adams was silent. James felt a drop of sweat fall from his forehead. Eric reached under his son's chin and turned him to look at his face. James' eyes were still monstrously dilated.

"James if you've done something, you need to tell me."

James twisted his face out of his father's hand to stare straight in front of him. "I told you there was nothing."

Eric turned away in pain and disappointment. They used to be the best of pals. So much had gone wrong in the relationship, so much had happened since the divorce, that now they were like casual acquaintances instead of father and son. Something had happened back there in that room. Eric felt it. And there was danger here, all around them. Eric felt that, too.

He suddenly reached and started the Jeep. "You're white as a sheet. We've got to get you back to the hotel. And if you don't start feeling better we're going to the hospital."

The rest of the trip was completed in silence, much to James relief. As soon as they were in the hotel Eric took James to their room and went and got ice and more water. "Keep hydrated." And he left to get them food.

When he returned James ate quickly and then laid down. He was beginning to feel better but sleep came over him so suddenly he seemed to pass out as soon as his head hit the pillow.

When he finally awoke, the sun was setting in the west and the room was bathed in its yellow glow.

His father was sitting in a chair next to the bed. "How are you feeling?"

"Okay, I guess," James replied. "How long was I asleep?"

"Four hours," replied his father. "You were talking in your sleep."

James felt a stab of fear run through him. What had he said? Had he given it away?

He looked at his father. Eric's face was blank.

"I always talk in my sleep," came James' lame reply.

"Really, I don't ever remember you talking in your sleep."

"It just started last year. What did I say?" and he swallowed.

"Nothing I could understand. Mostly gibberish," said his father. And then: "You said the word "Horus" one time, distinctly."

"Oh."

"Do you know who Horus is?"

"Yes. The god of war."

"He's also the god of protection and secret wisdom. Did you see him on the wall in the excavation?"

"No . . . I don't think so."

"You wouldn't," said his father. "He wasn't there."

"I need to go to the bathroom," James said abruptly. He got up from the bed and went to the bathroom closing the door softly behind him. He looked at his face in the mirror. Nothing seemed amiss. Maybe he had hallucinated after all. But his eyes were still dilated.

He didn't know how much longer he could stand up under his father's questions. He took his finger and pulled down the lower lids of both eyes and then repeated the same process with the upper ones. Nothing. What had happened in the dig had been so weird. There was no way it could have actually happened. It *was* a hallucination. His eyes were dilated because of the intense darkness in that room in the dig. That had to be it.

He finished up and went back into the room. His father was standing by the window talking quietly on his cell phone. The curtain had been drawn and Eric slowly pulled back the side of one of the drapes and looked out. When he heard James he dropped the curtain back into place, abruptly finished the call, and turned to face his son. "You didn't eat much lunch. Would you like to go and grab some dinner."

"Sure," said James. "Is anything wrong, Dad?" he asked.

"No," said Eric replied, shaking his head and sticking out his lower lip. "Everything's fine. Still a little bit worried about you, that's all."

"Okay. Can we go to the same restaurant we went to last night?"

"No. I want to go somewhere else."

"Okay."

Eric stowed his phone in the holder on his belt and they left the room, locking the door behind them. Once outside Eric led him down side streets, finally coming to a small café where they ate their dinner. It wasn't as good as the first restaurant but it would do. Afterward, they wandered around awhile stopping at a shop that was still open. They stepped inside and James bought his mother a necklace that the proprietor swore was genuine lapis lazuli the blue stone so valued in ancient Egypt. James smiled at his father, knowing it was a fake but bought it anyway. After that, they went back to the hotel.

Eric paused when they came to their door but inserted the key and reaching in turned on the light. His father walked into the room and didn't stop until he had checked the bathroom as if he was looking for something. James walked past him and went to the bathroom. When he returned his father said, "If it's okay, I'm going to turn in now. You can sit up if you like. It won't bother me."

"No, that's okay," said James. "I'm tired again. I think I'll sleep, too."

They got ready for bed and Eric turned off the light but James lay awake until he heard his father's soft snoring, then he too slipped into sleep.

Sometime in the night, James woke up. He felt hot and sweaty and when he tried to kick off the sheet he was under it became twisted. He rolled over and thought he saw his father sitting in a chair across the room watching him. But he couldn't keep awake and fell back into a troubled sleep.

When he awoke the second time, his father was leaning over him. The drapes were still drawn and the clock on the nightstand showed 4:00 a.m.

His father spoke to him," Get up, James, and get dressed. You have to go home."

CHAPTER 5

"Go home? What do you mean? I just got here."

"I know. But it's not safe here anymore," said his father, pulling him up in the bed and then to his feet.

"What do you mean? Safe from what?"

"It's just not safe."

"But . . . "

"No buts, James. Get dressed now and hurry. We'll miss the plane." His voice was tense, without any of the normal kidding around.

James stumbled forward, pulled on his jeans and t-shirt and reaching down pulled his backpack from under the bed, stuffing it with the few things he had brought on his trip. Then he went to the bathroom and finished up in there. The whole process took less than two minutes.

"Ready?" said his father who was already unlocking the door to their room. He didn't wait for James to answer but stepped outside and waited for James to follow. At this point, James realized that his father was carrying all of his own possessions as well. Eric would not be coming back to the room, either.

They quickly made their way downstairs and Eric told James to wait by the door while he paid for their room.

The man behind the counter looked sullen and suspicious but he plastered a thin smile on his face.

"Leaving so soon, Dr. Adams?" he said.

"Yes, we're moving to a room closer to the Pyramids. Sightseeing, you know."

"Of course. Thank you for staying with us."

Eric didn't answer but as he turned away James saw the man pick up the phone, his eyes following them as they turned away, and began to talk quietly into the phone as if he didn't want anyone to overhear his conversation.

Eric led the way outside and to the Jeep.

They climbed inside, closed and locked the doors, and backed out of the space. The streets this early in the morning were almost empty. A few shopkeepers were heading for their businesses but that was all. They drove in silence, his father nervously glancing in the rearview mirror several times until they were well away from the hotel.

"You know you could have let me sleep until morning," James blurted out.

"There was no time. I'm sorry," his father replied.

"And you're not going to explain why after one day with you I'm being sent home?"

"I will explain. I promise. Right now we have to make the plane."

James felt his face grow hot with anger. A wave of dizziness came over him and he closed his eyes as he leaned back in the seat. His pulse was racing and sweat came onto his face. From what seemed like far away, he heard his father's voice talking. Then for an instant everything became black. He didn't know how much time had passed until his eyes popped open and he was sitting calmly in the seat as if nothing had happened. His father glanced at him several times, studying his face as he drove.

He felt groggy and his eyes were heavy. What was going on? Should he tell him what he had found? He turned and looked out the window.

"Wait a minute. This isn't the way to the airport," he said.

"We're not going to the airport in Cairo. We're going to Alexandria."

"Alexandria?"

"That's right. The airport in Cairo didn't have a flight out soon enough."

"It's that important to get me out of here."

"I believe so. As I said I'll explain it soon."

They drove on through the darkness without speaking again. Before long, light began to appear in the East. They drove into Alexandria as the sun peeked over the horizon. Eric drove straight through the city and into the airport. He grabbed the pack back and handed it to James as they quickly made their way to the terminal. Dr. Adams stopped and scanned the few people inside the room. A man came up behind them and touched Eric on the arm. He swung around and the look of relief on his face showed he was expecting the man who stood in front of him.

James quickly took in his appearance. He looked younger than his father, maybe thirty. They were about the same height but the other man, who had short brown hair, had a slimmer build. He was wearing a pair of khaki slacks, a light cotton shirt, and a pair of sunglasses, which he quickly took off revealing his dark eyes. He hadn't shaved in a couple of days and his hair looked like he had rolled out of bed without bothering to brush it. The two men shook hands.

"Hello, Eric," he said.

"Philip. I didn't think we were going to make it." He turned to his son. "James, this is Philip Harrington. He's . . . my assistant. He's going to accompany you back to the States."

Philip turned to James and extended his hand. "Nice to meet you, James." Then, "We'd better get a move on. They're holding the plane for us."

They walked to the ticket counter. The clerk stamped their tickets and James and Philip walked to the security station. Dr. Adams stopped James and faced him. James half expected him to hug him, something his father never did. Instead, he handed him an envelope.

"Take this. Don't open it until you're halfway home. Understand?"

James nodded and looked at his father, "Dad . . .?"

"Yes?"

"Are you going to be okay?"

Dr. Adams smiled and hugged him after all. "Yes," he whispered in his ear. "Now go!"

James walked forward where Philip was waiting, turned and glanced at his father who held up his hand. James waved back as he felt Philip take his arm. They went through security and out to the steps leading up to the airplane. Once on board Philip guided James to their seats in the back. James stowed his backpack in the overhead but kept the letter his father had given him. He sat down by the window while Philip took the seat on the aisle leaving the center seat empty. The aircraft had few passengers, just a few men here and there. No women and no children. A voice came on the intercom telling everyone to fasten their seatbelts as the plane began to slowly pull away from the terminal. He turned the letter over in his hand. His father's handwriting spelled out "James" in clear block letters, all capitals. He felt so tired but he had to know what was going on. He ran his finger underneath the flap and tore the envelope open.

Again the same strong printing. It read:

James,
I believe you are carrying something you found in the excavation. I wish you had confided in me. But it may be for the best. I am unsure myself what all of this means. Stay close to Philip and do exactly what he tells you to do. When you get to Virginia a car will be waiting for both of you. Philip will drive you home to Arlington. Don't mention anything about what has happened to anyone, especially your mother. She has already been advised that you are returning early. I gave her an excuse so she will not be questioning your return. <u>*Do not tell her anything*</u>*. It's for her safety and yours. I will be returning home in a few days. I will explain everything when I get there.*

Again, speak to no one about what you are carrying.

I love you,
Dad

James suddenly felt cold. He got up and stumbled over Philip to the other side of the plane, looking out, hoping to see his father. But it was too late. The terminal was already behind them and the plane was turning onto the runway. He turned and scrambled back into the aisle and threw himself at Philip, grabbing the sleeve of his shirt. "Who are you? What's happening to my father?" he almost shouted.

Philip yanked his arm away, suddenly very angry, as an attendant began to make her way to them. Philip made an effort to control himself as he spoke. "Your father already told you who I am. I work with him at the dig."

"You're a damn liar! Make them turn this plane around, NOW!"

"It's too late to turn the plane around. Now get back in your seat and buckle up!" His lips were tight, his face tense.

"To hell with you! You tell them to turn around or I'll yell bomb!"

With that, Philip sprang up, grabbed James by the collar, and pushed him down into an empty seat.

The attendant reached them and said, "Is everything alright here?"

"Yes, yes," Philip replied calmly, "He's just a little sick. He'll be fine."

"Please buckle up and when we are in the air he can go to the lavatory."

"Thank you," Philip said as she walked back to the front of the plane.

Philip slammed his arm against James' chest so hard it took James' breath away.

"You snotty-nosed brat. Don't screw with me or I'll hurt you bad. I don't give a crap what your father will say. The last thing I want to be doing is babysitting a little punk like you and chaperoning your ass back to your mama. You mention a bomb one more time and you'll regret it. You understand me?" he spat the words at James as he released his grip.

With that, James lost all control. He felt his teeth clench and stood up about to lunge at Philip when he suddenly began to sweat and sway on his feet. A startled look came into Philip's eyes and he pulled back quickly glancing to the front of the plane where several of the men were watching them.

"Teenagers! What are you going to do?"

He pushed James to one side and yanked the lavatory door open. Take off or no take off, he stuffed James inside. James half fell but clutching the walls, pulled himself back up. The tiny space was alive with streaming symbols that danced before his vision. He closed his eyes several times, hoping they would stop but just like in the excavation they continued. He felt weak and just when he could not stand it anymore he felt his legs buckle. He slumped to the floor, his vision going black and he fainted.

When he came to he was back in his seat at the back of the plane next to the window. Philip was sitting in the seat next to him. He had a painful headache and felt sick to his stomach. It took several moments for him to get oriented. When he looked to the side Philip was watching him.

"Are you alright?" he asked

"What do you care?" James replied.

Philip grinned at that. "Now you sit here like a good little boy," he said.

If James had wanted to move he would not have been able to. His body ached all over. He reached inside his pocket and felt the talisman he was carrying. It felt hot to his touch. What was this thing? He was scared and now he wished more than ever that he had told his father the truth. Should he tell Philip? He didn't even know who he was and every minute he disliked him more and more.

"Are you hungry?" Philip asked, "Do you need something to drink."

"No."

"Well, you're going to drink something anyway."

Philip left him there and without asking an attendant went to the kitchen by the lavatory and picked up a soda. When he returned he said, "Drink this and I'll get you some more."

James looked at the drink and sat still.

Philip rolled his eyes. "What do you think, it's poison?" he said, sitting down.

James still hesitated.

"Well, here, let me," and Philip put the can to his lips and drank half of the liquid. "Man that was good." The words were barely out of his mouth when his body began to twitch and he clutched his throat with his free hand. "Oh, oh my god. You were right. I'm dying, oh . . . oh." He stopped and shoved the soda into James' hand. "Drink it, you moron."

James downed the drink and Philip got him another one, which he also drank. They were silent as the plane continued to climb and finally leveled off.

James turned to Philip. "Can you, at least, tell me if my father is going to be okay?"

Philip looked at him for a moment. "I don't know what you are talking about," he said. "He asked me to take you home. That's all."

James turned away but not before Philip saw the pained look on his face. He knew he should not say anything else. He should stop the conversation at this point and say nothing more until they got home. But after a moment, he continued:

"Why didn't you talk to your father?"

"How do you know I didn't?"

"Because I have a father and I was your age once. I never said anything to my father. I kept secrets like a dead man. But let's see if I can fill it in." He looked around the passengers in the front of the plane as he lowered his voice. "You don't get along too well with your father. I'm guessing maybe a divorce from your mother. Hence, my taking you back to a Virginia address that is not your father's address. You came over here to be with him for a few days but you didn't really want to come. You felt you had to. You had no way to know it but you could not have come at a worse time. That's not your fault but it's true just the same.

Your father invited you to come to the dig and see what he has been working on. But again, it could not have been at a worse time. Things were happening there – that morning – he didn't know about it until both of you got there. He took you to see the bas-reliefs deep inside the excavation. While he was talking to you, you gave him an insight, a clue that had been right in front of him the whole time. He realized suddenly what the answer might be but as soon as he knew it he also knew he had to get you out of there as soon as he possible. Other people were there, listening.

Acting completely unconcerned, he asked you to go and wait for him at the opening and you left. But you didn't go outside. You wandered into the rooms that had been blocked off: rooms that had been deemed unimportant, storage areas if you like, and therefore not worth any attention. But it turned out they were very important. Completely by luck, dumb stupid luck, you went into one of them and you found something there."

"No! I didn't!" James replied.

"After what happened to you in the bathroom just now, I'd say you did."

"I just got sick in the bathroom, that's all."

Philip smiled again. "Well, let's say it's natural for you to come out of the bathroom white as a ghost and with the pupils in your eyes as big as saucers. It doesn't change the fact that you did find something. What I'm sure you don't know is there are three of them. One of them may have already been found and has fallen into the hands of very desperate men who will stop at nothing to get the other two. One of the them is still lost and . . .." He turned and looked directly into James' eyes, "you're carrying the third one, probably in the pocket of your jeans."

James instinctively sucked in his breath as his body tensed. "No, I'm not," he said too fast and quickly looked away.

"Yes, you are. The thing is you're scared and confused. You've touched something of power and it's already beginning to affect you. You don't know how to control it and I'll bet you'd give your right arm right now if your father was sitting here with you instead of me."

James felt like he was going to throw up. He turned away as his heart began to race and his breath came in short little gasps. Everything began to go black again when Philip grabbed him, shaking him violently. "STOP IT!"

"I don't know how!" he gasped. "I don't' know how!"

"Look at me, *look at me!*" Philip's voice was hoarse and intense. "Now relax, relax."

James began to calm down and finally collapsed against the seat, the darkness leaving his vision. After a few minutes had passed he said: "If Dad knew all of this why did he send me away?"

"He believed you were in danger . . . and he didn't want the thing you are carrying to fall into the wrong hands. I believe he doesn't realize the power of what you have . . . yet. He loves you very much. He had to find a way to protect you."

"What do I do?"

"There's nothing you can do. You have to go home and, my advice, stay low and stay calm. It seems to turn on when you get upset or angry. We have to wait and see if your father can solve the riddle."

"Tell me what you know, please."

"I can't."

"What about my father? He said he would come home in two days. Will he?"

"If that is what he said, then you can bet he will try as hard as he can to be there. You have to wait and trust him."

"Do you think this thing is going to hurt me?"

"I think if it was going to hurt you, you would already be dead. Now try and get some sleep. It will be hours before we get home."

CHAPTER 6

  If it had been in Eric's power he would have gotten on the plane with James and escorted his son home to safety. As it was, there was nothing he could do but put him in the hands of Philip and stand and wait, watching as the plane taxied down the runway and took off. He walked outside when it was finally in the air and watched it until it became a dot in the cloudless sky and disappeared from view.

  He was not a man who was prone to superstition or fanciful flights of fantasy and he certainly wasn't a romantic. His ex-wife could attest to that fact. But there were times when he wondered if there was such a thing as fate or coincidence. Or perhaps he had just closed his mind to what seemed supernatural.

  He had studied the sculptures in that room in the excavation for months on end and the old saying had held true; sometimes you can't see the forest for the trees. James, walking up to the wall and looking at it with fresh eyes, had instantly seen what he had missed. The final clue to the puzzle, the final answer to the riddle. The thing that forced him to confront what he had been fighting since the beginning. But could it really be true? It was improbable but was it impossible?

He turned and walked back into the terminal, through the empty concourse, and out to the parking lot. He climbed back into the Jeep. James' jacket lay on the seat. He had left it behind. His father picked it up and squeezed it in his hands. "God, don't let anything happen to my son." He laid it back down and quickly pulled out of the parking lot. Once he was on the road, leaving Alexandria behind, he fell to thinking about what he now believed the hieroglyphs were trying to tell him.

From the moment he had walked into the excavation and looked at the walls, Eric knew he was in over his head. Many of the symbols on the wall were very common and easily read. But others were new and he could not make anything out of them. He had immediately thought of Dr. Stevens.

Dr. Stevens had been one of his teachers at university. He was a life-long scholar of the Old Kingdom, that period of Ancient Egyptian history that marked the dawning of civilization in the Nile Valley. Should he contact him? He had hesitated. Dr. Stevens had fallen into disrepute and had lost his tenure. He had not taught for many years. Instead, he had taken to writing rambling, scholarly articles that were almost never published and working on odd projects as an assistant in a museum in New York.

The reason for his dismissal from his teaching position was simple: his unceasing talk of aliens from outer space coming into the Nile Valley, laying the foundation for the Egyptian civilization, giving them the hieroglyphic language and helping them build the Great Pyramid. It was insane talk; the stuff of science fiction and sensationalist TV shows, with absolutely no basis in fact.

Everyone agreed Dr. Stevens was developing some form of mental illness, either bi-polar disease or more probably, dementia. He had resisted his dismissal of course: had told the university, and anyone else that would listen to him, that he could prove it. He had found a link to the distant past that showed beyond any doubt that aliens had visited Earth.

Under pressure to produce the evidence, he had refused, saying that if it fell into the wrong hands the power it possessed would be uncontrollable. Eric had not seen or heard of him for many years.

He wrestled with the decision and tried to put it out of his mind but the longer the work continued the more fruitless it became. He was going nowhere and needed Dr. Stevens.

One Saturday afternoon when the work at the site had been suspended he was sitting in his room searching the web for any kind of information he could find about Old Kingdom writing. Hardly realizing what he was doing, he typed the Professor's name into a search engine and tapped the return key.

A flood of men named Stevens popped up. As he scrolled down the list of entries none of them fit the Professor's background. He came to the third page and was about to give up when an entry appeared with aliens, Egypt, and Professors Stevens' name embedded in the copy of the entry.

Against his better judgment, he clicked the link and a page opened up with an article and Dr. Stevens' picture. He looked much older than what Eric remembered.

He glanced through the essay. It was a rehash of everything that had gotten him into trouble. Could he possibly work with a man who was mentally ill? Eric realized that he might be crazy but he could think of no one who possessed the knowledge of the Old Kingdom, its culture, and its symbolism like Dr. Stevens. He would simply have to sift through the Professor's crazy ramblings and try to decipher the information he needed to help him with the work.

He clicked the link taking him to Dr. Stevens' email and wrote a brief paragraph. He explained that he was sure Dr. Stevens would not remember him but he had taken all of the doctor's courses at the university and was now working on a small excavation in Egypt south of the temples at Karnak (he saw no reason to go into depth of how important the excavation was as the excitement might cause the Professor to go off on a mental tangent and not return). He explained that he was having trouble discerning some hieroglyphics and was wondering if the Professor would mind taking a look.

His finger wavered for a moment and then hit the 'send' key. He knew it was a wild goose chase. The Professor had taught hundreds of students over the years. Why would he remember him, especially in his mental state?

Suddenly, as these thoughts ran through his head there was a message. Looking at the screen, he was amazed to see that the Professor had responded.

He opened the email and read:

Eric!

I can't believe it! Of course I remember you! Whenever any of my colleagues would ask me who was going to be the next Indiana Jones I always told them, Eric Adams. You just had the bug. I could see it in you from the beginning. I knew one day I would pick up the paper and there you would be, giving all of us insights into the discoveries you had made. God, it is so good to hear from you.

And Egypt! Has there ever been anything like it? So amazing, so exciting. It never disappoints! Believe me, I know.

I would be HONORED to assist you in any way I can. Just tell me what you want me to do.

George Stevens

Eric had sat back, stunned. Not only from the Professor's praise but that he had actually found him and had gotten his reply so quickly.

Now what? How should he proceed? He couldn't back out now. He would just have to be careful how he phrased things and more importantly, he needed to take his time. This could not be rushed. He also made the decision to, in the beginning at least, only show the Professor the standard symbols, not the strange ones he couldn't read. Not for a while, anyway. He also made a deal with himself. The minute anything was said about aliens he would shut off the correspondence, no matter how much the Professor was assisting him.

Eric wrote back and thanked Professor Stevens for his words, gave him a very brief description of what he was doing and told him he would contact him in a few days with the first of the symbols.

The Professor had immediately responded and said to send the documents as soon as he was ready.

Eric waited two days and then picked some symbols at random. He could translate them himself but he wanted to start off with something simple to see how the Professor would react.

As before the response was almost instantaneous with an indication that he was surprised that Eric could not decipher what any first-year archeology student would be able to do. Eric had smiled at that and sent a sequence of harder ones. Again he could read the symbols himself but was still unsure, still feeling his way, into this new relationship with his old teacher.

This time, the response came back with a question at the end: *"Are you testing me?"*

Eric had responded: *"No, sir."*

"Then why are you asking me to translate things that are so elementary?"

"I need you to verify my own translations. Some of the patterns, the groupings of the symbols, are different than usual."

"I understand. How are they different?"

Eric paused. He couldn't give too much away. *"The pattern of how they are presented on the wall?"*

"Are they paintings or carvings?"

"Carvings."

"Can you send me an image of the wall?"

Eric lied. *"Not at this time. Red tape with the government and the ministry."*

"Understood. Can you send me a longer sequence?"

"Yes." Eric pulled up a string of hieroglyphic drawings from his computer, edited out the unknown symbols at the bottom of the image, attached it to the email, and sent it back.

After a long pause, the translation returned: *The people rose up: There was war (rebellion?) against the gods. The stars fell (were?) silent . . .*

This had been Eric's translation, as well, although it made absolutely no sense to him. As he sat thinking a new email popped up on his screen.

"Eric – what have you found?"

This was moving too fast. He had to slow it down. He wrote: *"Not sure. Have to go. Be in touch soon."*

A week went by where he did not correspond with Professor Stevens at all. One evening, after returning to his room, he opened his computer and found an email from Professor Stevens.

Eric:

I believe my reputation proceeds me. I know you are aware of what happened to my job at the university. In this profession, you would have to be living under a rock not to have heard about the situation. I'm also sure you have heard the various diagnoses that have been made concerning my mental state. There is nothing I can do to change people's opinions, or your personal belief, about the situation. And I don't really want to try. As I told you when you first contacted me I will do anything to assist you if I can. But I also understand your reluctance to engage me in your work. I'm here if you need me, with no further questions asked.

Your friend,
Professor Stevens

Eric sat back in his chair, ashamed. He had been rude and insensitive to someone whose lectures had set him on fire with the desire to become an archeologist.

He clicked "Respond" and wrote:

Dear Professor Stevens,
You are right. I know everything about what happened concerning the end of your relationship with the university as well as the insinuations that were made about you. I also know there is no one that I consider a higher authority on Old Kingdom hieroglyphics and their meanings. If you can't solve it, nobody can.

Forgive me. I'm just a little overwhelmed at the moment with the scope of this.

Here is what I propose. I will begin sending drawings of the sections of the wall I need to have you look over. The ministry won't allow any kind of photography. It will be laborious but it can't be helped. If you will agree to simply look at them and give me your best interpretation without any further inquiries on your part we can begin.

However, knowing what both of us are like, I also realize that at some point it will become unfair to you to not let you in on what is happening. I promise you that when the time comes, I will provide you with all the answers you desire.

Eric

Professor Stevens replied:

My dear boy,
I agree to rules of the game. When do we begin?

In the days that followed, Eric sent, on an almost daily basis, random sequences of the symbols.

Most of them came back as verifications of his own interpretations. He made sure none of the other symbols were sent during this time. But there came a day when he felt he had to show the Professor some of the other icons on the wall. So he sent him a set of drawings but left in the band of strange geometric shapes at the bottom.

He expected the Professor to respond immediately but instead he went silent. He did not respond for a whole day and when he did it was with a cryptic reply with an attachment to the email.

Eric:

Review the attachment and don't send me anything else. I believe our correspondence is being monitored. I must speak with you face-to-face. I need to show you something. It's vitally important. How do I find you?

Professor Stevens

Was this paranoia? Were the accusations that had been leveled against the Professor true?

He opened the attachment. It was a rough sketch of a pie shaped piece of metal with a curve with a serrated edge and a hole off-center at the bottom. To someone who had not seen the carvings on the wall of the excavation it would have meant nothing. To Eric, it was like a thunderbolt.

He forwarded all the information his old teacher would need to come to Egypt and find him. He also offered to wire him money for the ticket, which the Professor declined. That was the last conversation they had.

He had tried repeatedly to contact the Professor but with no success. The email account had been shut down. What had happened? He was very concerned but did not know how to begin to find him again. James had arrived one week later.

Now James had gone home and, unless Eric was wrong, was carrying something that was another piece of the puzzle. He drove back to his permanent lodgings. He waited until evening, changed his clothes, got into his Jeep, and headed south out of Cairo.

When he arrived at the dig all seemed in order. He greeted the guards at their station and descended into the excavation. As Eric passed between them the guards gave each other a knowing look; then resumed their stance.

He picked up his helmet on the way in, switching on its light as he progressed down the darkened corridor until he had come to the room. He turned on the large lights on their stands, went to the far left corner of the wall.

His plan was simple: open his mind to all the possibilities no matter how impossible or bizarre they seemed, use Professor Stevens' translations and his own, avoid the foreign symbols.

He looked at the first symbols in the upper corner and using James' translation began to read:

From the stars we come . . . to this world . . .

Twenty minutes later he had finished and stood shaking, not from cold (the room was stifling hot even at night), but from amazement tinged with fear.

He finally turned away from the wall and walked back into the main corridor. He needed to get away and back to his apartment. And he needed to call his son.

He glanced toward the front of the dig where the electric lights illuminated the rectangle of the entrance. As he walked along, a figure suddenly appeared out of a side hallway and began to approach him, his shape backlit by the lights at the front. He didn't have to wonder who it was. The tall, erect figure could only be one man.

Eric stopped, switched off his headlamp, took a flashlight out of his pocket and waited until Raza stepped close to him and into the small circle of light.

"Dr. Adams," he said in a flat tone and then he stopped, waiting for a response, his black eyes searching Eric's face.

"Raza," Eric replied, trying to sound calm and unconcerned as if meeting the assistant director so late at night in the dig was the most common of occurrences.

"It's rather late to be working is it not?" Raza inquired without any inflection in his voice.

"I . . . wasn't working. I realized I had left some of my papers here and wanted to retrieve them before tomorrow."

"It was my understanding you would be taking off several days to be with your son. During his visit to our country, I mean."

"That was the intention. Unfortunately, James had to return home this morning."

"How sad. He must have been terribly disappointed. Egypt can be an amazing place to visit. So many things to see . . . and discover." His eyes never left the doctor's face. "Nothing serious, I hope."

"No, no. Nothing like that," said Eric. He stopped.

Raza pursed his lips and paused as if in thought. Then: "He seems a very intelligent, insightful young man. Someone who could see through a clutter of information and discover . . . well, discover many things, if he chose to do so."

Eric felt himself go tense. Raza was no fool and he was searching for something, a clue perhaps of what James had discovered looking at the sculptures or the thing he had found in the unexamined room.

There was an uncomfortable pause while each of them waited for the other to speak.

"Yes, James is a very smart kid. I'm very proud of him. Well, I need to get back," Eric said finally. "Have a good evening."

"Of course. Have a good evening," said Raza and slowly stepped aside.

Eric had only gone a few steps when Raza called to him. "Dr. Adams?"

Eric turned to face him again. The light of the flashlight cast his figure in a pale spectral light, making him appear ghostly in the darkness.

"Yes?" Dr. Adams asked.

"This excavation is very important in ways you might not be able to discern. I'm sure if you discovered something, something important, you would tell me what you had found – tell me before you told anyone else."

Eric could not decide if it was a request or a command.

"I'm . . . not sure what you mean." Eric walked back until he was facing the man eye to eye. They were roughly the same height but Eric had never been this close to the archeologist before. The black eyes gleamed with a strange light in their depths, a light that made Eric want to turn away as if he was staring into something not quite human. No matter. He was not going to be intimated by the man. Now it was Eric's turn to become the inquisitor.

"Is there something *you* need to tell me about this dig, Dr. Raza."

Raza took a small step back, away from Eric's intense gaze.

"I came here at your, and your government's, request," Eric continued. "To decipher the symbols is all I was asked to do: not to try and explain who created them or even why they were created. Obviously, there is more to this than I've been made privy to. Would you like to explain what you know?"

Raza looked at the doctor. "I only know what you know," he said, giving an answer that was not an answer at all. "I just need you to understand that I am your friend. And a friend to your son if it ever comes to that."

Eric's face fell and he opened his mouth to speak but before the words came, Raza said good night and turned down the tunnel toward the room with the carvings.

Eric watched as his shadow was swallowed up in the darkness. He realized he was sweating and not from the heat of the corridor.

"You're the last thing I would confide anything to," he whispered under his breath and then made his way outside.

He ascended the steps and when he reached ground level he discovered he was alone: the guards had deserted their posts.

He called out. No response. He felt himself tense.

He turned and looked down into the dig but there was no one there and Raza was still inside.

When he swung back around, he gave a gasp and stumbled back onto the edge of the steps. A man, flanked by two soldiers, was standing directly in front of him. Eric had never seen him before. He was heavy set with dark features. He smiled but the smile was sinister.

"Dr. Adams. How nice to meet you . . . at last."

"Who are you?"

"That's not important. What is important is we have a mutual friend. A friend who would like to see you tonight."

"Mutual friend?"

"Yes. And we were wondering if we could escort you to him."

Eric looked at the soldiers who flank the man. They were carrying high capacity rifles in front of their chests. They did not speak but they didn't have to. This was no invitation. He was being kidnapped.

"What if I refuse?" asked Eric.

"I'm afraid that would have unfortunate consequences especially for your friend."

For a wild moment, Eric thought of calling to Raza. But the thought died as soon as it came into his head. Raza was one of them.

"Who are we meeting?"

"Someone you know very well," came the reply.

Eric felt panic rising up in his throat. Had they gotten to James?

A van pulled up with a crunch of gravel under its tires.

"Shall we go, doctor?"

There was nothing he could do but go with them. After blindfolding Eric, they took his cell phone, removed his watch and wallet and took him to a van. They opened the door and helped him climb inside. Moments later they left the site.

Inside the excavation, Raza had switched on one of the electric lamps sitting on the sand-covered floor. The sculptures sprang to life, their forms thrown into high relief. He looked all around the space, admiring the art once again. So beautiful. So serene. So full of danger. He stepped before the large figure of the winged man with the head of a cheetah. Reaching up, he touched its surface. He sighed and hung his head. He recited a prayer that had come down through generations of his family. Then he turned and abruptly walked away leaving the lights burning.

CHAPTER 7

James had experienced jet lag when he had landed in Egypt a few days before. It had not felt good. Now it was brutal.

He felt like he had hardly seen his father before being put on another plane and sent home. By the time he got back to Dulles International Airport his normal sleep pattern was messed up.

He stumbled off the plane with Philip right behind him. They boarded a shuttle that carried them to the main terminal where they entered the concourse. His only luggage the whole trip had been his backpack so there was no need to go to the baggage claim. Once they had picked their way through the crowds in the concourse they went to a car rental station. As his father had said, a car was waiting for them. Philip left him standing on the sidewalk facing the main parking lot while he went and retrieved the car. He returned momentarily and after James got in, they left the airport and headed east toward Arlington.

Philip had been silent after the incident in the plane and he remained silent until they came to Falls Church. He turned, glanced at James, and said: "You need to listen very carefully to what your father told you. Follow his instructions to the letter. Do you understand?"

James nodded without saying anything.

"As to what you are carrying, whatever it is, my suggestion is to find a place where you can lock it up and never touch it again. Don't let anyone else touch it either. And don't, whatever you do, talk about what happened to you in Egypt. Your father will handle it in his own time. And don't try to call your father. Are you listening?"

James was looking out of the window. "Yes," he said shortly and fell silent. He didn't like Philip Harrington.

Twenty minutes later they pulled up in front of James' house. Philip reached into the backseat for the backpack, pulling it into the front of the car, but James snatched it away.

"I can do it myself," he snapped.

"I'm sure you can but it will look odd if I just drive away. Now give me the backpack!"

James stuffed it into Philip's hands and opened the door, stepping out onto the sidewalk. At that instant the door of his house opened and his mother appeared. She walked down the sidewalk, a look of worry and concern on her face. It had only been a short time but he was glad to see his mother again.

"Oh, honey, I've been so worried. Are you really okay?" she said, lifting his face up and studying it. She put her hand on his forehead. "Well, no fever at least."

His dad must have told her he had gotten sick. "It was probably just a bug but your father was right to send you home. You never know what you are going to pick up in a foreign country. I made you a doctor's appointment just in case."

She turned to Philip who extended his hand smiling. "Hello, Mrs. Adams. My name is Philip Harrington. I'm Eric's assistant."

"So pleased to meet you, Philip. You'll come in for some coffee before you leave?"

"I appreciate that. But I have to be getting back."

"It was so nice of you to bring James home. All that way."

"Not at all," he said. James thought he was going to pat him on the head but instead he touched him on the shoulder. "He's a great kid. We just wanted to make sure he was okay." And he smiled a fake smile at James who curled his lip in disgust. "Well, I better be getting on." He walked back down the sidewalk to the car.

James called out to him. "Philip?"

Philip turned and looked at him, his face questioning.

"Tell dad . . . I'll be waiting."

Philip nodded, "You bet," he said. "Goodbye." He got into the rental car and drove away.

His mother took him by the shoulders and turned him around. She said: "Honey, is everything okay? You seem really upset. What are you waiting for your dad to do?"

He avoided her face: "I'm just tired. I'm fine, Mom. Dad is going to call me that's all," he fibbed. He couldn't let on about anything that was going on.

"I was worried sick when your father called. Come on in and let me fix you some dinner. What would you like?"

"Actually," James said, "some pancakes."

His mother didn't question him, just nodded, and James followed her inside and went upstairs, telling her he wanted to wash up. When he got to his room he went to his desk. The bottom drawer had a key. He opened it and fished the talisman out of his pocket. He tried not to look at it but couldn't help himself. It seemed dull in the light and looked like some old piece of metal found on the street or a player's piece out of a board game. He held it up turning it over and over in his hand. Whatever power it possessed now seemed spent and would not repeat itself. He didn't wait any longer but quickly dropped it inside the drawer, closing and locking it up in one swift motion.

He took a deep breath, went and washed his face and hands, and headed back downstairs.

He could smell the pancakes at the head of the stairs. A plate of crispy bacon was sitting on the table along with warm maple syrup and a glass of orange juice.

He surprised his mother by asking for a cup of coffee. He had never liked coffee but he knew enough about jet lag to know that the last thing he needed was to eat and go to sleep. He had to stay up as long as he could and then go to sleep and begin to reset his internal clock.

He was hungry and quickly ate a large stack of pancakes, four pieces of bacon, along with two cups of coffee and the juice. Then he refilled his plate and did it again.

Mrs. Adams watched him without interrupting him but when he was finally through she asked him if he felt better.

"Yes, very much. Thanks, Mom."

"Of course. Can I get you anything else?"

"No but thanks."

"Sure. Did you get to do anything at all while you were there?"

James sat back and answered as honestly as he could. "Not much," he said. "We ate at a restaurant the first night and went down to the excavation he was working on the next morning."

"Is that when you got sick?"

"Yeah," that's when I got sick." He didn't like lying to his mother.

She picked up his plate. "How is your father doing?" she asked casually.

"He seems okay. He's just wrapped up in his work. You know how he is."

"I'm sorry the trip didn't work out. Maybe you can go back later – once you're feeling better and after you've rested up."

"Yeah. Listen, mom, I'm feeling a lot better *now*. I don't really think I need to go to the doctor."

"Well, let me take you just the same. We need to make sure you haven't picked up something that needs treating. Do you want to take a nap?"

"No. I need to stay awake and try to get back onto some kind of schedule."

"Okay."

The next afternoon he went over to Larry's house. Larry Chen had been his best friend since grade school and lived down the block from James. He was an avid computer geek, passionate video game player, and president of the science club at school. Larry was short and completely lacking in athletic ability. But he made up for it with boundless energy and a brain that seemed too big for his little head.

Mrs. Chen greeted James at the door, asked how he was doing, and yelled for Larry to come down.

James heard Larry's footsteps pounding overhead. He bounded down the stairs two at a time, jumping over the last three, and landing in front of James. "Man, what are you doing here? Something happen? You look like crap."

"I don't want to talk about it."

"What was Egypt like? What did you do? Did you dig up any mummies?"

"I don't want to talk about it."

"Okay . . . Well, I've got the new *Death Squad*. Wanna play?"

"Okay."

They went downstairs to the basement and Larry switched on the game console. Once settled in they played for a couple of hours, had some lunch, and played some more. James finally went home at 4 o'clock and hung around until it was time to go to bed.

In the night, he began to dream but it was unlike any dream he had ever had. The symbols reappeared and were streamed across his vision even though his eyes were shut. He suddenly came out of sleep, sitting up in bed, sweating, and breathing hard.

But the dream wasn't a dream at all. It was real. The symbols were streaming in the darkened air. He felt himself begin to panic and tried to remember what Philip had said. "Calm down," he kept repeating to himself. "Just calm down." And after a minute, it worked. He felt himself relaxing and as he did the symbols stopped moving so fast and slowed up to the point that he could actually look at them for the first time.

He slipped out of bed, went to his desk and grabbed a pen and some paper and without looking at the paper began to write down as many of them as he could. As he did they slowed down to the point that he could transcribe what he was seeing almost exactly as they appeared. The same two symbols repeated themselves but in random patterns, over and over again. This was followed by other symbols, different and varied, but those, less in number, did not repeat themselves.

After several minutes, the symbols faded from his vision and the room fell back into darkness. He looked down. He had written a whole page and somehow felt better that they were at least physically down on paper. They were not some kind of hallucination. They were real.

He crawled back into bed, exhausted, and fell asleep again.

The next afternoon he went to the doctor who found nothing wrong with him, as he knew he would. When he returned home he went to his room and glancing down at his desk saw the paper with the symbols he had transcribed.

What could it mean? He still couldn't believe what had happened in the dig. He folded the paper and put it in the pocket.

He thought of Larry. Nerd was his middle name: a walking encyclopedia. Maybe he would have an idea what they were. Later that day, he went over to Larry's house and showed the paper to him.

"Have you ever seen anything like this before," he asked. "Do you have any idea what they mean?"

Larry studied the paper and said. "Noooo. Should I?"

"No. I guess not."

"Where'd you get them? Maybe they're Chinese. My mom might know."

"No! That's okay. I just saw them somewhere."

He didn't say anything more. They played some more video games and James went home.

Friday morning found him sitting in his room alone. It had been several days since he had returned and his father had still not contacted him to let him know when he would be returning to Virginia. He looked at his watch. It was 10:00 o'clock, which meant it must be around 4:00 o'clock in the afternoon in Egypt.

Philip had told him not to call his dad.

He hesitated. What would be the harm? He just needed to speak to his father, hear his voice, so he would know that everything was okay. But should he? Was there a reason Philip was so adamant about waiting until his father contacted him.

His mother had gone out for the morning so if he was going to call he had to do it now. He picked up his cell phone and began the complicated routine of calling overseas. He remembered trying to call out of the Cairo airport when there was no signal. It all depended on where his father was if the call would work. If his father happens to be in the dig it would be impossible to get a connection.

He waited while the call went through. After a long pause, a recording came on the line that said: "We're sorry the number you are trying to reach has been disconnected or is no longer in service."

James clicked off the phone. He had been holding his breath the whole time and now let it out with a little gasp. He tried again. Maybe he had misdialed. But the same thing happened again. Something was wrong. His father always made sure he could get in touch with the people he worked with or with James or his mother.

Something was wrong.

What could he do? Philip had told him to stay put and wait for his father to contact him. And his father had told him the same thing in the note he had given him.

He decided he would have to wait.

But that evening after dinner he went back to his room and flopped down on the bed. He couldn't shake the fear and worry, no matter how hard he tried. He had thought about it all day and he had two choices: do what he had been told and wait until his father contacted him . . . or go back to Egypt.

Suddenly his mind was made up: he was going back to find his father. Dr. Adams had told him to wait but that was before, in James' mind, something bad had happened to him. As for Philip, he didn't know what he was talking about. He was a jerk.

He got up, went to his computer, and Googled as many airlines as he could think of. Most of them flew out of Dulles but only two had flights going to Egypt. One was leaving in five hours, at 11:00. That was the one he would be on.

His mind began to race with his plan. He would sneak out after his mother had gone to bed and go to the airport. He would be in the air while she was sleeping. If his plan worked she would hardly know he was gone before he called her.

He would walk to the subway and take it to Falls Church where he would connect with the shuttle, which would take him to the airport. But he would have to hurry. Everything would close down for the night and he would be stranded. He went to the closet, retrieved his backpack and began to fill it with clothes. His mother had washed the ones he had worn on the first trip and he simply stuffed those back inside the backpack.

In the middle of his packing the doorbell rang and after a moment he heard his mother open the front door. He hardly noticed. He finished with the clothes, leaving the backpack open on his bed. He went to the desk and found the key. Bending down, he unlocked the bottom drawer and reaching inside retrieved the talisman. He held it up to the light turning it over in his hand.

There was a pounding on his door and he jumped, dropping the metal piece on the floor where it landed halfway under the desk. He fell down fumbling to pick it back up so he could hide it again.

Larry didn't wait to be invited in but opened the door and bounded inside.

"Hey! My mother gave me some money to go to the movies. Wanna come?"

He stopped, looking at the bed with the open backpack. He looked at James. "Where are you going?"

"Nowhere!" He walked around Larry and quickly closed the door. "I'm not going anywhere. I'm just unpacking from when I got back."

Larry was too smart to swallow an obvious lie. "Okay, if you don't want to tell me."

"It's the truth . . ." James stopped, sighed, and looked at his friend. "You can't tell anyone until I'm gone, okay. Promise. I'm going back to Egypt."

"Back to Egypt? But you just got home!"

"I know. But I left some stuff over there and I need to go back and get it."

James was not good at lying.

Larry set his lips. He walked back to the door. "Do you want to go to the movies or not?" he said with no inflection in his voice.

"Larry . . ."

"*It's* fine. Do you want to go or not?"

"*Okay*," James said. "I'll tell you. Something's happened to my father. I have to go back."

"Wow! Does your mother know? Has she called the police?"

"*Nooooo*! He's just . . . in trouble."

"How do you know?"

"I just know, alright. I have to go back."

"Is your mother going with you?"

"No! And don't let on. I have to go by myself."

"Why?"

"I just do! Now go home."

Larry didn't move. "You don't have to go back by yourself . . ." James knew what was coming next. "I can go with you!"

"NO!"

"*WHY NOT?*"

"Because it's too dangerous and your mother would skin you alive not to mention what she would do to me!"

The doorbell rang again.

Larry's mouth drooped down again. "I thought we were *friends*."

"Larry, *come on*! You could get hurt."

"So could you!" He frowned. "I wouldn't leave *you* behind!"

Someone pounded on the door. They both jumped and froze.

58

"James? Larry?"

They looked at each other in shock and both said the same word at the same time. "Sharon?"

"God, it's like I-95 in here!" James exclaimed.

"What can she want?"

"I don't know!"

"James? Larry? *Are you in there?*"

"Yes!"

"*Well*, can I come in?"

"What do you want?"

They could see her fold her arms and twist her lips into a tight little knot even though they were on the other side of the door. "My . . . mother . . . wanted . . . me . . . to . . . drop . . . something . . . off . . . to . . . *your*. . . mother?" she said sarcastically. "Of course, I can always go back downstairs and tell your mother that you were rude and wouldn't let me in. She was the one who wanted me to come up and say hello."

"She drives me crazy!" James whispered.

Sharon Baxter had known both James and Larry since the first grade. She was cute but she was always acting superior and sticking her nose into their business. James had to admit he had on occasion felt sorry for her: her parents were divorced, like his, and she spent a lot of time shuffling between them. They were always busy with their careers leaving little time to show any attention to Sharon.

"Well?"

"Just a minute."

James walked back over to the desk where he had dropped the talisman. He found it on the floor and picked it up.

"What's that?" Larry asked.

"Nothing!" James went to his backpack, unzipped the side pocket, and stuffed it inside. Then he went and opened the door.

Sharon was standing there just like they had pictured her: arms folded, head tilted back like a teacher who had caught them smoking behind the school, looking at them from under her eyelids.

"What's going on?" she asked.

CHAPTER 8

"Nothing," said James looking at Larry.

"Yeah, we're just hanging out," said Larry

"Really?"

"Yeah. We're just hanging out. So how have you been?" asked James.

"Fine," Sharon replied. "Where are you off to now?"

"What do you mean? I'm not going anywhere."

"So why are you packing?"

James glanced back down at this luggage.

"That's not his stuff, it's mine," said Larry suddenly. "I needed to borrow his carry on and some of his clothes. I only have a few clothes at home. That's all. I'm going to Egypt, not him!"

James stared at Larry, his mouth falling open.

Sharon looked at Larry like he had lost his mind. "Egypt? Who said anything about Egypt? Didn't you just get back from there?" she said, turning to James.

"Yes . . . and that's why I'm not going back. It's hot and there are lots of bugs and there's . . . " He stopped, glanced away, sighed, and gave up. "It's none of your business," he said shortly. "It was nice of you to drop by and say hello. Now go home and do me a favor and, for once, keep your mouth shut."

Sharon paid no attention. She wasn't going to be sent home like some six-year-old kid. She walked over and sat down. "So why are you going back?" she said calmly. "Just tell me that and I'll go home and I won't say a word."

James and Larry looked at each other.

"Really," she said. "Besides I might be able to help with whatever it is you're planning. Your mother knows, right?"

James knitted his brow. "Yes . . . no."

"Which is it?" she asked.

"She doesn't know. I just have to go back, that's all."

"Okay. I understand." She paused. "Just . . . is your father okay?"

James looked at her. She was no dummy. "No," he said flatly.

"What happened?"

He suddenly wanted to tell her everything. "He was supposed to follow me home in a few days. He didn't and he didn't call me. Something happened when I was over there. I can't explain. I just know he's in trouble."

"Have you tried to call?"

"Yes. Several times."

"Shouldn't you tell your mother?"

"I can't. I was told not to get her involved."

"So what are you going to do?"

"I'm going back."

"When?"

"Tonight."

"How are you going to get to the airport?"

"The subway and then the shuttle."

"It's getting late. You better get a move on if you want to make it before the subway shuts down for the night."

"I know. That's why you need to go home and let me finish."

"Of course. I'm holding you up." She got up to leave but at the door she stopped and said, "You do have your ticket, right?"

James froze and looked at Larry. "I didn't order the ticket!" he gasped.

"Go online and order it now," said Sharon calmly

James swallowed and looked at Larry. "How much money do you have?"

Larry looked at Sharon and back at James. "The movie money my mother gave me."

"Oh man . . ." James sank down on the bed.

"Well, that's a start," said Sharon. "Now all you need is about $1,500 dollars more and you're all set."

"Oh, shut up and go away!"

61

"I'm kidding! Look, I understand, and as a friend I happen to be in a position to help you."

"How are you going to help me?"

"I have a car, a driver's license, and a credit card with a $5,000 credit limit."

"YOU DO NOT!" said Larry.

"Yes I do!" said Sharon. My parents gave it to me in case I need things for school and to buy my clothes. It's simple," she said turning to James. "We go online, order the tickets, drive to Dulles, and take off."

"I can't take you to Egypt! And besides, you don't have a passport."

Sharon folded her arms. "What choice do you have? And I do have a passport. We went to Europe last year."

"You drive me . . . "

"I know . . . crazy."

Larry's mouth flew open. "YOU'RE NOT GOING TO TAKE HER AND LEAVE ME BEHIND?"

"Lower your voice! I don't have a choice, Larry!"

Larry's face twisted up.

"Oh, don't start crying, baby. You can come, too," said Sharon.

"Really?" said Larry. "Okay, let's order the tickets!"

"NO. Both of you can't come back with me. And Larry *you* would need a passport, too." said James

"I *have* a passport! I got it when we went to visit my grandparents!"

"Passports or no passports they're going to let you just walk into the country and say, hey, here to see the pyramids."

Sharon shrugged her shoulders, "Basically, yes, you can walk right into the country. We already have our passports and James you already have your visa. All we have to do is land at the airport and apply for a tourist visa. We get thirty days to screw around in the country, and then we leave."

"How do you know stuff like this?"

"I read a lot."

"Right! Well, it doesn't matter. We can't all go. What will your parents say?" said James.

"The same thing your mother will say when she finds out we're taken a plane to the other side of the world," Sharon responded. "WHEN YOU GET HOME I'M GOING TO KILL YOU AND AFTER THAT I'M NEVER LETTING OUT OF MY SIGHT AGAIN!"

"It will never work!"

"Yes . . . it . . . will!" said Sharon. "Boys are so slow. Larry will call his mother and tell her he wants to spend the night with you. He says he'll be coming home to get some clothes, or video games, or whatever. You tell your mother that you're going over to Larry's house to spend the night. That way you've covered each other's tracks. You meet up outside and then meet me. We drive to Dulles. By the time they discover we're gone we will have landed in Egypt. We can call from Cairo. Yes, they're going to be pissed but what can they do? I don't know what's going on but it's obviously important if your father is in danger. Now let's order the tickets! We can do it!"

James looked at Larry who was nodding his head so hard it was about to fly off. "It will work, James."

James looked down. "Neither of you get it," he said. "It's *dangerous*."

"All the more reason that we go along. Wouldn't you like some friends with you when things start going down?" asked Sharon.

"I don't want you to get hurt."

"We won't get hurt, James. It's almost eight o'clock. If we're going to do it we have to start . . . *now*!"

She turned to Larry. "Call your mother and ask if you can spend the night with James. I'll order the tickets." She flopped down in front of the computer and James gave her the password. "What airline did you use?"

She quickly accessed the page. After Sharon had typed in the ticket information for three to Cairo the price appeared.

James gasped. "$4,500 dollars!"

"We're buying tickets *three hours* in advance! What did you expect?"

"I don't know. But $4,500! Oh, my god."

"Why are you so upset? It's my money! Look over the information and help me make sure everything is correct. We will only have one chance at this.

James scanned the page. "It's one way!" he said.

"Yeah, we don't enough money for round-trip tickets."

"We'll be stranded in Egypt."

"No, we won't. We can get back home. Our parents will send us money for the return trip tickets."

She turned to Larry. "What did your mother say?"

"She said it's okay to spend the night."

"Good. Go say goodnight to Mrs. Adams, go home, get your stuff but do not come back over here. Understand?"

Larry ran to the door.

"Wait a minute. Don't you want to know where to meet?"

"Oh . . . yeah."

"Meet up with James down the street and walk over to the bus stop on Highland. I'll pick you up there."

He ran to the door.

"Larry!"

"*WHAT?*"

"Don't run out of here like the house is on fire. Mrs. Adams will think something's wrong."

"Okay, okay." He left and they listened at the door while he went downstairs. They could hear him say goodnight to James' mother and the front door open and close.

Sharon went to the bed. "Is this everything?"

"I think so."

She zipped up the backpack, took them to the window, and threw it outside.

"What did you do that for?"

"James, we have to hurry. We're already out of time. When was the last time you flew? We'll be at the airport forever. You can't just walk onto the plane! And besides you can't go downstairs with those. What would your mother say? And what would you say? "Oh, I'm going over to Larry's FOR A WEEK, MOM!"

"We need to print out the boarding passes and then I need to go home," she continued, going to the computer and hitting print. "Give me fifteen minutes, then go downstairs, and go to the kitchen to get a drink. Take your cell phone. I'll call you pretending to be Larry. Tell your mother he wants you to spend the night. Then walk outside, pick up your bags and join Larry. Call and I'll pretend you're a girlfriend. Ask me to come over and spend the night. I'll ask mom. She won't care. She never does."

The last boarding pass came out of the printer.

He hung back.

"What's wrong?" Sharon asked.

"I don't want to lie to my mom."

"James if this is as bad as you say it is, you don't have a choice. She won't let you go if you tell her what's going on. She'll understand why you did it when you call from Egypt and explain. Okay?"

"Okay."

Sharon opened the door. "It will be fine. It'll work," she said. She left and suddenly like a storm had quickly passed, he was alone.

James stood for a moment, then went and turned off his computer. He waited for the time Sharon had indicated and walked downstairs. He went to the kitchen and just as he was opening the refrigerator his cell phone rang.

"Hey."

"This is Larry," said Sharon. "Can you come over and spend the night. We can call *girls*!"

"Hey, Larry." I don't know. Let me ask my mom."

He dropped the phone to his side. "Hey, mom. Would it be okay if I went over to Larry's and spent the night?"

"Sure, honey."

He put the receiver back to his ear. "She said okay."

"Alright, I'll see you in a few minutes." And Sharon hung up the phone.

James walked into the living room where his mother was sitting watching TV. She looked up at him. "Have fun, sweetheart. If you need anything call."

He had the overwhelming urge to tell her everything and they could go to Egypt together. But all he said was okay and walked to the door. His hand was on the knob when he turned back.

"Mom?"

"Yes, honey?"

"I love you."

She smiled. "I love you too, sweetheart."

Five minutes later he had retrieved his bags and joined Larry on the sidewalk.

"Ready?"

Larry nodded enthusiastically. James called Sharon's number as they walked along and the final part of the plan fell into place.

It didn't take them long to reach the bus stop on Highland and a few minutes later Sharon pulled up in her car.

They quickly loaded everything into the trunk and took off. Sharon drove out of Arlington at a normal speed but once on the toll road to the airport she began to speed.

"Aren't you going a little fast?" said James.

"We're not going to make it if I don't. Just help me look for cops."

It turned out that cops were the least of their worries. An accident halfway to the airport caused them to lose fifteen minutes.

"We're not going to make it," James said.

"Yes, we are. Just hold on."

Once past the crash Sharon hit the gas again and ten minutes later they swung into the airport. Sharon dropped them off and went to leave the car in the extended parking lot. Then she rejoined them and they dashed into the terminal and through the concourse to the gate. The attendant was getting ready to walk away when Sharon, who was in the lead, ran up to her.

"Is this the flight to Cairo?"

"Yes, but you're too late. The shuttle left ten minutes ago."

"Please, we've got to get on that plane!"

"I'm sorry but there . . ."

"You don't understand!" said Sharon gasping for breath.

"What?" the attendant asked.

"Our mother!" Sharon blurted out. "Our mother . . . our mother is in the State Department she is assigned to the embassy in Cairo she was bitten by a snake she'll be dead by the time we get there but we have to try and make it to say our last goodbyes my brothers are devastated please don't make it worse for them. *We have to get on that plane . . .!*

The attendant looked at James and Larry. James was staring at Sharon with his mouth open but Larry suddenly put his hand to his face and starting sobbing "Oh, mama!"

"Okay, honey," said the attendant, sympathetically. "I'll see if they can hold the plane."

She went to the phone and ten minutes later they were on a shuttle out to the runway.

"Nice save," Sharon said to Larry.

"Thanks!" Larry replied.

"Yeah," said James. "Considering our brother is Chinese."

Sharon shrugged her shoulders. "He's adopted."

The shuttle eased into its parking space and they quickly got off and ran to the security check in. It was so late no one else was in line.

As they were going through the ropes James suddenly froze. The talisman! It was in his backpack!

"I can't go through?"

Sharon ran back. "What do you mean?"

"I . . . I can't go through."

"Why not?"

"I just can't."

"Listen! I just told the biggest lie in the history of the world not to mention I'm paying for this trip, not to mention I broke all the speed limits getting here. Now! You're going through security and we're going to Cairo!" She slipped under the ropes behind James and pushed him through until he came to the attendant at one of the metal detectors.

"Please remove the contents of your pocket, any metal objects and your shoes," the man said without emotion.

James reluctantly placed the backpack on the belt and put everything else in a plastic tray. He watched the backpack as it disappeared into the scanner. He held his breath as he walked through and stopped on the other side. The woman who was watching the monitor called her supervisor over and they stood there looking at the screen. The monitor was malfunctioning.

"What's going on with this?"

"It was having problems this morning I believe."

The screen suddenly cleared as the backpack slipped by. But the supervisor had seen something inside.

The supervisor looked up and motioned James over.

"Could you open your backpack, please."

It was all over.

James unzipped the bag and the man rummaged through its contents until he found the talisman.

"Could you tell me what this is?"

"I . . ."

Sharon walked up behind them. "James, what are you doing with that stupid thing? Will you never grow up? Sorry," she said, looking at the security guard. "It's part of a toy he had as a kid. It doesn't matter. Just throw it away. They're holding the plane for us!"

"No . . . !" said James. "I . . ."

"It's okay," the man said to the Sharon. "Let them through."

James was shaking as he put on his shoes and picked up his stuff. As they quickly made their way onto the plane Sharon asked, "What is that thing?"

"I can't . . ."

"I know, I know. You can't tell me!"

They got on board and quickly found their seats. Everyone was glaring at them.

"Sorry, sorry," said Sharon to the passengers. "Dying mother."

Once settled, the plane began to move, backing up and taxiing to the runway. Once they were in the air and a flight attendants had given them safety instructions one of them came to them and said how sorry she was about their mother.

"Thank you," Sharon said. "Can you tell me when we can get some food?"

Somewhere over the Atlantic, after they had all fallen asleep, Larry suddenly woke up, lurched forward and loudly proclaimed: "Base 2!"

There was an immediate chorus of "SHHHH!" coming from all around them in the semi-darkness of the plane's cabin. Mercifully, Sharon did not wake up and remained gently snoring by Larry's side.

James, however, came immediately awake. He turned to Larry and grabbed his arm. "What's wrong?"

"Base 2."

"Base 2? What are you talking about?"

"Base 2. It's binary."

"What's binary?"

"The paper you showed me. It's a binary code. But it's using two unknown symbols. Do you still have the paper?"

"It's in the overhead. I don't think I can get it without waking up Sharon."

"I can do it," Larry said.

"It's in the pocket of my jacket."

Larry stood up and leaned across Sharon's seat. He opened the overhead and fumbled around until he grabbed what he thought was James' jacket. Instead, it was the pink jacket the old woman in the seat behind them had worn onto the plane.

He stuffed it back inside and tried again. Finally, he found what he was looking for and pulled it down. Then he flopped back into his seat. They both looked at Sharon expecting her to wake up but she only mumbled something unintelligible, twisted around, and went back to sleep.

James removed the paper and turned on the overhead light.

"See?" said Larry. There are only two symbols and they appear randomly across the page. Like the binary code."

"You mean the binary code a computer uses?"

"Yes. You know." And he rolled off: "11000101111100111101110000111100 . . ."

"Okay, okay. And what does the binary code do exactly?" he asked.

"It encodes the data we put into the computers. People use the decimal system – one to ten – because we have ten fingers and that's how everybody learned the decimal system based on 10. The computer can't do that. It's all binary – two numbers – zeros and ones. All data stored in a computer is based on code strings of 0 and 1. When the computer reads the sequences of those two numbers we see pictures and words on our monitors. Get it?"

"I guess. But it doesn't matter." He looked down at the paper. "What you're saying is this is some kind of information, some kind of data. But we can't read it because we don't know what the two binary numbers are, or whatever these symbols are anyway?"

"Yeah. But what do you think they are?"

"I have no idea.

Larry's eyes got big. "It could be anything. It could be the map to a treasure!

"Or it could be something bad.

"Why do you say that? Don't you want to know what it says?"

"Maybe."

"If we had the computer it was written for we could do it," Larry said.

James sat back in his seat and looked out at the darkness beyond the window.

"Where did you see these anyway?" Larry asked him.

"I saw them in Egypt." James quietly replied.

Nine hours later the plane touched down in Cairo.

CHAPTER 9

Eric knew the direction they followed when they left the excavation area because there was a depression right before you would pull onto the highway. Right after the van hit the bump he tilted to his right. The van had turned left; they were heading north toward Cairo. He sat hunched in the second seat between the two men with rifles. It was hot in the van, even with the windows down, and the smell of sweat and unwashed bodies was strong.

Time had no meaning and there was no way of knowing how long they drove before the leader said one word: "Here."

Eric felt himself tilt left. This meant they were probably heading due east across the Nile and toward the Red Sea. To Eric's knowledge, there was nothing out there except small, scattered villages. They were taking him away from the dig, away from Cairo, away from everything and everyone and making sure he would stay hidden or worse.

He didn't know exactly what was going on – yet – or what his captor's plans were. He had known from the beginning there were people in the dig that were not archeologists: their lack of experience was very obvious. He had assumed they were part of the Egyptian military making sure nothing was stolen. Now he wasn't so sure.

There was one person on his team who wasn't an archeologist, either: Philip Harrington. Eric had been with the CIA for many years. He had been recruited right after college to observe, while on various excavations in different countries, anything he saw that was suspicious or out of the ordinary and report to Washington. He wasn't a secret agent, or anything that dramatic: just an observer. This dig had been suspicious and out of the ordinary from the beginning. Philip had been assigned to work with Eric and be his liaison with Washington. He had not met Philip at the agency, but when they did meet he had liked him immediately and, more importantly, had trusted him. This was why when James needed to be sent home, Eric had begged Philip to take him and make sure he was safely back with his mother.

He had kept Philip up-to-date on everything that was happening in the dig and everything else that had been going on, including his work with Professor Stevens. But tonight, when the pieces of the puzzle had fallen into place, there was no way to let Philip know. The carvings had revealed an evil that had befallen the world before history began: horrific events hard to believe. The one thing Eric couldn't understand was why something that had happened at the dawn of human existence could have any bearing on mankind now at the beginning of the 21st century. But it had to have a bearing or why else was he being kidnapped. He had gotten too close to something, but what?

The wall seemed to indicate some kind of power source. Was it the disc the creature was holding in his hands, a seeming gift to the man figure on his left? Was that what they were looking for? The wall did not say where to find it or how to use it as far as Eric could tell. At the moment this, like so many other things, was unknown. There were many panels he had barely glanced at.

A part of his mind refused to accept what his eyes were telling him. It had to be a hoax. But if it was a hoax, it was the greatest deception ever conceived.

His mind jumped to James. He had found something in that room in the excavation. Eric was sure of it. He knew the pieces lying on the sand when he was helping James out of the room were papyrus. Was that all? Papyrus could not carry any danger surely. Had it been tainted with poison thousands of years before? Again there was no way to know.

They had been so close his whole life. The divorce had caused a wall of anger to grow up between them. A wall he now regretted more than ever. He missed his son, and truth be told, he missed his wife but didn't know how to get back to them. Regardless of how difficult it was to have a meaningful conversation with James, he should have stopped on the road to the airport this morning and demanded to know what James had found. Whatever he had touched, god forbid it was a part of what was happening now. Eric was grateful for one thing: James was safely home in Arlington. Whatever happened he didn't have to worry about his son. And he had called ahead to tell Maria that James was sick and he should see a doctor. If it was something like poison they would find it.

He felt himself dozing on and off while the van bumped along the road until it suddenly turned once more to the right before coming to a halt. The doors opened and he felt the guard on his left grab his arm and begin to pull him, stumbling, out of the van. The other soldier joined them and together they guided him forward. He stumbled along for several minutes until they stopped. He heard a knock on a door followed by a grating sound as the door was opened. He was marshaled inside and the door was closed and locked behind them.

The van had been uncomfortable but it was nothing compared to the heat and lack of air inside the building. Eric was thirsty and hungry and wondered what was waiting for him here at the end of his journey. He didn't have long to wait.

They walked forward until he was pushed inside a room where his restraints and blindfold were removed. There was a pale, naked light bulb hanging from the ceiling whose light was so dim it barely illuminated the small bare room made of mud bricks. A cot held up by a rusted bed frame and a bucket were the only accessories. There was a hole at the top of the facing wall, presumably a window. It had no need of bars. It so small a grown man would never be able to crawl through it.

The guards withdrew leaving Eric alone with their leader.

"I hope the accommodations are to your liking, doctor," he said.

"Exactly what I had expected," replied Eric, sitting down on the cot. "Would you like to tell me why you've kidnapped me and brought me to this place. I was invited by your government to help your country in the greatest archeological discovery since Tut. This is quite a display of hospitality."

The man chuckled. "King Tut." He walked into the middle of the room and looked down at Eric. "King Tut will fade in the world's eyes when the true meaning of this discovery has been revealed. And you, good doctor, are going to help us in that revelation."

"After what you've done to me, I will never willingly help you do anything."

"Oh, I think you will. In good time," he said. "Well, I won't keep you from your rest. Someone will bring you food and something to drink momentarily. We wouldn't want you to die from hunger or anything." He paused at the door. "And in the morning, everything will be explained to you. Sleep well."

Eric watched him go and then got up and went to the window. He could see the night sky, a few stars, and the tops of dark masses across the way that had to be buildings: but buildings where no lights burned. He walked back to the cot and removed his shirt, sitting down again.

He heard shuffling outside the door. A small man opened it carrying a tray. He didn't look at Eric but set the tray down on the cot next to him. There was a plate of grilled meat that turned out to be lamb along with some stewed vegetables. It also contained a large pitcher of water. The water wasn't cold but it was water and Eric drank it down. As the man was leaving the room Eric asked for more water but the man did not reply, instead closing the door and locking it behind him without ever saying a word.

Eric tasted the meat and ate some of the vegetables but the food was salty which would only make his thirst that much more difficult to bear. He ate only enough to alleviate his hunger and slowly drank the rest of the water. Then he lay down to try and sleep.

When he awoke, the tiny cell was bathed in bright sunlight that was shining directly in through the little window. He got up and shading his eyes, looked outside. A man appeared briefly on the roof of the building directly across from him and then disappeared. He knew he was in a village of some kind because he could hear the early morning activity on the street as people got up and came outside to start their day.

The sun was directly in front of him so he was facing east. But this information was of little use to him. He returned to the cot and waited for his captor's next move. When he had sat for a while he heard the same scuffling of feet outside his door and the same sound of a lock being thrown aside as the night before.

The little man who had brought his food then now reappeared with breakfast. Eric didn't wait to even look at the food but held up the first water pitcher and asked, in Arabic, for more water to be brought. The man blinked but gave no indication that he would bring what had been requested. He placed the tray down in the same spot he had placed it before and retreated.

Eric drank out of the new pitcher and turned to his food. He was very hungry and as before the food was tasty. The meal also included a cup of strong black coffee. He ate everything on the plate and drank all of the water but avoided the coffee. He was hot enough without making it worse.

The man returned and to Eric's surprise carried another large container of water. After he had gathered the dishes he waited for Eric to drink again then took the water jug, placed it on the tray with the other items, and disappeared, locking the door behind him once more.

The morning was still young but already the heat was building. By noon, it would be unbearable. Was that the plan? Whatever they were trying to get out of him they would get by roasting him alive?

He leaned back and rested his head against the wall and waited once more.

He must have dozed off because the sound of someone calling the faithful to midday prayer outside his window brought him fully awake. The bolt of the door was suddenly thrown. It opened and a man appeared, an Egyptian, very well dressed even in the heat. He was of medium height with a slim build. His black hair was neatly combed and the brown eyes looked out of a face that showed the scars of childhood acne. His white cotton shirt was damp from perspiration but his linen slacks were neat and tailored reaching down to a pair of polished black shoes. His linen jacket was slung across his arm and his hand was holding a briefcase.

He came inside, staring unblinking at Eric, and stood across from him. He reached into his back pocket and produced a handkerchief with which he mopped the perspiration off his forehead. A soldier came in with a chair for the visitor, placed it beside him, and silently withdrew.

The man carefully draped his jacket across the back of the chair and sat down. Eric expected him to speak in Arabic but when he did speak, it was in perfect English.

"Good morning, Dr. Adams," he said.

"For you maybe," Eric replied, "As you can see it's not so good for me."

"Your . . . ," he chose his words carefully, "invitation was unfortunate but necessary. I believe you would not have come any other way."

"I don't go in for abductions as a general rule. So yes, I would not have come with you any other way."

"I'm sure you are wondering why you have been brought here."

"You are correct. I am a guest of the Egyptian government, as I have already told your co-conspirators, and was invited to Egypt to assist in the analysis and interpretation of the discovery south of Thebes. Is this your government's idea of hospitality?"

"This has nothing to do with the government."

"Really? I'm so surprised."

"Allow me to introduce myself. My name is Amil. Like you I am a scientist; an astrophysicist. I am an Egyptian by birth but I was educated in England and also worked in America for a time at Cal Tech." He paused and pursed his lips. "The organization I work for needs your help. If you can provide the information we need you will be allowed to leave."

"An astrophysicist. Now *that* is fascinating. What would an astrophysicist be doing at an ancient archeological site?"

Amil ignored the question. "You will be allowed to leave without harm," he repeated.

"Leave without harm," said Eric and he smiled. "You've already caused harm. And as for leaving and letting bygones be bygones we both know that will never happen. For one thing, I would go directly to the authorities and tell them what you have done to me. So let's just cut the crap as we say in America and put the cards on the table. You will never let me out of here alive. So why should I help you do anything?"

"Because."

Eric furrowed his brow and looked up at his visitor. "Because why?"

"There are people you care about."

Eric felt a stab of fear but kept his voice steady. "Like who?"

"At the moment, I am not at liberty to say."

"I see. So an empty threat."

"Not empty I assure you. I came here because I know about you, and as a fellow scientist, I respect what you do. I asked to talk to you first. I want to help you avoid any discomfort. Any pain. But in order to do that you have to help me," he said

"What exactly are you fishing for?"

Amil was confused by the saying, "Fishing for?"

"What do you want me to tell you?"

"We need three things." He got up, reached into his jacket pocket, and turned to Eric.

"Tell me what this is." He dropped a piece of metal into Eric's hand. It was what looked to be one-third of a circle with a hole off center and symbols, like circuits, covering its surface. One of the sides was serrated. He felt himself go tense.

"I have no idea," he said calmly.

"But you've seen something like it before."

"Yes."

"On the wall. In the excavation."

"Yes."

"But you have no idea what it is for."

"None," Eric answered.

"Can you guess what it might be?"

"No," Eric lied.

"Do the wall inscriptions explain what it is and what happened to the two other pieces shown on the wall that complete the circle?"

"No."

Eric handed it back and Amil seated himself again and studied Eric for a moment.

"So what's the second thing you need?" Eric asked.

"I believe you have completed the translation of the inscriptions. We need you to tell us what you know."

"Why do you think I've completed the translation?"

"That doesn't matter. What matters is you have completed your work and you will now transcribe what you have found."

"I haven't completed anything. I was in the dig last night still trying to figure out what it all means."

"I'm afraid that is a lie."

"It's the truth. Go ask your fearless leader."

"Fearless leader?"

"Raza. He found me there as I was leaving and he was coming in."

"You refuse to let me help you I see." He paused and then slowly said: "Perhaps Professor Stevens would be of more assistance. We could always ask *him*."

Eric felt his jaw clench. "Professor Stevens is a doddering old fool, half out of his mind and totally discredited by every member of his profession. He would not be able to tell you anything that would be of any use to you or that you could trust. Believe me, when I tell you that he will not be able to help you."

"Then why were you corresponding with him so intently? Let's see," and he took a handful of papers out of his briefcase and begin to read:

'I need you to verify my own translations. Some of the patterns, the groupings of the symbols, are different than usual.

I understand. How are they different?
The pattern of how they are presented on the wall?
Are they paintings or carvings?
Carvings.
Can you send me an image of the wall?

And later the Professor Stevens replies, '*The people rose up: There was war (rebellion?) against the gods. The stars fell (were?) silent . . .*'

"So he was right. You were hacking into our correspondence. Those emails are not what you think. Professor Stevens was one of my favorite teachers while I was in university. I heard through various colleagues that he was struggling with depression and health issues from the stress of his theories being rejected by others in our field. I reached out to him to help him take his mind off his troubles. That's all. The things I reference in the emails were all made up of bits and pieces of what I was working on at the time. It was all gibberish."

"I see." Amil shifted in his chair. "It's odd then that he told us just the opposite."

"He told you nothing. You've never even spoken to him."

"I'm afraid we have and he did. It took some convincing if you will, but he did tell us a lot. Unfortunately, he is withholding the information we *really* need from him. That's where you come in and that is my third and final request. That you impress on the Professor how important it is that he give us the information we need."

"How would you like me to contact the Professor; telepathy?"

"That won't be necessary, Dr. Adams. The Professor is just down the hall.

Eric studied the man's face trying to discern if this was true or a ruse to draw him out. The eyes staring back at him revealed nothing at all.

"Professor Stevens is in New York."

The man rose, opened the door of the cell, and stepped outside. Eric heard the sound of footsteps and another door opening. Two guards came into the room and lifted him up, bound his hands in front of him and led him from the room and down a narrow hallway with doors on either side. They came to another cell whose door stood ajar. Amil walked into the room and the guards pushed Eric inside. He turned to Eric and said: "As you can see, we are taking very good care of your friend."

He stepped aside and Eric drew in his breath. Professor Stevens lay slumped on the floor, his head resting against the wall. He was bare except for his underwear and his face was caked in blood.

Eric sank down by his side. "Oh, god, Professor. Are you alright?"

The Professor stirred and turned to his former student. "Eric? Is that you, Eric?"

"Yes, it's me. I'm so sorry I brought you into this."

"Sorry?" he smiled faintly. "For what? You've validated everything I have been saying for years. You don't know what it's like for people to call you crazy and laugh at you behind your back because you're trying to show them the truth. You're the last person I would wish to feel sorry about anything. You've saved me, Eric. Saved my reputation. Saved my life. Everything I said was true."

CHAPTER 10

Eric angrily turned to their captors. "He needs a doctor!"

"He needs to tell us what we need to know and he can have a doctor," said Amil calmly. "Until then he can die as slowly as he cares to."

Suddenly Professor Stevens, whose head was resting against the wall of his cell, began to laugh loudly.

Eric turned, "Professor . . ."

Professor Stevens looked up at the man above them. "Don't let them fool you, Eric. They're not going to let me die. If they wanted me dead they would have killed me long ago. They want something I've got, something in my head, something they need."

He looked at Eric. "They've brought you here to see if you can give them more information about the inscriptions on the wall . . . and to use you as leverage to make me talk. But death? That's the last thing on their minds."

"There are worse things than death, my dear Professor," Amil's voice came out in a hiss. "Much worse."

He turned abruptly and left the room. The guards followed, shutting and locking the door behind them.

Eric turned to Professor Stevens. There was nothing in this cell: no bed, no furniture. He half lifted his old teacher into a sitting position on the floor leaning him against the wall, making him as comfortable as possible. The professor closed his eyes.

"Are you in pain, Professor?"

"No . . . well . . . yes somewhat. But it's nothing I can't handle."

Eric looked around the bare cell. "There's nothing I can do. There's nothing here, not even water."

"It's alright. They gave me a little food and some water before they brought me here." He looked at Eric. "Who are these people? What are they after?"

"I don't know. It's something in the excavation." Eric looked down. "The wall speaks of things, things that happened long ago. Those things were evil. but I'm still trying to figure out what it has to do with us here and now, although I have an idea.

But . . . I believe everything is connected to the disc, the carving in the middle of the wall. This man Amil showed me one-third of the actual disc just now, a piece of dirty metal."

"Like in the drawing I sent you."

"Yes. The drawing you sent shows one-third of the disc. I believe that's what they're after."

"They have more."

"What do you mean?"

"They have a second part of the disc. They took it from me," said the Professor.

Eric twisted around and sat down, his back to the wall next to the Professor. "Where did you find it?" he asked in disbelief. "How did they know you had it?"

"They were hacking into our emails and they put two and two together. I think they have been watching me for some time because of my work and what I have been saying all these years. I'm sure they thought I was a crackpot like everyone else did but they weren't sure so they monitored my correspondence. I suspected someone was watching me. I just didn't know how far to go once you had contacted me because I was desperate to find out what you were seeing in the dig, what you were translating.

If I had known I was putting you in danger I would have stopped immediately. I just never thought I would ever find any concrete evidence, other than what I had found myself, that my theories were correct. In fact, I had given up ever convincing anyone that what I had discovered was valid. I thought I would die with people believing I was just a senile, delusional old man.

And then one day I turned on my computer to find an email from my favorite student: an email that opened the door to proving what I had been saying for years was true. At first, I thought you had stumbled onto a tomb of some kind. But when you sent me the symbols I was dumbstruck and found I couldn't breathe from excitement.

I told myself to stay calm and help you as much as I possibly could. But the longer our correspondence went on the more dangerous it became. I made a mistake by sending you the drawing of the portion of the disk I had in my possession. They saw it and knew. They came to my apartment to take me. I thought I was a step ahead of them. I had planned my escape but didn't help. They anticipated my moves and caught me in the museum. There was a place there where I planned to hide the relic and hopefully get a message to you where it was hidden. But before I could they took it from me."

The Professor took a ragged breath. "As to how I found the relic can only be described as the greatest stroke of luck, fate, or a miracle; possibly all three. As you know I worked with the museum for years in New York; went on numerous excavations for them. I took my students on field trips to the museum if you recall."

Eric nodded.

"The museum's collection is small but important in its own way. I was so involved in the work at the museum they allowed me to handle the artifacts at will, with no one bothering me even though I wasn't a curator.

A small statue of a seated god that I had never seen before was put on display. Its base was covered with hieroglyphics. One day I was in the exhibition area where the statue was on view. It was after hours and I opened the case to look at a sandstone fragment that was also there. At random I picked up the statue. I was turning it around in my hands when I saw something on its base. The bottom edge on the back had been broken off but on one side there was part of a hieroglyphic that I had never seen before. There was only a tiny fragment left. But the carver who had done it had deviated from style and it didn't match the other symbols. It was of a geometric shape.

I felt like I had stumbled onto something unique. But I put my thoughts aside and told myself it could have been damaged when the statue had been broken. I was busy with my teaching and other things were on my mind, so I put it back into the case and left it there.

I left it. But it didn't leave me. It stayed in the back of my mind and I would think about it at random times and tell myself to go back and look again. Finally, one day I did. I picked it up and studied the base. Nothing, of course, had changed. The mark was still there. But now I looked at the statue itself.

The little god was seated on his throne in the same pose you've seen a million times: rigid, staring straight ahead, arms flat on his legs. But this time, I looked at his face and was surprised to see that it looked like the work of Armarna – the city of the heretic. The face also looked like Akhenaten's statues with big slanting eyes and elongated features. I went to the front of the case and looked at the information on its card. It said it was a statuette from the Old Kingdom. How could that be? Akhenaten's reign was in the New Kingdom. Surely the artwork had been mislabeled.

And . . . how had the museum acquired it? I didn't want to draw attention to what I was seeing until I knew for sure if there was anything more important than a mislabeled artifact. So I waited and at random asked one of the younger curators about the piece and its origin.

He was busy and told me it had arrived the year before in a box of fragments that were purchased by the museum. The crate was still being examined and he directed me where I could find it. I went to the storeroom and it was sitting in a corner in the back of the room; obviously not considered of much importance. I opened the case and, after hours of sifting through what amounted to a box of shattered sandstone pieces with the usual markings, I came to the same conclusion as the rest of the staff: the statuette was the most important piece and the box contained nothing further of importance. I was getting ready to seal the crate back up when I saw something odd: a piece of metal, oddly shaped with strange markings on its surface. I picked it up and looked into the circle it contained.

What happened next can only be described as life changing. The metal began to glow and then . . . it began to download information into my head. I know it sounds insane but that is exactly what happened. It took maybe ten seconds. Then it went dark. I stumbled back as I became dizzy, nauseous, and disoriented. What had just happened to me? I sat down, trying to catch my breath.

I tried to calm myself. After a few minutes, I felt better but I was scared because I knew something had happened to me that doesn't happen every day. Something unknown and I wasn't sure what that unknown would lead me to."

"Did you call anyone to help you?"

"No I didn't. At first, it never occurred to me and, as I said, it was after hours. Even if I had called no one would have probably come."

"Did you tell anyone afterwards?"

"No. I thought about it when I had finally gotten my wits about me again. I could have told the director of the museum or, at least, the head curator of the Egyptian collection. But I did neither. Something, I can't explain it, told me not to. If anyone found out I would never see the talisman again. It would simply disappear into a vault or worse the government would get wind of it and it would disappear forever. Somehow I couldn't let that happen especially after what occurred next.

After a time I tried to stand but when I got up and started to walk the dizziness began again and I felt hot like I had a fever. I took a couple of steps and fell, hurting one of my knees. The pain was bad and as I sat there holding it something came over my vision. At first, it was a blur but it quickly began to come into focus and I could see what it was: symbols racing across my vision like one of those old jerky, silent movies where you can almost see the frames going by.

"Now I was truly frightened, breathing hard while my heart raced. But as I sat there I began to calm down and the flow of the symbols began to slow down as well. I willed myself to relax and as I did they became so slow that I could see them plainly. After a time, they faded from my vision and I told myself that was all that was going to happen.

Then, after I had stumbled to my feet once more, I did something I thought I would never do: I stole the relic. I put it in my pocket, replaced the cover on the crate making sure it looked as if no one had disturbed it and I went home.

I still felt unwell. I went to the bathroom to splash water on my face. My eyes looked funny but it barely registered on my mind. I was so exhausted. I collapsed into bed without even eating dinner. In the night it would come in waves: nausea, fever, and when I would open my eyes in the darkness, the symbols would flow across my vision.

The next morning I woke up and reached for the talisman. I had not even taken off my clothes before going to bed. It was still in my pocket. I held it up, expecting it to do something. But it did nothing. I turned it over and over in my hand, took it to the window and looked outside through the hole: nothing. It was as if it had downloaded the data into my head, like a computer, and now it was empty.

The day is a blur. At some point, I placed the relic on the table next to my computer. I came around and turned on the computer but something was wrong. It looked like it was malfunctioning so I rebooted it again and again. Nothing helped. That's when I noticed the talisman. It looked odd and when I picked it up it was hot to the touch and the computer was going crazy. I looked through the hole but again nothing. I took it to the other side of the room and laid it down. When I returned to the computer it was functioning normally, as if nothing had happened.

Besides what it did to me, I believe it also has the power to connect and communicate with our own technology. I had always believed the earth, at the dawn of time, was visited by an alien race, which somehow interacted with early humans. Was the relic from that? I believed it was and I knew I had to tell others in our field; an alien race had come to us at the beginning of recorded time. I tried but they were blind to it and I couldn't show them what I had found. I just couldn't. I was afraid it would be taken away from me. The result was years of ridicule and people telling me I had lost my mind, had dementia, or gone crazy."

Eric sat silent while the Professor concluded his story. "Eric, are you alright. I know this sounds insane even now . . ."

"No . . . not anymore. I couldn't believe what the wall was telling me. But I'm not concerned with the wall or what they did or anything right now. Your description of what happened to you . . ."

"Yes."

Eric turned and held his mouth close to the Professor's ear: "When you went into the bathroom at home after you have found the relic, you said your face looked funny. How . . . how did it look funny?"

The Professor looked at Eric. "My eyes were dilated to an enormous degree. I looked like something evil. The pupils were so large the iris were almost completely gone."

Eric closed his eyes and hung his head.

"Eric, what's wrong?"

"I think my son has the final piece; the final part of the disc."

The Professor sucked in his breath. "Oh my god!" the Professor whispered. "How do you know? How did it come to him?"

"He found it in the dig."

"Tell me what the wall says. Tell me what the disk is for?" the Professor entreated.

"It's fantastic, the parts I can figure out. I don't understand it all myself." He looked down at the floor. "I believe . . . I believe they're trying to figure out how to make contact with the other world – the alien world – the creatures who came here before."

"That's insane. That's mad. Why . . .?"

"I don't know. But we have to try to get out of here."

"How?"

"Dr. Mohamed. I have to try and get a message to Dr. Mohamed."

"Who is he?"

"The director of the Ministry of Antiquities. He doesn't know what's going on. I'm sure of it. He can help us but I have to get word to him first."

"At that moment the door opened without warning and Amil stepped back into the room followed by four soldiers.

"Shall we go?" was all he said.

"As if we have a choice?" said Eric. "Where are you taking us now?"

"You'll see."

They threw their clothes at them and Eric helped Professor Stevens get dressed. Once that was accomplished they were quickly bound and blindfolded, marched out of the room, and taken to a waiting van. In the distance, Eric heard someone call for the *Asr*, the afternoon prayer. The van pulled away from the building and the next journey began.

When the van finally stopped an hour later they were forced out and pushed forward until they found themselves inside some kind of building. They heard the swish of an electronic door and once inside of that were stunned to discover they were in an air-conditioned space.

The cold air made the Eric and the Professor gasp and gulp in the cool air.

Their blindfolds were torn off and they found themselves in what looked like some kind of office building but one whose windows were blacked out. They were marched down a short hallway and through double doors where they were confronted with a large room full of men who sat behind desks aligned in rows, each with a computer monitor in front of him. The men made no attempt to talk to them or acknowledge them. They simply stared at them without expression. Eric noticed a room full of computer servers on one side and dry erase boards on which some of the symbols from the wall had been written. They didn't have much time to see anything else but were taken through double doors at the back of the room and into another hallway. Momentarily they were ushered inside individual rooms and the doors locked behind them.

Eric was alone once more. The room was unlike his first prison. This one was clean with a new bunk, a toilet, and running water. He went to the sink and splashed water on his face and washed his hands and torso.

Then he sat down on the bunk. He was so exhausted he could hardly sit upright. He wished they had let him stay with the Professor but that was obviously not something that was going to happen: at least not yet.

"What am I going to do now?" He said to himself as his head leaned back against the wall. Eventually, they brought him food and water. Afterward, he sat, not feeling sleepy, staring into space. He finally laid down and when he awoke a man came with his breakfast. He counted the meals as they were brought to him and roughly discerned that he sat in the room for almost two days.

After the noontime meal on the second day the door opened and a man appeared.

Eric smiled ruefully. "So what took you so long?" He said. "I was expecting you hours ago?"

CHAPTER 11

"Now what?" asked Sharon.

Their plane had landed an hour before and, after going through customs, Sharon and Larry had gotten their temporary visas. Now they were standing in the concourse of the Cairo airport.

"I don't know," said James.

"What do you mean you don't know? We need to find your father. Let's go to where he's staying."

"I don't know where he's staying. We stayed in a hotel room when I came. I'm not even sure where he's been living while he's been here."

"Well, we could start at where he was the last time you saw him. Maybe the hotel would be able to tell us where he's at."

"Maybe," said James. He had no desire to return to where he had been staying on his previous visit. But if all else failed they could go there. Was there anyone else he could ask? There was only one person he could think of – Philip Harrington. And the thought of asking him anything was completely out of the question. If Philip found out he was back in Egypt it would only take a few hours before they would all be on a plane back to America. Plus, like his father, he didn't know where Philip could be located.

"I'm hungry." It was the first time Larry had spoken.

"I am too. We can get something," said James. "But first I want to try and call Mom."

"Yes," said Sharon. "You should get the yelling, screaming, and bloodletting over with as soon as possible."

"Aren't you going to call home?" asked Larry.

"I'll call later. My mother won't even miss me until next week."

James and Larry walked in opposite directions away from Sharon. James dialed the number. The call went through but the phone on the other end rang and rang with no one picking it up. I must have dialed the wrong number, he thought, and carefully dialed again. As before it rang out and stopped. He tried again and again with the same result. He walked back to where Sharon was standing with Larry.

"She didn't answer," he said.

"My mom didn't answer, either," said Larry.

James looked from Larry to Sharon. "Something's wrong."

"How do you know that? She might be sleeping."

"She would have woken up and answered the phone."

"Maybe she's outside with the garbage or feeding the birds."

"We don't feed the birds and I take out the garbage."

"What time is it at home anyway," asked Larry.

"Who knows? I get it confused. We'll try again in a little bit," said Sharon. "It'll be fine, both of you, it'll be fine. You'll see."

"No there's some . . ." James stopped, sucked in his breath in a sharp little grasp, and grabbing them both turned them roughly around and began to push them into a hallway off the main terminal.

"What are you doing?" said Sharon sharply.

"We have to get out of sight!"

"Why? Did you see somebody we could ask about your father?" she said as she tried to pull out of his grip and turn back.

"NOOOO! We have to hide!"

He suddenly began to steer them toward the men's room.

"Whoa! I'M NOT GOING INTO THE MEN'S ROOM PAL, NOT EVEN FOR YOU!"

"God! You're not going to see anything! You're such a girl. Now . . . get . . . in . . . side!" and he pushed them both inside where they scattered into different stalls bolting the doors after them. Luckily no one was using the facilities at that moment so they sat, breathless, and listened.

Momentarily they heard the door slowly creak open. James closed his eyes and prayed. Then . . . there was a sound of a zipper going down and the unmistakable sound of a man using one of the urinals.

He finished and the door opened and closed again with a little tap as he left the room.

"Well, that was lovely!" said Sharon, dryly. "And he didn't even wash his hands."

"Please be quite," said James.

"May I, at least, ask who we're hiding from?"

"Philip Harrington. I thought I saw him in the concourse."

"Who's Philip Harrington?" asked Larry.

"He works with my father: his assistant or something. He was the one who took me home before. If he finds us here we're done for."

They all fell silent and as time passed no one else came into the room.

"We've been sitting here for fifteen minutes," said Sharon finally. "What do you think he's doing out there? Getting ready to break down the door and take us prisoner before we can hurl rolls of flaming toilet paper at him?"

"Okay, okay. Maybe I didn't see him," said James and he unbolted the door to his stall and walked out. "But he could also be waiting for us to come out."

"Fine, I'll go out and see. What does he look like?" asked Sharon.

"He's around 34 or 35, medium height, brown hair. The guy I just saw was wearing shorts and a t-shirt. At least, I think that's what I saw the guy wearing."

"Okay," Sharon said. She slowly opened the door, peeking outside as she did so, and walked out of the room.

After a few minutes, she reappeared and said: "Nothing. No one looks like that out there. There are a couple of women in robes and some men in the concourse but none of them look like you described."

"Okay. I think we should grab a taxi and go into Cairo. If everybody can wait, we can eat when we get to the city. Then, I guess we go to the only place we can go which is the hotel we stayed at before."

They slowly opened the door and peered out. No one was outside the door and Sharon was right; there was no one in the concourse that looked remotely like Philip.

James breathed a sigh of relief and they made their way outside, got a taxi, and piled inside. James told the driver the name of the hotel and without speaking, he put the car in gear and pulled out of the airport parking lot.

As the taxi drove away they didn't notice a second car pull out of the parking lot and follow them.

As they approached the city, Larry leaned out of the window and said: "Wow. Look at that!" Both James and Sharon followed his gaze. The pyramids sat on the horizon dominating everything in the desert around them.

"I never thought I would see anything like that!" Larry said.

"They're amazing," James agreed.

"Did you go to see them, up close I mean, when you were here before?"

"No. There was no time to go to them or much of anything else. Everything happened so quickly and before I knew it I was on a plane back home."

"Do you think we can go and see them before we go back home? Can we?"

"If everything's okay with my father and he doesn't kill me for what I've done, then yes we can go see the pyramids."

By now they were approaching Cairo. The taxi slowed down as the traffic picked up and once the driver had turned off the main road they found themselves in narrow streets amid the bustle of people going to work or opening their stalls in anticipation of the tourists that would be coming soon.

James recognized the area where he had bought his mother's present during his first visit and made a sudden decision. He leaned forward and spoke to the driver: "Can you let us out here, please?"

The car slowed and pulled to the side. They quickly got out of the taxi and stood on the street corner.

"How much?" James asked the driver, who told him the amount.

James pulled out his wallet. "Dang! I don't have enough money." The taxi driver scowled.

"Here," said Sharon rummaging around in her bag. "I'm like the First National Bank of Sharon."

James paid the driver and turned to Sharon. "Thanks."

"You're welcome. Now where can we eat? I'm dying."

"There are restaurants in here. I saw some of them when my dad and I came into this part of town before."

They walked to the opposite corner and down a side street until they came to a little café tucked between two market stalls. "Let's try this one."

They stepped just inside the door and waited. A short heavyset man approached them from the back and directed them to a table against the wall on their left. Most of the early morning clientele were men. They stared after them until they were seated and continued staring until the waiter brought them a menu. He stood waiting while they looked over their choices for breakfast. They didn't notice the man who quietly stood up and exited the café.

"I can't read any of this," said Larry.

"Me either," said Sharon.

"It's Arabic," James said as he turned to the waiter. "Eggs . . . eggs?"

"Yes, yes," said the man in halting English. "Eggs."

"And coffee?"

"Coffee yes," the waiter repeated and he turned and walked away toward the kitchen.

Sharon made a face. "Wow, what kind of eggs do you think we're going to get?" she said.

After about fifteen minutes the man returned bearing a large platter on a tray with their coffee. He sat everything down on the table. The dish was fresh slices of tomatoes with cooked onions, eggs, and spices mixed together.

"Shakshouka," he announced. "Good."

"Okay . . . thanks," said James.

"Could we also have some water?" asked Larry.

"Water," the man repeated and disappeared once again.

They were very hungry but even that could not be the reason the dish tasted so very good. They ate without talking and when the man had returned with the water they ordered another serving of "Shakshouka."

93

Finally, they were full. Sharon paid for their breakfast and they all stepped outside.

"Which way is the hotel?" asked Sharon.

"This way."

"They followed him back to the place where the taxi had dropped them off before. James turned to his left. They walked by several shops until James suddenly stopped and turned around.

"What is it?" said Larry.

James looked back up the street from where they had come and at the buildings on either side. There were a lot of people milling around and he looked at each of them carefully.

"I don't know."

"Do you think someone's following us?" asked Sharon.

"I don't know. I don't think so. I don't know. It's just a feeling. That's all. Let's go."

They walked to the next corner and James pointed ahead. "There it is."

The hotel was small and rather nondescript with only two stories. There were some men standing outside the front door talking.

"I don't think I should go in there."

"Okay, Larry and I will go in," said Sharon. "What do you think I should say?"

"Just ask if they know anything about Eric Adams: where we might find him."

Sharon and Larry walked up to the door and disappeared inside. The lobby was dark and small and smelled of cigarettes. They made their way to the front desk and waited until the man sitting behind it looked up and noticed them.

"Hello. A man named Eric Adams stayed in your hotel a little over a week ago. Do you happen to know where we might find him?" Sharon asked.

The man looked at her for a moment and said in a thick accent: "Did he have a young man with him?"

"Yes, he did."

He got up and made a pretense of looking through the hotel register, turning back a page and looking at the past week's guests.

"Yes. They were here but checked out without leaving any information as to where they were going."

"Do you know by chance, where Eric Adams is staying in Cairo, his apartment, I mean."

"No."

"Okay. Thanks." Sharon and Larry turned to go but were stopped by the man.

"Did his son return to America? To Vir-gin-ia?"

Larry looked at Sharon who glanced back at the man. "No," she said. "I don't know where his son is. I just need to find Eric Adams." And she quickly turned around and taking Larry by the arm they walked back outside and down the street to where James was waiting."

"What happened?

"We need to get out of here.

"Why? What did he say?"

"He remembered your father but asked about you, where you had gone, if you had gone back to Virginia.

"How would he know I was from Virginia? How would he know that?"

They all looked back at the hotel where the men who were on the sidewalk were watching them

"Like I said we need to get out of here," said Sharon.

They began to quickly retrace their steps only glancing back when they had moved several blocks away from the hotel. When they did look back they saw that several of the men who were outside the hotel were now following them.

James looked all around them trying to figure out where to go to lose their pursuers. They darted into a shop that had another door in the back. They quickly walked out the door and found themselves on a small side street. Moving as fast as they could without arousing suspicion they quickly moved down that street into another and another. Nothing seemed to help. However hard they tried they couldn't shake the men following them.

The streets were confusing and James began to panic. Without meaning to he lead them straight back into the street that ran by the hotel. It was only a block away from the corner they were standing on.

"This way," Sharon gasped as they darted across the street into another maze of shops. Suddenly they came to a dead end. The street led directly into the back of a building that had no exits: just some doors. They lunged forward and tried to open each one but they were all locked. Before they could try the last one they heard running feet and knew they were trapped for good. They froze: unable to move.

At that instant, the door behind them flew open and a man grabbed James, pulling him into the darkness of the interior. Sharon and Larry were quickly dragged inside as well. They were slung against the back wall and told to keep their mouths shut. The door lock was thrown and everyone stood or crouched where they landed and didn't make a sound. Outside the running feet suddenly slowed and began to walk around the ally. They could hear the sound of the doors being tried.

They came to the door behind which James and the other huddled in the darkness. The knob of the door was grabbed by someone's hand that it began to turn this way and that. Someone spoke in Arabic and the door was released. The sound of running feet was heard as the men disappeared again out of the street.

James leaned against the wall and was finally able to breathe until he was hit full force. A cloth was torn off of the only window as he was physically lifted to his feet and slammed against the wall.

"You little shit! I'm gonna kick your ass till Monday!"

"Oh god, Philip. I'm so glad to see you!"

"You're not going to be glad to see me when I'm through with you!"

"That's enough! Let him go!" Sharon yelled and came after Philip. He dropped James and slung her back. "Who the hell are you!"

"I'm not afraid you!"

"You'll be frigging afraid if I open that door and throw you to the wolves.

He turned back to James. "You just couldn't control yourself could you? You just had to come back. *And* bring your little friends with you!" And he smacked James against the wall again.

"We're not so little, you prick. We're old enough to take care of ourselves," Sharon yelled.

"Ooooh, *excuse me, ma'am*! I didn't have time to notice your maturity, as you were standing shitless in that alley just now. We were too busy saving your ass."

"EVERYBODY STOP!" James almost screamed the words.

He looked at Philip. "I'm sorry! Okay! I'm sorry. I had to come back. I had to!"

"You didn't have to do *anything* except stay at home where you belong. You have no idea what a mess you're in now. You show up when you've been told to stay away and what do you do? You go to the one place where you're going to be seen, the one place they'll recognize you. Walk right into it like the fool that you are. And now they know you're here: you and these two. Do you think they won't be hunting for you now in every nook and cranny, every back alley and hotel room in Cairo: hunting you like bloodhounds on a scent until they find you and take it away from you?"

"Take what away from him?"

They had been so busy yelling at each other that they had barely noticed the other man in the room. He stepped further into the light. He looked to be the same age as Philip but taller. He was wearing similar clothes: cotton t-shirt over jeans and hiking boots. But that was where the similarities ended. He wore black horn-rimmed glasses that looked dusty in the light of the window and his hair, even at a young age was already beginning to thin. He looked like what he was: an academic whose field of study was ancient languages.

"Take what away from him," the man repeated.

"It's nothing. Something unimportant."

"Are you hiding something from me?"

"You *WERE* in the airport!" said Sharon accusingly from behind them.

"Yes. We were in the airport," Philip said turning to her.

"Then why didn't you stop us then. None of this would have happened!" said James.

"We thought you knew where your father was. We thought you could help us find him; that he had gotten a message home to you. We never thought you would come back *here*."

James looked like he had been struck. "What do you mean help you find him? What happened to him? What happened?"

Philip took a breath and his face relaxed. "We don't know. He's gone: disappeared."

James looked away. "Oh, god. I knew something had happened to him. He never came home like he said he would. I couldn't get him on the phone. Oh, god. He might be dead." And he sank down on the ground.

Larry sat down with him followed by Sharon: "He's not dead, James," said Larry.

"He's not," said Sharon. "We'll find him no matter what it takes. We'll find him."

"*You* won't be finding anybody. *You're* going home . . . !"

"Oh, like you're doing such a great job. If you know so much why haven't you found him already instead of lurking around airport terminals hoping somebody will show up to help you," said Sharon.

"So help me if you don't keep your mouth shut . . ."

"What are you going to do start smacking me around, too?"

The second man spoke: "Philip . . . they can't go home. You said it yourself. They already know they're here. They will be watching the airport, the flights, even the roads to the airports here and in Alexandria. They're here to stay until this is over."

Philip shook his head. "And how do you suggest we get them out of here and to some place where they can hide?"

"I don't know. I'm making this up as I go along just like you. But one thing is certain: they need to stay in here until it's dark outside or until we can get them into some kind of disguise. We all look like what we are: Americans. And they will be looking for Americans at every turn."

"No. There has to be a way to get them out: into the Sinai or into Israel."

"How?"

"I DON'T KNOW! We have to find a way. I'm not going to sit around babysitting a bunch of bratty kids with everything that's going on. If those men lay hands on them there's no telling what they'll do."

"Why do they want the relic?" James asked suddenly. "Why do they want it so badly?"

"What relic?" Sharon and the other man said together as they stared at Philip.

"I don't know what they want it for. I don't know really what's even going on. All I know for sure is your father disappeared suddenly. We found his notes and his computer. The written notes, and the information on the computer are so complex and confusing we can't make anything out of them. Everything points to some . . . it's crazy stuff," he finished curtly.

"Why didn't you tell me this?" said the man. He turned to the others. "I'm Nathan by the way, Nathan Bedford. Why didn't you tell me?" he repeated turning back to Philip.

"I honestly didn't think it was important. The translations are important. And we can't get anywhere with those."

"We can't help with that. But we can solve the symbols on the relic!" said James.

"You?" Philip stared at James with a look of disgust but James went on.

"You already know information has been well . . . downloaded."

Nathan blinked and looked at Philip. "Downloaded where?"

Philip didn't respond and James went on. "I can transcribe those symbols and Larry can tell us what they say!"

All eyes turned on Larry whose eyes got as big as saucers. "*Whaaaaat*? I don't know anything about this?"

"Yes, you do! You told me on the plane."

"All I said on the plane was . . . "

"STOP! Don't say anymore," James said and he turned to Philip. "You keep us here, with you, and we'll tell you what we know. If you try to send us away you'll never find the solution."

"You're a liar."

"No. I swear."

"You're a liar," he repeated. "How could you possibly know anything? Nathan can't solve it. How can you?"

"You don't know what we know."

"We don't really have a choice, Philip," said Nathan, his lips set. "We need to wait here a few hours and then one of us needs to go into the bazaar and buy some clothes. We can disguise ourselves and I can take two of them with me and you can take the other. We can go to the safe house. Let them see what we have, what Eric was working on, and they might be able to help. And . . . you can explain this relic."

Philip had never taken his eyes off of James. He said: "Okay, I'll take you with us. But if you're lying to me, the men who are looking for you won't get a chance to kill you. I'll do it myself."

Sharon pulled James' arm. "What disc?" she asked again

"I'll explain it later," said James

"It downloaded information," she persisted. "So it's like a computer.

"Yeah . . . you could say that." James replied.

CHAPTER 12

Raza stepped into the room where Eric was being held and quietly closed the door behind him. He lifted the one chair and moved it in front of where Eric sat on his cot.

"Again, what took you so long, Raza?" Eric repeated. "I would've thought you would have come running out of the dig that night and assist them in my kidnapping."

Raza looked at Eric: "I'm here to help you, Eric – if you'll let me."

"Ooooh, I see. You're my best friend in the whole world. But you'll need something in return won't you. All I have to do is . . . what?"

"As Amil has already told you, if you give us what we need, you and the Professor can go. We just need the data. It means nothing to you."

"It means nothing to me," Eric repeated and shifted on the cot. "Really? Which data are we talking about here? Do you want my translation of the wall or do you want what's in Professor Steven's head. Or both? But wait, that can't be right.

If I were guessing I would bet you already know what the wall says. You've known from the very beginning. I would hazard to say that you walked in and started translating on the spot. But for some reason, you decided to keep quite about what you knew. In the meantime, the ministry sends for help – me – even though I'm not needed. Was it a smoke screen or a way to stall for time: keep up the appearance that this dig was being executed like any other archeological discovery would be executed. Only you can answer that one."

"You give me too much credit."

"Really? I don't think I give you credit enough. I have a habit I've had since childhood. When I read, my lips move, forming the words silently as I go along. Everyone laughs at me about it. I came into the dig one day and you were there. You must have missed something from an earlier visit and had returned to double-check yourself or perhaps to continue your translation. Your lips were moving as you scanned the wall. I didn't think anything about it at the time. It occurred to me in the last few days, after talking to Professor Stevens. But the big question is how did you pull it off: translate a 5,000-year-old alien inscription using unknown symbols. It was like your native language; like you were reading a newspaper or a book."

"If it appeared that way it was simply the hieroglyphics I was trying to understand. And who said anything about aliens?" Raza shifted in his chair.

Eric ignored the last remark. "Let's not be silly, Raza. This is too important a discovery, don't you think, for us to pretend what is obvious. Your kind would know how to read everything; hieroglyphics and all."

Raza smiled for the first time Eric could remember. His teeth were perfectly white, straight and slightly pointed. "You think I'm an alien?"

Eric's eyes never left his captor. "Aren't you?"

The smile faded.

"I'm not the subject of discussion here. You and the Professor, and the information you carry, are."

Eric ignored that. "You know I expected more out of my first alien encounter: Bigger eyes, larger head, little gray body. You look almost normal."

Raza's face became like stone. "Don't you dare play games with me, Eric! I can hurt you in ways you can't even imagine."

"Oh, I'm not playing any games. I'm dead serious," he said. "Why should I tell you anything? We're not going to get out of here alive. Why would I help you phone home? That's what you're trying to do, isn't it? Contact the mother ship!"

Raza leaned forward in his chair. "Maybe I am. What's it to you – *HUMAN*!" he spat the word like it was an accusation. "That's nothing to you."

"What's mom and dad going to do once their spaceship lands. Spend a few days with you and the little woman and then retire to a condo in Florida."

Eric was a big man but what happened next left him stunned and disoriented. Raza sprang from the chair and grabbed him with a strength Eric had never felt before. He was dragged bodily off the cot and slung onto the floor like a doll. Raza held him down with superhuman strength, his hand clutching Eric's throat cutting off his air. Eric struggled to resist but found all his strength was gone.

Raza's enraged face hovered inches above Eric's own and he couldn't look away. The door suddenly opened and guards rushed in but were repelled as Raza screamed for them to leave.

He turned back to Eric, his words like venom.

"Americans! You're so smug. You think you know everything; can control everything. You know nothing – NOTHING – babies just learning to walk. You sit here insulting me when you're in so much trouble you can't even imagine its scope."

He suddenly released his grip on Eric's throat. Eric gasped for breath and rolled to his side. His throat felt like it had been crushed. Raza grabbed him and lifted him up and slammed him onto the cot.

"Now will you help me or not?"

Eric was shaking all over but his words came out strong and without hesitation. "I will never willingly help you do anything!"

Raza stood over him and spoke through clenched teeth. "We'll see about that!"

He walked to the door and opened it, speaking to one of the guards outside. "Bring her in," Raza stood by the door and never took his eyes off of Eric.

There was a shuffling in the hall outside and then a woman with a covering over her head was forced, stumbling into the room. The covering was ripped off and Eric gasped, as he leaped off the cot to grab her before she collapsed to the floor.

"Marie!" He held his wife against his chest while she sobbed his name.

He looked at Raza who was now leaning casually against the wall by the door as a smile played across his mouth. "The little woman," Raza said, mocking Eric's words.

"You son of a bitch," Eric spat at his captor. "I'm going to kill you!"

"Someday, perhaps," Raza responded easily, "But not today. I'll leave you alone for a few minutes to get reacquainted." And without another word he left the room, closing the door behind him.

Marie continued to sob and tremble against Eric's chest. He led her over to the cot and they sat down together. He pulled her into his arms.

"Oh, god, Marie. "God. How did they get to you? Where's James?"

"Eric!" she sobbed, "James has disappeared!"

"What do you mean?"

"He's gone; gone. I couldn't find him. They came and took me away. I couldn't find him! He's disappeared."

"Slow down," he said, brushing her hair away from her face. "Tell me if they've hurt you."

"No. They've just pushed me around. They haven't hurt me."

"Can you tell me what happened? Slowly. And don't leave anything out. Can you do that for me?"

"Yes," She sat up as Eric held her hand. "Your friend brought James home."

"Philip."

"Yes. I took James inside. He seemed fine to me but I made an appointment for him to see a doctor anyway. Everything came back normal and for a couple of days, he seemed perfectly fine. He would go over to Larry's house or Larry would come over to ours. The only thing that seemed out of the ordinary was he was distracted like something was on his mind. I didn't press him too much to tell me what he was thinking. I just let him rest up and try to get back to his normal routine.

One night at the end of the week, Larry came over and they were in James' room. Sometime after that Sharon, his other friend, came over. They were all upstairs for a while. Then Larry and Sharon came down separately to say goodnight and both of them went home. James asked if he could go and spend the night with Larry and I said yes. He told me he loved me and left.

The next morning, I got up as usual. I felt like I should call over to Larry's house to make sure everything was okay. When James had left the night before he seemed strange like he was not saying goodnight but saying goodbye. I went into the front hall where my phone was charging. I picked it up and dialed. Mrs. Wu answered the phone and I asked if I could speak to James. She seemed confused and said James was at home: Larry was spending the night with *him*, not the other way around. At that moment, there was a loud knock on the front door. It was so loud I jumped. I told Mrs. Wu there was someone at the door and I would call her back. I laid the phone down and went to the door. I peeked out of the spy hole and there were three men standing there.

They were tall, heavyset, and dark. They looked middle-eastern. They knocked again but I was afraid to open the door. They didn't wait any longer and broke down the door. I was standing there and they rushed in closing the door behind them. One of them grabbed me and forced me into a chair. They crushed my phone on the floor. The other two fanned out and started going through all the rooms. They came back and said James was not there. The one man stood over me and demanded to know where James was.

I was so scared and I told them I didn't know. They took me upstairs and began to tear everything apart. They had found James' room and drug me inside. His closet was open and his backpack was gone. His computer was on and there was airline information like he was going to take another trip. But that was all. They said something in Arabic and then made me get dressed. They took me outside and put me in a car and we sped away."

"Did anybody see what happened?"

"I don't think so. I don't know. It happened so fast. They drove me to Dulles where a private jet was waiting. They told me if I cried out they would kill me and when they found James they would kill him too. We got out of the car and they took my arm and pulled me into the plane."

"What markings were on the plane?"

There were no logos, no markings, just numbers. They pushed me to the back of the plane and another man sat next to me. After that, we took off. I kept trying to ask them who they were; what they wanted with us. They wouldn't answer. We flew for hours, landed somewhere and then took off again. When we landed again they blindfolded me and put me back into a car. I don't know how long I was in the car before it stopped and I was taken out. When the blindfold was removed I was in a room like this one." She paused to catch her breath. "Where are we, Eric?"

"Egypt."

"Egypt?"

"Yes."

"What's going on? Why have they brought us here? Is this something to do with your work; the dig you're on? What happened to James? Do you know what's happened to James?"

"I don't know for sure but if I were guessing I would say he's back in Egypt, too."

"Did somebody take him like they did me?"

"No. I don't think so. Maybe but I don't think so. They would have brought him to me by now." Eric looked down and bit his lip. "I told him I would follow him home, that I would be there in a couple of days. I promised. When I didn't he probably tried to call me and when he couldn't get me, decided to come back and find me. Because of what you just told me I would also bet that his friends came along with him."

"Oh, no. How will they be able to get by? He doesn't have any money; nowhere to go, nowhere to stay."

"They must have figured out some way to do it. Whatever the case, they will be in danger. These people mean business and they're watching everything. Pray they don't find them."

She started crying. "I'm scared."

Eric pulled her into his arms. "I know you are. I am too. But we have to keep our wits about us. They're going to try and use you for leverage to make me talk just like they are trying to use me to make Professor Stevens talk."

"Professor Stevens?"

"My old teacher from New York."

"What will you do?"

"If it comes to it, tell them what they want to know. I can't let them hurt you."

"What do they want?"

"Information."

"About what?"

"What's in the dig? There's something in the dig; something bad."

At that moment, the door suddenly opened and Raza stepped back into the room followed by guards who marshaled Professor Stevens inside. The Professor stared back and forth between Eric and Marie.

"I don't know if you've ever met Eric's wife, Professor. But let me introduce her to you. Marie, isn't it?" he said.

Professor Steven's face fell. Raza turned him around until he was facing him.

"It's your choice, Professor. You can give me what I need or let us do to her what we've already done to you."

The Professor looked at Eric. "I don't have anything you want? Anything that would be helpful."

"You have the information from your part of the disk. Isn't that right?" Raza said patiently. He took Professor Stevens by the shoulders and pulled him forward until their faces were inches apart. "It downloaded the information into your head," he continued as he thumped the Professor's forehead with his finger. "Then it went dark. There is no way to get the information anymore unless you give it to us.

"I don't know . . .

"Guards!" Raza yelled as everyone jumped

The guards reentered the room

"Take her," Raza said indicating Marie.

Eric jumped up, pushing Marie behind him. One of the guards quickly approached, pulled a gun and smashed it into Eric's head, grabbing Marie as Eric fell. She was hauled to the door.

"Stop!" Professor Stevens cried. "I'll give you what you want."

"Very wise," Raza said. He turned to Eric. "And you, Eric? What would you like to do?"

Eric paused and said: "I'll tell you what you want to know if . . . you let Marie and the Professor go."

"No negotiations, Eric. I think it best we keep the family together, don't you? All we're missing is your son. And it might interest you to know that he is back in Cairo. It's only a matter of time before he joins us here." Marie gasped and her startled face turned to Eric.

Raza turned back to Professor Stevens. "You will be taken to a room and given a pencil and paper. You will transfer the symbols. Take your time. It is important and I don't think I have to tell you to transcribe them exactly as you see them. If you try to manipulate the symbols or leave any of them out I will discover what you have done and you will pay the consequences. Do you understand?"

Professor Stevens nodded his head and Raza motioned to the guards to take him away.

Raza turned to Eric and Marie. "Come with me."

They got up and followed him down a hallway to another room. It was about the size of the room Eric was being held in. It contained a table, some chairs, a notepad and some pencils. Raza indicated where they were to sit and they took the chairs he pointed to. He called out in Arabic. A man brought in several large rolls of paper, put them on the table in front of him and silently left the room, waiting outside the open door until Raza told him to close it and leave him alone with Eric and Marie.

Raza looked through the rolls, turned one around and unrolled it in front of Eric. It was a full schematic of the wall and all the symbols.

"I need you to answer some basic questions today. In the days that follow I will need you tell me everything you know about your translation. Raza's gaze never left Eric's face." What is the overall meaning of this section?" Raza asked and pointed to the left-hand side of the drawing.

"The diary," said Eric.

"The diary? What do you mean?"

"I called that section the diary. It's an account of what happened when their ship became disabled and they crashed here."

"And what happened afterwards," Raza said almost to himself.

"Yes," Eric replied.

108

"Here?" And he pointed to the far right side of the wall.

Eric paused and twisted his lips. "How to enslave the people; make them do their bidding." His eyes never left Raza's face. "How to use the women to get to the men who would resist, how to torture them into submission . . . by killing their babies."

Eric expected Raza to go to the central panels about the figures and steeled himself for that eventuality. But Raza seemed deep in thought.

"Was this your take on it as well?" Eric said breaking the silence.

Raza didn't bother to deny it any longer. "Yes. But I need you, and the Professor, to verify my own interpretations. I need you to help me understand everything you can. It's very important. We have to understand the hieroglyphics in order to break the code of the other symbols." He picked up the pad of paper that was still lying on the table and began to doodle on it as his voice dropped lower. "In the days ahead, I will be meeting with you privately. It is vital that you not communicate anything that you have told me today or anything you will tell me in the future to anyone but me. You will speak to me and me only. Do you understand?"

"Yes," said Eric.

Raza looked at Marie.

"Yes," she repeated.

He finished his doodle and pushed it roughly across the table at Eric. "Good! We're done here for today." They watched as he stood up, gathered the rolls of drawings, and without another word, left the room.

Marie collapsed against Eric's shoulder, sobbing softly.

"It's alright," he comforted her. "Everything will be alright."

They sat silently for a few minutes, holding each other and thinking about James. Marie felt Eric's body stiffen. She glanced up at his face and then at what he was looking at; the notepad Raza had been doodling on. It showed a single hieroglyphic.

"What's that?" said Marie.

"The Eye of Horus."

"The Eye of Horus?"

"Yes," Eric replied, slowly. "The Egyptian symbol for protection."

CHAPTER 13

"Please! I've got to stop for a minute!"

Philip slowed down and glancing behind him pulled James into a doorway. The alley they were moving down was narrow and littered with debris. Old cars stood on one side while electric wires crisscrossed helter-skelter above them. The lines ran between the darkened buildings like the broken strands of a spider web. James leaned against the mud brick of the wall and closed his eyes trying to catch his breath. Then he sank down onto one of the rough steps that led up into the darkness of the building.

They had stayed in the storage area for most of the day, afraid to venture out until it was dusk. Philip and Nathan had taken turns going into various bazaars to find the clothes they would need to cover what they were wearing. It had been slow going getting everyone ready to leave and the day had seemed to go on forever.

There had been one scare while they had huddled inside the space. Someone in the front of the building had come back to get something out of the storage room. Everyone had crouched down, hiding in dark corners and behind the crates that filled up most of the room. Luckily, the man had stopped just inside the door, found what he was looking for, and disappeared toward the front once more, locking the door behind him.

When the day finally ended and everyone was ready to depart, the decision was made that Nathan would take Sharon and Larry with him and Philip would escort James. There had been some argument over who would go with who, with Philip insisting that James, and no one else, go with him. Nathan had finally given in to Philip's plan and him, Sharon, and Larry were the first to leave and make their way to the safe house. They were now some distance ahead of James and Philip in the darkening city.

They had waited fifteen minutes after the others had gone and walked out into the streets once more. At first, they had ambled along, lingering on the street and walking into shops. Philip did not want to draw any attention to them by appearing to be in a hurry. But after leaving most of the shops behind their pace had increased until they found themselves in what, to James, was a maze of alleyways and small shadowy courtyards.

Along the way, they would run into people, some of the men casting a suspicious eye their way. But James noticed they only looked at Philip and not at him. No one stopped them, however, as they moved along and James was glad when all the foot traffic ceased and they were alone.

More than once he would have sworn they were lost but Philip seemed to know his way around and never hesitated as they came to a turn or struck off in a new direction. Exhausted and out of breath, James had finally called for a temporary halt so he could rest.

"How much further?" he asked.

"We're about halfway there," came the reply.

"God."

"You'll make it and then you can have something to drink and some food. We just need to move as fast as we can. It's dangerous as long as we're outside."

James nodded his head, "Okay. Do you think everybody else is okay?"

"I'm sure they're fine. The most dangerous part was when we came out of hiding. It's so active around there. You never know who's watching. The further away we get the better."

They waited a few more minutes until Philip said: "Let's go."

James got up without a word and followed Philip as he quickly moved down the alley. From that moment on everything was a blur to James. The buildings, the streets, the alleys all looked the same and he had no idea even which direction they were moving in.

After what seemed like forever, Philip stopped in a small courtyard. James had no way of knowing but they were now in one of the poorest sections of Cairo.

Philip looked around, scanning all the buildings. Pale light shown in a few of the windows but that was all. There was no one around. Apparently satisfied Philip moved to a doorway with a set of stairs very similar to the one where James had rested before. There was no light coming from this building; every window was dark.

They felt, rather than saw their way up the steps and once at the top walked down a hallway, with various doors opening on either side. James expected Philip to knock on one of the doors. Instead, he walked to the end of the hall and turned left into another hallway. They followed this zigzagging pattern until they came to another flight of stairs leading down to another street. There was another small courtyard here with no exit except the one they had entered by.

Philip walked across the space to a door with a sign in Arabic that James could not understand. He didn't knock but pulled a key out of his pocket, inserted it in the lock of the door and turned it, allowing them entrance into a totally dark interior. Once inside Philip ran his hand across the surface of the door looking for the keyhole so he could lock them in. When it was done he walked through the darkness to a door on the other side and softly knocked.

There was a pause and then man's voice in Arabic said, "What do you want?"

Philip answered, also in Arabic, "Entrance."

The door opened and James blinked, blinded by the light that streamed out of the interior room. He turned his head away from the light as he was pulled inside and the door was shut and locked behind him.

"You made it," said Nathan.

"Yes. Everything alright here?" Philip replied.

"Yes. We got here about thirty minutes ago. It was pretty uneventful. You?"

"We did fine. Where are the others?"

"Inside. They've been upset that you haven't shown up 'til now."

"We waited a few minutes before we left the storage room. Let's get inside."

The room they had been standing in could have been another storage room. Crates and boxes were stacked against the walls with an old table in the middle of the floor. Everything was covered in dust.

They quickly walked through the inner door, which was shut and locked behind them by Nathan.

"James! Finally!" said Sharon with relief. "We thought you were right behind us. We got worried when you didn't show up."

"We didn't leave right after you did. We waited and then I had to stop and rest for a few minutes. Are you guys okay?"

"Yes, we're fine."

James looked around the space. Two fluorescent lights hung from chains attached to the ceiling that illuminated a small room sparsely furnished with old folding chairs, which were sitting around a long table. It was covered with papers, file folders and clipboards. Two computer monitors sat side-by-side, data streaming across their screens. Cables snaked off the tabletop onto the floor and into generators placed against the facing wall. Two other rooms opened off of this one: one with a refrigerator that James could see through the empty doorframe and one that presumably was the sleeping quarters. There was a small window in that room but it was shut even though it was warm and stuffy.

"Let's get you something to eat," said Nathan. "You haven't had anything all day. He led the way into the kitchen which turned out to have a small table and chairs, a hotplate and a few wall cabinets with no doors.

"There's fruit there in the bowl and I'll put on some soup," He retrieved two cans of soup from the cabinets, opened them and poured the contents into a pot which he placed on the hotplate. "You'll find some crackers up in the cabinet and something to drink in the fridge." He left them there and went back to converse with Philip.

As they prepared their dinner they could hear them talking together in the other room but their voices were so low they couldn't understand what was being said.

When everything was ready they pulled the chairs up and sat down to eat. It was soup out of a can but the best soup they had ever had.

"Did Nathan say anything when he was with you?" James asked.

"Nothing," said Larry. "We came straight here and he hardly said anything."

"What about Philip," asked Sharon.

"No. Nothing. But something did happen. It was small but weird."

"What was it?"

"We kept running into people at first, mostly men. They would look our way but would only look at Philip. Nobody would look at me."

"Well, that was a good thing, right?" said Larry.

"Yeah, I guess so. It was just . . . it seemed odd. I felt like they knew who we were, where we were going."

"Just be glad you got here in one piece. I was scared the whole time we were outside," Sharon said.

"I wonder where we are," said James. "In Cairo, I mean. I got so turned around I don't think I could find my way out of here if I tried."

"Yeah, me either," said Larry.

"What's going to happen now?" said Sharon.

"Larry will have to tell them what he told me on the plane," James replied. "That's all we can do. I'm sorry to have put you on the spot like that," he said to Larry. "I couldn't think of anything else back there to stop Philip from sending us away again."

"It's alright. I think it would help if I knew what was going on."

"What exactly did you tell him on the plane?" said Sharon.

At that moment, Philip called them. "Are you done yet?"

They quickly finished their small meal and went back into the outer room.

Philip and Nathan were sitting side-by-side at the table watching one of the computer screens. The streaming codes had disappeared to be replaced with some of the symbols that had downloaded into James' head.

"Aren't those what you showed me?" Larry whispered. James nodded, never taking his eyes off the computer monitor.

"Yes, or ones just like them?"

Both Philip and Nathan turned at the same time to look at them.

"All finished?" Nathan asked.

James nodded.

"Good," said Philip shortly. "What have you got?" he said looking at Larry.

"I . . . umm . . ."

"Just tell him," said James.

Larry looked at James and back at Philip. "It's a binary code."

Philip stared. "A binary code?" he said in disbelief. "A binary code? I hope you've got something else besides that!" His voice was getting louder.

Larry slowly shook his head. "That's all I've got."

Philip shook his head. "What the hell good does *that* do? You frigging lied!" he said turning to James.

CHAPTER 14

"I *didn't* lie. It is a binary code."

"Ooooh," said Philip. "And what good does that do us if we don't know what the binary code consists of?" He was yelling now.

"Philip!" said Nathan. "Calm down. It's some place to start at least?"

"It's no place to start! How are you going to break a 5,000-year-old alien code if you don't know which numbers to use?"

Nathan's eyebrows shot up. "*What* are you talking about?"

"There's an indication that . . . it's crazy," Philip stopped and looked at Nathan. "There's an indication that the odd symbols on the wall and in James' head are alien in origin. I thought maybe Eric had said something to James about it. That's all."

"That's all?" said Nathan incredulously. "That's *all*. Really? And you didn't think to tell me?"

"Like I said," Philip replied. "It's crazy."

Sharon's eyes got big as her mouth fell open. "*What* alien symbols in James' head?"

They ignored her.

"He didn't say anything to me," said James. "I sorta figured it out that day in the dig. The odd symbols on the wall are like the ones in my head."

"And, again, what does it matter if we don't know what the binary code consists of! " said Philip.

"*I'm sorry*," said Sharon sarcastically interrupting them again. *"BUT WHAT ALIEN SYMBOLS ARE YOU TALKING ABOUT?"*

116

"The geometric symbols – the odd symbols – in the dig and in James' head, may be alien in origin. And that's a big maybe. We're trying to figure out how to read them."

"She doesn't know about the symbols," said James.

Sharon folded her arms across her chest, pursed her lips, and looked at James.

"I'm sorry," James said. "Everything happened so fast. I didn't have time to explain." He took a breath. "When I came over the first time to visit, Dad took me to the excavation. We were inside the main chamber when something happened and he sent me away suddenly. I wandered into a section of the dig that had been blocked off and I found something there, embedded in one of the walls. It was a little piece of papyrus that fell apart in my hands and a small piece of metal. When I looked at the piece of metal it sorta rebooted itself and . . . and downloaded stuff into my head. Symbols . . . all these symbols."

Sharon's face froze. She closed her eyes and shook her head. "You're kidding me! You're kidding me!" On the last "me" her eyes popped open again. "And I suppose *you* knew about this?" she said turning to Larry.

"I . . . I knew about the symbols . . . on the plane. I didn't know they were *ALIEN*?"

"Oh my god! Oh my god!" Sharon suddenly exclaimed turning back to James. "That's what you were carrying in the airport. How did we get through the airport? How did we get through security?"

James shook his head. "I don't know."

Larry froze. "We could be sent to prison for transporting alien technology across state lines," he said breathlessly.

"Oh, SHUT UP!" said Sharon.

"STOP!" Philip's face was red. "We didn't say it *was* alien. We said it *might* be! It could be anything. None of that matters at the moment because we're right back to where we started, which is nowhere. I'm sending you home first thing tomorrow if every thug in Cairo chases us to the airport."

"No, no. Please let us help you. If it will help find Dad, please let us try."

"It's not as crazy as it sounds," said Nathan. "If it's a binary code there could be a correlation with our own mathematics."

Philip shook his head. "And how is that even remotely possible?"

"If it is binary, two of our numbers in the right sequence could break it."

"That would require the 'aliens,'" Philip said making air quotes, "to be using our own numbers. What? Their ship came down and they gave us *math*?"

"Look, all I'm saying is it's possible because of base 10."

"Base 10?"

"The ancient Egyptians invented base 10; all of our basic numbers from 1 to 9. They were using them at least fifty years after the Great Pyramid was built. We know this because there are artifacts that show them. They could have been used fifty years earlier, as well. It sounds farfetched and nuts, I know. But all of this is farfetched and nuts. It's improbable but . . ."

"That *can't* be true."

"It *is* true. The ancient Egyptians created our basic number system. What if something, or someone, gave it to them. It would explain the Great Pyramid: a perfect pyramidal shape because geometry made it so, mathematics made it so. How did the Egyptians, at the beginning of civilization, master math to that extent? Maybe they had help."

"You're sounding like one of those ancient alien nuts," said Philip

"Did Dad say anything to you about the aliens?" James asked.

Philip shook his head. "Not in so many words. He suddenly sent me all of his research. Everything he was working on before he disappeared. Some of the writing implies it. But I can't make any sense out of the information he provided. It's so confusing I'm having a hard time figuring out anything it says."

"Well, it's worth a try Philip," said Nathan.

"Do you know how insane this sounds?"

"At this point Philip, what else do we have?"

"I don't know," Philip replied and got up to walk across the room.

"I'm not going to tell you this will be easy. It's not."

"How many combinations of just the base ten numbers are there?"

"I don't know off the top of my head," Nathan said. "It can be a hell of a lot depending on what you're doing."

"And if, by the wildest coincidence in the history of mankind, the supposed aliens used the base 10 numbers, we can take that, and using our computers find out what all of this means?"

"Roughly . . . yes. Maybe. I don't know! But again, what else do we have?"

Nathan followed Philip as he walked to the other side of the room. Nathan lowered his voice so the others couldn't hear. "I know how this sounds. But it's all we've got. The symbols and what they are trying to say, whoever created them, may never be understood. In fact, I doubt it will ever be cracked. But we have to try. It would have never occurred to me that this is a binary code because we're too close to this. Why would the symbols repeat like this unless it's some kind of coded message? The kid figured it out and on some level it makes sense.

Having said that, you need to call Washington. These computers here are not powerful enough to make this happen. We need help. You need to call Washington."

"No. We can't call for help."

"Philip . . . Eric is missing. Something major is going on here. These kids are in danger. You know it's true. We need help! Call in the cavalry."

"No. It's way too early. You get everyone involved and there's no telling how this will turn out."

"Philip, please."

"No. Not yet. Just give me a little time. I need to make sure of the lay of the land before I call the agency. Just give me a little time."

Nathan shook his head. "I don't know if we have any time left. At least, send the information to Washington. We can show them what we have, explain the binary code connection, tell them we need a computer to run these sequences to try and figure this out. Their computers could run thousands of sequences in no time."

"That would have the same effect as if I called for help. They would be on this in a millisecond."

"Okay, so what do we do if we're going to try and figure this out?"

"We need the symbols that are in James' head. That's the first place to start."

"Agreed. I can make nothing of Eric's work with the stuff he sent you."

They turned to James. "We need you to write out the symbols."

"I already have," he said and walked to where he had dropped his backpack on the floor. He pulled out the paper he had shown Larry on the plane and handed it to Nathan.

"Is this all of them?"

"No," said James. "They have appeared at various times but I can't tell if they are in different order or not. Also, there are other symbols, different symbols, but not as many as the main ones. Those symbols appear less frequently."

Nathan studied the paper. "These two symbols are like some of the ones Eric sent you from the walls of the excavation," said Nathan.

"Yes, that was the first time I ever saw them. They were on the wall," said James.

"I wonder if these say the same thing as the ones on the wall?" said Philip.

"I have no idea."

"Okay. Let me think." Nathan walked back to the two computers on the table and sat down. "If we try to do them all at once it's going to become insane. We need to take a certain number of the symbols and assign each of them one of the base numbers.

We'll start with 24 symbols and feed that into the computer. There are so many combinations we could be here till the end of time. That's why we need bigger and faster computers to try the various combinations."

"How would you feed in the code?" Larry asked. "HTML?"

"We're not building a website!" Philip snapped.

"No. We need a binary to text converter," said Nathan.

"A what?" asked James.

"We need a way to convert the binary codes into something we can read if that's possible."

"Where are you going to find something like that?" asked Larry. "We're on the other side of the world?"

Nathan looked at him questioningly. "The Web."

"They have a binary converter?" asked James.

"Yes," said Nathan, "We just have to find the best one to use."

Five minutes later Nathan had what he was looking for. "Ok, let's begin . . ."

Before Philip could respond everyone jumped. Philip's cell phone was ringing.

"Who the hell would be calling you?" said Nathan. "Nobody knows you're here."

Philip looked at the phone. "It's the Ministry of Antiquities?"

"How did they get your cell phone number?"

"I have no idea." Philip paused.

"Answer it," said Nathan.

"What would they want with me?"

"You won't know until you answer it."

Philip pressed the illuminated keypad. "Hello?" he said as he walked to the other side of the room.

They watched him walk away. "Is there anything I can do to help you?" James asked Nathan.

Nathan looked back at the computer screen. "Nothing except to begin assigning numbers. Take this pencil and count until you have 24 symbols. Then mark that spot. Those are the ones we will use to begin. After that, continue and group them in sections of eight. All of you can help me assign numbers to those symbols. This is a total crap shoot so it doesn't matter what is assigned where."

"Like trying to pick the winning numbers in the lottery?" said Sharon.

"Exactly," said Nathan.

James counted the 24 symbols and transcribed them onto another piece of paper leaving a lot of space between each line so the various binary combinations could be written above them.

At that moment, Philip returned.

"What did they want?" Nathan asked.

"It was Dr. Mohammed. He is aware that Eric has disappeared and he's concerned. He wants me to come in tomorrow to meet with him and sort out what we need to do."

"You know Mohammed?"

"Yes. From the dig."

"Why didn't he call the police?"

"I don't know. Eric is from another country. Maybe there's some kind of protocol they have to follow."

"I met him when Dad took me to the excavation," said James.

"Yes. I met him there as well. Along with that other guy, Raza."

"When do you have to go?" asked Nathan.

"In the morning."

"It may be a good thing. Maybe he can help find Eric."

"Maybe. But something is fishy. He may be hiding something."

"They're all hiding something. They're keeping all of this under wraps. No one knows anything about this excavation except their people, Eric, and us. It's never even gotten into the press. The dig started out like any other dig. Now it's an armed camp. Plus, the Great Pyramid is closed."

"What does that have to do with anything?" asked James.

"The Great Pyramid is never closed," answered Nathan. "Suddenly six months ago it was shut up for 'restoration.' But what needs to be restored? It's a pile of stones. There are no carvings, no paintings, nothing inside at all. What are they restoring – rocks? Didn't Eric even comment on it?" he said, looking at Philip.

"That has nothing to do with this," Philip remarked. "They are always shutting up temples and stuff to keep the tourists away. What's happening with the dig is completely unrelated unless I'm badly mistaken."

"Well, it's just weird," answered Nathan as he turned back to the computer. "But that's neither here nor there. Let's see if we can win the lottery."

While they had been talking Sharon and Larry had been assigning number combinations to the symbols. Nathan took the paper and inserted the code they gave him into the converter.

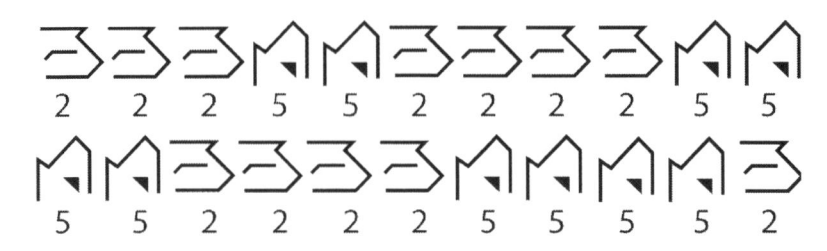

```
ᗱ ᗱ ᗱ ᜋ ᜋ ᗱ ᗱ ᗱ ᗱ ᜋ ᜋ
2  2  2  5  5  2  2  2  2  5  5

ᜋ ᜋ ᗱ ᗱ ᗱ ᗱ ᜋ ᜋ ᜋ ᗱ
5  5  2  2  2  2  5  5  5  2
```

They waited, staring at the screen for several minutes.
Nothing happened.

They tried another pattern and another and another until at the end of an hour they all sat back in their chairs, staring at the blank monitor. Nothing had appeared.

"This could go on forever," James remarked.

"Yes, it could," agreed Nathan.

"I'm going to bed," said Philip and disappeared into the bedroom flopping down onto a cot and falling asleep.

"Maybe it's not just the numbers of one to nine. What about the prime numbers? Maybe it's just the prime numbers," Nathan said. They started trying those numbers but again with no success.

Suddenly Nathan exclaimed, "What are we thinking? Our computers can only read zeros and ones. No wonder nothing's appearing. The numbers we have been using mean nothing to the computer. If this has any chance of working, it has to be zeros and ones. And that means that one of these symbols is a zero and the other one is a one," He stopped and stared off into space and spoke again as if to himself. "But how can that be? The ancient Egyptians didn't really have a zero."

"They didn't?" asked James.

"Well, I guess it depends on who you ask. Some people say yes, some people say no. Either way, it wasn't a zero as we think of a zero. It was a different symbol. But that's our best bet; if we can figure out which symbol represents 1 and which represents 0. Maybe Philip is right. This is nuts."

They quickly regrouped and began again. They assigned the 0 and 1s and took turns giving the combinations to Nathan who would code them in. Information began to appear on the computer screen as the converter began to work but it was just gibberish, meaning nothing.

By 3:00 a.m. they were no closer than when they started.

"The order in which we place the zeros and ones in relation to each other is endless," said Nathan, as he turned to them.

"Well, at least, something is appearing now. It was hard when it was just a blank screen."

"Yes, something is appearing but it's garbage with letters mixed in with it. Unless I'm really off track I don't think the aliens would be speaking English. If it appears at all it will be some kind of mathematical communication. They would only be using the numbers, or at least, that's all that we would be able to understand."

Larry had already fallen asleep at the table. Nathan got up and shook him by the shoulder, waking him up. "Time to go to bed pal." He led him into the small bedroom where Larry fell into the second cot and immediately fell back asleep.

"Maybe they were writing backwards," Sharon said jokingly as she continued scribbling. "Like a secret decoder ring or something."

"Yeah, I'm sure that's the answer," Nathan said dryly. He was beyond exhausted. Sharon tossed her last codes onto the table, as did James.

"So we're giving up?" asked James.

"Without more computer power there's no way to run through the combinations. We could be here till the end of time," Nathan said as he picked up one of their last codes and entered it in.

```
ƎƎMMƎƎƎƎƎƎMM
0 0 1 1 0 0 0 0 0 0 1 1

ƎMƎMMƎƎƎMƎMƎ
0 1 0 1 1 0 0 0 1 0 1 0

ƎƎMMƎMƎƎMƎƎƎ
0 0 1 1 0 1 0 0 1 0 0 0

MƎMƎ
1 0 1 0
```

James stood up, disappointed. "I have to go to bed."

"I know," said Nathan.

"Me too," said Sharon. They both walked into the other room. Sharon lay down next to Larry and James took the floor. Philip was snoring gently on the other cot.

Nathan watched them go then sat back down at the computer.

"Screw it!" He cursed under his breath. He laid his head down on his arms and closed his eyes.

There were so many papers on the table that his movements created an avalanche with the sheets falling to the floor followed by a half empty soda can. As Nathan lurched to grab them the soda spilled out and ran across the papers blurring the codes. He didn't bother to pick them up but laid his head down again.

The computer cursor continued to flash for several minutes, like an eye forever blinking and getting no rest.

Then . . .

It disappeared from the screen to be replaced by a fragment of code that had been created 5,000 years in the past; a fragment of code from another world light years away from earth.

But no one was there to see it. They were all fast asleep.

CHAPTER 15

"Sharon! Sharon! Wake up!"

"Whaa?" she mumbled and pulled away, trying to roll over again.

Nathan shook her harder and spoke louder in her ear. "You have to get up!" And with that Sharon came fully awake. She blinked her eyes and pulled herself partially up off of the cot. Larry was still curled up, pressing himself against the wall next to her.

"What do you want?" she hissed. "I'm tired."

"I know you're tired. But you have to get up and help us. You have to give me the last codes you gave me last night before you went to bed."

Sharon sat up and rubbed her eyes, looking up at Nathan and James who was standing behind him. Philip was standing by the door but did not speak.

"What codes?" she said. "I wrote them down. I gave them to you."

"I know you gave them to me but they're lost."

Sharon swung her legs off the cot, which finally woke Larry up. He sat up and said, "What's going on?" No one paid him any attention.

"I wrote them on a piece of paper. Go look at the paper," Sharon snapped.

Nathan stepped back. "There was an accident."

"What do you mean?"

"I accidently spilled soda on them. They're gone."

Sharon was finding it hard to understand him. "Why do you need them? They're like all the others. Nothing worked."

James spoke, "No they're not, Sharon. We broke the code but now we don't have what you wrote and can't go on."

Her mouth fell open. "You're kidding."

James shook his head as she got off the cot and went to the computer. The small code was sitting there on the binary converter.

05☐ 12☐

Sharon stared at the screen and shrugged. "It's some numbers and empty boxes. So what?"

"Yes, it's a couple of numbers! Don't you see? It's working."

"It's just a coincidence," said Philip. "You accidently typed in the code that gave you the numbers."

"Maybe," said Nathan, "And maybe not. We have to test it and that's why I need you to tell me what you were doing right before you went to bed," he said looking at Sharon.

"I was . . . I don't know. I was tired. I don't remember."

"You were sitting next to Larry," Nathan said. "We were using zeros and ones. We had stopped using the prime numbers and switched to the zeros and ones."

"I was inserting them at random. Just at random," said Sharon.

Nathan picked up the paper and showed it to her. Everything was smeared and unreadable. "Oh my god," was all she could say, again.

"You HAVE to remember, Sharon," said James.

"I don't remember anything!" she exclaimed. "I was so tired. I was just scribbling numbers on the paper."

"Everybody stop!" It was the first time Philip had spoken. "You're only going to confuse her and then we'll never find the numbers again." He pulled a chair to her side and made her sit down. He pulled another chair beside her and sat down next to her.

"They're in your memory," he said. You just need to relax, think back to the moment before you handed Nathan the paper; before you went to sleep. Relax and they'll come back to you. Where were you sitting?"

"On Nathan's right. Larry was sitting on the other side of me. James was behind us."

"Okay. What else do you remember?"

"I remember how tired I was. How sleepy I was. I was scribbling on the paper, doodling really. I knew we were about to stop for the night. I was just doodling."

"Okay, that's fine. What grade are you in?"

She looked at him like he was crazy. "What?"

"Don't think about the numbers. They're there. They'll come out. You need to relax and think about other things."

Sharon's eyebrows went up. "Okay. I'm about to be a junior in high school."

"Are you a classmate of James and Larry."

"Yes."

This line of questioning went on for five minutes until Sharon suddenly exclaimed: "I can't do this! I can't! I don't believe this is happening. It was there. They were there and now they're gone. I can't believe this."

"Sharon," said Nathan. "It's okay."

"NO IT'S NOT!"

"Wait, you said something about trying them backwards like it was a decoder ring. We should just try the numbers backwards," said Nathan.

"I said it but I never did it. It wasn't me."

Philip had said nothing during all this activity, standing to one side and watching.

"When is your appointment at the Ministry?" asked Nathan suddenly, turning to him.

"Ten o'clock. I'll have to leave in a few minutes," he responded, glancing at James who stared back at him.

James gasped. "*I did it!*"

They all turned and looked at him. "What?" asked Nathan.

"I did it!" Sharon said to do it backwards and I did. It was the last code I gave to you. I just did it without thinking. We need to find *my* paper."

"Here," said Nathan, as he pulled it from under the codes they had worked on during the morning. "This is your handwriting." He handed the sheet to James.

"The codes are smeared but we may still be able to read some of them."

"How?"

"Backlight. If we hold them up to a bright light we might be able to pick out the two numbers at least. If we just had the two numbers in correct order . . ."

James took the paper and held it up to the florescent lights hanging above their heads. Everyone gathered around him. But there was nothing to be seen; the cold blue light shown through the paper, illuminating nothing.

"What about sunlight?" asked Larry. "The sun is shining through the window in the bedroom."

James took the paper to the window and held it up to the sun. At first, he could see nothing except the smear of the drink and a symbol in the bottom right corner that had no numbers assigned to it. Then as he eyes became accustomed to the glare he could see them, zeros and ones faint but still visible.

They went back into the first room. Nathan sat at the second computer and took the first of James' numbers. He carefully fed them into the converter and everyone stood waiting to see what would happen.

They waited two minutes, staring at the screen but nothing appeared.

"Wait!" exclaimed James. "Look!"

As they watched the exact numbers appeared again.

"We read left to right," said Nathan. "In the Arabic world, they read right to left. These codes must be reading right to left! That's why it worked."

Sharon was still not impressed. "Okay, but it's still just boxes and numbers."

"Yes, but more importantly, we now can figure out what symbol represents zero and what symbol represents one," Nathan said. "Show me where you started James."

James showed him the paper. "See this symbol is 1 and this symbol is zero. Give me some more of the code."

James did.

"Is this actually possible?" said Philip behind them.

"We're about to see," said Nathan. He paused and they waited once again.

The next section of the translation appeared.

"Wait a minute," he said. "This may be some kind of coordinate. See those empty boxes? That means the computer can't read that code. It's an unknown symbol to the computer and to us – an alien symbol. But . . . pick a star or a constellation as an example, let's say Andromeda." He quickly searched for Andromeda on the second computer. The website came up and he pointed to a set of codes. "This is the beginning of the right ascension of Andromeda."

"The what?" asked Larry.

"It doesn't matter. Take the beginning of Andromeda's right ascension, leave the numbers but remove the unknown symbols, the boxes, in the coordinate." He began to draw on a piece of paper. "Now look, if I insert the actual symbols we use to define a location of an object, what do you have?"

23 25 48 6945
23h 25m 48.6945

James looked at it and said, "It could be the same thing except the symbols we use are different. Are you saying it's a star?"

"I don't know. But I believe it's a coordinate of some kind – the beginning of the position of something."

"But of what?"

"I don't know. Something out there."

"So which sheet was it," asked Philip, calmly.

James handed it to him. Philip studied the opening lines of the codes for several minutes. "Hand me that pencil," he said. Larry handed it to him and Philip marked the paper. "We don't want to lose this again."

"So what do we do now?" asked Nathan.

"Continue," said Philip, "And see how much more of the code you can break."

Nathan looked at him blankly. "We broke the code *maybe* but that doesn't mean we can go much further with this. We need faster computers. We have this little fragment but we could still be here forever trying to get the rest of the info. We need faster computers!"

Philip looked at his watch as he picked up a pad of paper and a pen. "I have to go. We'll discuss this when I return from this meeting." He looked at James. "We have to try and find Eric first before we do anything else. If Mohammed can help us do that we can move on with this."

He turned to go but Nathan came after him and stopped him at the door. "Philip let me call some people I know. They're hackers but they're really good at what they do. They can help us with this and they'll keep their mouths shut."

"NO! Don't call anybody until I get back. Okay? Let me deal with Mohammed and we'll call when I get back. Okay? I promise."

"Okay," Nathan said quietly, backing away. He watched Philip as he walked out of the door, closing it behind him.

CHAPTER 16

A guard escorted Eric into the room they had sat in the day before, the diagrams of the wall had been returned and were sitting on the table.

Marie had been allowed to stay with him during the night, which had relieved his mind for her safety. But guards had appeared at the door of their room early the next morning and had indicated that Eric was to go with them. He had taken Marie by the arm but they had pushed her back and he had been forced to leave her there alone.

He sat down at the table and waited.

Momentarily, Raza came into the room along with a guard who closed the door behind them and took up his place by the entrance. Raza walked to the table and sat down.

"Good morning, Eric."

Eric did not return the salutation but instead said, "Why can't Marie be here with me."

"What we are discussing doesn't involve your wife. Or your ex-wife in this case."

"I . . ."

"She is safe," he continued, "I guarantee you she is safe. As long as you give us what we want no harm will come to her."

Eric glanced at the guard. "Where is the Professor?"

"In his room. He is safe as well. He will be joining us momentarily."

Eric shifted in his seat and looked at Raza. "How do you know what I give you, what the Professor gives you, will be true. I've studied Egyptology for years and the Professor is an expert in hieroglyphics. We could mislead you in so many ways, throw you off . . ."

"That would not be a good idea, Dr. Adams," Raza interrupted. He paused and stared directly into Eric's eyes. "Trust me," he said shortly.

Before Eric could say more the door opened again and a second guard escorted Professor Stevens into the room. He came silently to the table. Eric stood up and pulled out a chair for him to sit in. When the Professor was seated Raza turned to the guards and said, "Leave us."

One of the guards protested.

"I said to leave us!" His tone was sharp and dismissive and the men turned and left the room.

Raza turned to Professor Stevens. "You have transcribed the symbols from your part of the disc?"

"Yes."

"All of them?"

"Yes."

"Thank you," Raza said as he moved a schematic into position so all of them could see it.

"Who are you?" Eric said suddenly.

Raza looked at him and said, "Who I am doesn't matter."

"It does to me," said Eric.

"I am what you see," Raza said. "An archeologist, a lover of the past and its secrets, just like you."

"Archeology serves mankind by helping mankind understand where it came from, the mistakes our ancestors made before us. And that understanding shines a light on the future. It helps us understand so we won't make the same mistakes they did. What you're doing doesn't serve mankind. It threatens its very existence. Why are you doing this?"

"Doing what?"

"You know very well what. Who do you think you are that you can attempt this?"

Raza looked at Eric. "A believer," he finally said.

"In what?"

"Destiny," he said shortly.

"Destiny? Putting the whole world at risk so you can be the savior when they come back? So you can be the chosen one when they return? Is that it?"

"When who comes back? When who returns? I'm afraid your imagination is running away with you again, Eric."

Eric replied calmly. "Oh, okay. These pieces of the relic that can download information into your cerebral cortex: I must have imagined that. What . . . do you think I'm a fool? That we're all fools."

"Not at all. A fool is the last thing I would think of you."

"Both of us know what the wall is saying. Not everything. But we know enough to see who built it and what you're trying to do with it. Why in god's name would you try to connect them?"

"Shall we begin," said Raza.

"Does Dr. Mohammed know what you're doing?" Eric persisted.

"Shall we begin?" said Raza again.

For the next thirty minutes, they moved over the sections of the wall discussing various interpretations. For the most part, they agreed on the translations but Eric noticed that the discussion seemed cursory and without direction. The things they discussed were fragments that in the big picture meant nothing. In this manner, they quickly moved across the drawings to the panels directly above the large central figures that were holding the disc. There were two sections, one on top of the other. He pointed to the one at the top.

"What is your interpretation of this panel?"

"Nothing," Eric said. "I took it to be decorative only."

Raza sat back, his lips pursed as if he was trying not to smile. "Decorative."

"Yes."

"What else?"

"Nothing else."

"It doesn't strike you as a star chart?"

"No," Eric said flatly. "I hardly looked at those sections. I was too involved in the other panels."

"So, looking at it now, it still strikes you as just decorative."

"Yes."

"Professor," Raza said turning to Professor Stevens, "Do you agree? Because I see a star chart."

The Professor looked at the panel and back at Raza. He paused and then said, "Yes, I believe it is."

"A certain constellation, perhaps. If I were guessing I'd say a section of Orion. Wouldn't you agree?" said Raza.

"It's not exactly like Orion," Professor Stevens observed.

"Well . . . Orion 5,000 years in the past perhaps," Raza replied.

"How would you know? These symbols could mean anything," said Eric.

Raza sat back and spoke to Professor Stevens but kept his eyes on Eric. "Professor, when you first began to study the ancient Egyptian hieroglyphs what was one of the first ones you learned? What was one of the easiest to know and understand because of its shape, because of paintings found on the ceiling of say the tomb of Thutmosis III?"

"A star," the Professor said quietly.

"Very good. So if this symbol is a star then we can deduce a lot from their relative positions in the panel." Raza began to point to various stars, "Orion's belt. Betelgeuse. Bellatrix. Rigel. Sirius."

"All the stars are the same size," Eric observed. "The stars in Orion are different sizes. It can't be Orion."

"On the surface that statement is silly and a feeble attempt to mislead me. It is also incorrect," and he pointed to a symbol on the right-hand side. "What star would you say that is?"

"I'm not an astronomer."

"I never said you were. But if I were guessing I would say Rigel. It's larger than the others."

Eric didn't respond so Raza continued, carefully. "Why would they make a star chart like this Eric? Please give your opinion."

"Why would who?" Eric said," mimicking Raza's words. Raza didn't respond but sat waiting. "Whatever I say would be mere conjecture," Eric said finally.

"What do the hieroglyphs say in this panel? Since you only saw it as "decorative" I'll give you and the Professor a chance to study them now. Professor . . ."

135

Raza waited while Professor Stevens studied the panel. When he was through he looked at Eric and then at Raza. "It's Orion."

"What else?"

"The destination. The home world."

Raza glanced down at the drawing. "Precisely. That was my interpretation as well."

He sat for some minutes staring at nothing.

Abruptly he turned to another section: the second panel directly under the first. Raza pointed at it and said, "I need you to tell me everything you know about this section."

Eric glanced down and away. "As I've told you I don't know what it says. I focused on the other sections. That was the section I paid the least attention to when I was working in the dig. I really don't know anything about that inscription."

"Odd that you would do that. This panel is completely unique in my experience. Have you ever seen anything like this before, Professor Stevens?"

The Professor looked and shook his head. "No."

"Tell me what the two hieroglyphs represent, Professor."

"As far as I can tell, the number 1 and *nefer*."

"Yes. That is what I see as well. The number one and the hieroglyph for 'beautiful.' Very peculiar. How do we explain it except to say that it's a code? Is it not a code, Eric? Look closely. It's a code, is it not?"

Eric glanced at the drawing for a moment. "It's obscure. I . . . ," he trailed off

"I what?"

Eric looked back at Raza. "I'm not sure. It's obscure to me."

"You're a liar," said Raza flatly. "And you Professor?" he said suddenly turning to Professor Stevens once more. "Are you going to lie as well?"

The Professor shook his head. "No. I'm only seeing this for the first time. I don't know what this is?" the Professor protested.

"Look at it again," Raza said shortly and pushed it closer to the Professor.

Professor Stevens took up the drawing and spent several minutes studying the markings. "It's possible," Professor Stevens said and pushed it back to Raza. "But how would you possibly know what it says, it's just garble."

136

Raza moved to an inscription inside the panel where disc hung between the two figures.

"Does this speak of some kind of power; some kind of weapon?" he said. "Look! Does it speak of a weapon?"

"Why are you doing this?" Eric suddenly asked again.

Raza leaned across the table, lowering his voice menacingly, his mouth curled into a snarl. "We're *out* of time," he hissed. "This is very important. I'm running out of patience. Would you like me to call the guards or would you like to help me?"

He violently pushed his chair back so hard it hit the wall behind him. He stood and turned toward the door, which opened suddenly. The two guards rushed inside. Raza looked back at Eric.

Eric rose out of his chair. "Okay, okay," Eric shouted. "Okay. I'll tell you."

Raza motioned to the guards to leave. He pulled his chair back to the table and sat down. "One more time, Eric, or I swear I'm done with you! I don't care what happens to you or anyone else. This is too important. Do you understand me? Now, does it speak of a weapon?"

"YES! *As you well know!*"

"What kind of a weapon?"

"I have no idea? The description is obscure and confusing. Their technology bears no resemblance to our own. Why would it? Why don't you give me *your* interpretation for a change?"

"Decipher this phrase," and Raza pointing to three symbols in that section.

"Blue light," said Eric without hesitation.

"Is it some kind of laser?"

"I don't *know*."

"What about the disc?"

"What about it?"

"Is it talking about the disc. Can it be weaponized?"

"Again . . . *I don't know!*"

Raza sat back and shook his head. "You're never going to cooperate."

"I'm cooperating like I said I would. I can't decipher something this complex! I'm telling you the truth! Why won't you tell me what you think it says?"

"You're so childish. You sit here playing games with me, stalling for time, while so much hangs in the balance with the people you love."

"I love other things too, Raza," Eric said.

"Well, so do I! Which is why I'm sitting here dealing with your obstinacy!"

The Professor looked at the two men, picked up the corner of the drawing and pulled it to him. He studied it for a moment and said, "I will tell you what I believe. After that I would ask that you return the favor and tell us what you think it says. Do you agree?" Raza looked back and forth between the Professor and Eric, then slowly nodded his head. The Professor began.

"It speaks of power, yes, and possibly a weapon. The disc either becomes a weapon when all the pieces are joined or it is part of another kind of technology that can become a weapon. But the disc is more than a weapon or the part of a weapon. The individual pieces can connect to human intelligence as we have seen. In that state it can also interact with our own computers."

"And you know this how?"

"Because I saw it happen in New York before your people took the piece I had from me."

"Go on."

"It contains many pieces of information, I'm guessing now, data about their origin, their experience here on Earth and how to reconnect to the mother world.

I believe if all the pieces were to be joined it would become, for lack of a better term, a microcomputer although its creators would, I'm sure, not have used that term. The microcomputer would carry all the information, everything about them, what happened, what they hoped to achieve.

I believe the disc is part of a failsafe. If one person, or being, had all the knowledge and they died, all the knowledge would die with them. But if everything was downloaded onto the disc then three beings, three people if you want to use that term, would each have a piece of the information so if something happened everything would not be lost. In my interpretation each part of the disc contains the same information and each piece has the same ability to download content. But when they are joined something else happens."

"It becomes weaponized," Raza said.

"It becomes more powerful. That's all I know. And yes the possibility is there for it to become a weapon or weapons. Individually, the pieces of the disc cannot be used that way: only when they are joined can the power be accessed. This is my conjecture."

"This failsafe. You're telling me there's a redundancy across everything?"

"Across everything?"

"Between the wall and the disc. The same information that is on the wall is on the individual pieces of the disc?"

"That would be my interpretation," said Professor Stevens. "That and possibly more information that we cannot see. The disc is everything."

Raza turned to Eric. "Do you agree? Is that true?"

"Anything is possible with this. We've never seen anything like this before. And as far as I can tell, even with your advanced knowledge, neither have you," said Eric. "But if I were guessing as well I would say yes. The disc, the wall, the information the piece downloaded with the Professor all say the same thing. They made it redundant to keep the information safe."

Raza looked disturbed as he wiped his hands across his mouth. "The weapons? Can you give me any information about how to use the disc to build the weapons?"

Eric looked away, disgusted.

"Professor?" asked Raza.

"I honestly can't, although it speaks of something that I'm assuming is some kind of housing. The disc has to be together and locked into some kind of device."

"But you can't discern what that device might be?"

"That's correct."

"Is there anything else?"

"No."

They fell silent. Raza sat staring at the drawings until Eric finally said, "Well? Is that what you see? Is that your translation?"

"Basically, yes," Raza replied without looking up. He sighed and glanced at the Professor. "You are as certain as you can be that all pieces of the disc are needed for any kind of weapon?"

"As far as I can see," the Professor replied.

"Lucky for the people of Earth, you only have one piece of the disc. Gosh, sorry! No alien weapons today," Eric said sarcastically. "And — I'm just guessing here — it'll take years to build some kind device to send your little message home. By that time your scheme will be discovered."

Raza stared across the space between them, hatred etched on every feature. "The device, as you call it, is already built," he spat back. "The transmission can be sent in a matter of days *if* we so choose."

Eric face fell but he said, "Now who's lying?"

"Not I," said Raza.

Eric looked at Professor Stevens and back at Raza. "It's impossible: an enterprise that large, that complex. People would know."

"People, as with everything in the world today, know what we wish them to know. People are stupid and blind. Why, it could be built in plain sight and they still wouldn't realize what it was." Raza looked insane.

"It would never work! Orion is light years away from us. You don't have the power to send something across that distance."

"You forget our own technology, Dr. Adams. For instance you could bounce microwave signals off of one of the communication satellites. The first message would arrive faster than you might think. Then another and another, pulsing across space until they hear us and respond."

"The nebula inside of Orion—just the nebula—is twenty to twenty-five light years across. You could be sending signals till the end of time and nothing would ever hear you."

"You're forgetting *our* destination, *our* home world." And his finger stabbed down onto the star drawing and the largest star, Rigel.

"How do you even know they're still there? It was five thousand years ago!"

"We're still here! Why not they?" Raza shot back.

"My god, Raza. Do you know what you're saying?"

"I know perfectly well what I'm saying!"

"They're monsters!"

"They're *GODS*!" Raza smacked his hand down so hard everything on the table jumped.

Eric suddenly realized that he was sweating. "Well, one thing's for sure," he said, "you'll never build any kind of a weapon. You only have one piece of the disc."

Raza looked at him calmly, his anger suddenly gone. "I'm afraid that is not the case. We have two pieces of the disc. The first piece has been with us for years. The second piece was taken from Professor Stevens. And the third piece is now within our grasp."

"That's impossible!"

"Why do you think so? Do you believe your son, a mere boy, can hide it from us forever?"

Eric steeled himself to not react, to keep his voice steady. "James has nothing to do with this."

"I'm afraid he does. He stole the third piece out of the dig."

"That's not true."

"We both know it is. What you don't know is James is back in Cairo. We are aware of this because we are aware of everything. Our people, you see, are everywhere. It's only a matter of time before he is here with you and his mother. At that point, we will take from him the part of the disc he carries."

Raza stood up and leaned over the table, his voice dripping with menace. "Let's hope he doesn't resist."

CHAPTER 17

Retracing the steps he had made when he brought James to the safe house, Philip Harrington made his way back toward the center of the city.

He only stopped when he felt there was enough distance between himself and the others so he would not be seen. The city had been awake for hours now and the streets were full people. But no one observed him as he took the pad of paper and pen that he had brought with him and began to write.

He carefully transcribed as many of the symbols he had seen when he had glanced at the sheet Nathan had given him. He also wrote the corresponding binary code beneath each one. He knew he might make a mistake but he had to try and get as much of the information down as he could before he forgot it. When he was finished he tore the page off and discarded the pad of paper. Then taking his cell phone he searched for the number of the Ministry of Antiquities and hit redial.

After a few seconds, there was a short click and a man's voice came into his ear. "Yes?"

"This is Philip Harrington," he said. "Please tell the minister that I am on my way and will be there as soon as possible."

"I will inform him," was the terse reply.

Philip didn't respond but broke the connection and placed the phone back in the holster on his belt. He walked to the edge of the street and hailed a taxi that was going by. The driver saw him in time and pulled over. Philip slid into the back seat, as the man waited for directions.

Philip said, "al mathaf almasri," in perfect Arabic and the taxi pulled away from the curb.

The Supreme Council of Antiquities was housed in the Egyptian Museum. When the taxi pulled up to the entrance Philip stepped out, paid the driver, and walked through the front doors. He made his way into the east wing of the building, past the great ßinto the Ministry where he was quickly shown into the office of the Director.

Dr. Mohammad was finishing up a piece of correspondence with his assistant. When they were through the assistant exited the room without speaking or looking at Philip.

The door closed silently behind her before Dr. Mohammad finally spoke to his visitor. "Mr. Harrington, so good of you to come," he said as he indicated a chair. Philip sat down as the minister continued.

"Our plans are quickly coming into focus," he continued. "I'm sure you are aware that we have Dr. Adams."

"I had assumed as much."

"But that is immaterial at the moment. The more important question is do you have his son?"

"Yes."

"And does he still carry the artifact."

"Yes."

"You have seen it?"

"No. But after the events of last night, I know he still has it. But that isn't the most important thing. There's something much more pressing, at the moment than the last part of the disc."

Dr. Mohammed's eyes grew wide as he looked intently across the desk at his visitor. "What do you mean? What has happened?"

"We followed them into the city from the airport. As was our plan, they were to take refuge in the storage area behind the shop in Khan el-Khalili. I threatened them by saying I was going to send them away. James begged me to allow them to stay and if I did they would help us decode the alien symbols from the wall."

"Did you believe him?"

"No, not at first. He said the other boy, his friend who is with him, had made a discovery that would help us decode the symbols. I continued to play along with him and in the evening, we helped them 'escape' to the safe house."

"Go on." Philip had the minister's full attention now.

"Once there, James told me the boy called Larry had discovered that the alien symbols were a kind of binary code, like the ones that our own computers use. They spent most of the night trying to break the code."

"And . . ."

"And this." He placed the paper with the symbols he had drawn in front of Mohammed.

The minister picked up the paper as if it was the most ancient and precious of documents. "What happened then?" he said breathlessly.

"A tiny part of a schematic appeared on the screen, a fragment of something larger."

"What was it? Could you tell?"

"No."

"But you are positive what appeared on the screen came from the code the boy gave you."

"Larry didn't provide the code. He only provided the binary code connection. James provided the final combination by sheer accident. They were all trying to break it."

Dr. Mohammed sat back, stunned while Philip waited for him to speak.

"All this time, we have been laboring on the hieroglyphic record. All we have accomplished has been based almost solely on that and that only. Do you know what this means? If this works, it will provide the key to everything we haven't been able to understand. We will know everything. Most importantly, it will give us the coordinates we need."

"You still need to complete the disc."

"Yes but that is close at hand. At the moment, this information is much more important. Dr. Adams' son returning to us was unexpected. It was not our plan. But the gods," he said, pointing at the ceiling, "the gods continue to guide us. Don't worry about the disc. All the power it possesses will be revealed to us in time. The boy is safely in our hands and he still carries what we desire. The last stage of its journey is at hand."

"What are you going to do?"

"That depends on our scientists. The satellites will be in place within twenty-four hours for a first test of the system. If they can utilize the information you have provided in time, we can send the first signals with even more certainty that they will reach the exact destination we so desire."

"What about the boy and his friends."

"It's time for him, and the artifact he is carrying, to join us – dead or alive."

"Shall I return to them."

"Yes. It's important for you to appear as if nothing is amiss. We will talk to the priests before you go. The final pieces of our plan will fall into place."

Back at the safe house, James wandered into the little bedroom and sat down. Ever since Philip had walked out of the door that morning he had felt uneasy. At first, he had put it down to being exhausted, not having a decent meal in days, or nerves. But the feeling continued to grow until he felt like something was slowly closing in around him.

After Philip's departure they had continued, over the course of the day, to try and get more of the code to work. But nothing they tried produced anything. The converter only produced more garble. Everyone had slowly dropped away, exhausted. Larry had come into the bedroom before James and was now on the small cot opposite him sound asleep once again.

Philip had returned in the middle of the afternoon. Dr. Mohammed had been of little help. The only information the minister had provided was his belief that Eric had been kidnapped and his assurance the ministry would do everything it could to facilitate his return: they were already in touch with the authorities and the ministry would take it from there. He could hear Sharon talking quietly to Philip and Nathan in the other room. Everything else was silence.

The fact that the ministry was now actively searching for his father should have made him feel better. But it didn't. He leaned his head against the wall and closed his eyes. He thought about his mom and what she must be going through right now not knowing where he was or what had happened to him. He had tried over and over to call her but could never get through. She would have called Larry's mother long before now, found out that he wasn't there, found out he had lied to her and was missing. He felt a strong sense of guilt.

But what else could he have done except come back and try to find his dad?

On a whim he reached into his jeans pocket and pulled out the piece of metal, turning it over and over in his hand. For the first time, he wished he had left it in the dig where he had found it or at the very least given it to his father as soon as possible. He pictured himself walking back to the room where the wall stood bathed in the artificial light from the electric lamps. He could see the disappointment and anger on his father's face. He had disobeyed him and gone into the rooms of the dig that were blocked off plus he had touched an ancient and important artifact, possibly damaging it, not to mention the papyrus that had crumbled in his hands.

It would have been better had he chosen that path no matter what his father's reaction would have been. If he had, maybe none of this would be happening now.

He opened his eyes to stare at the small square in the opposite wall that was the window. It stood open, letting in the only source of fresh air. At that moment, Sharon walked into the room.

"Do you realize that is the only way out of here except by the front door," James said to her.

Sharon looked at him blankly. "What?"

"The window is the only way out of here except by the front door."

Sharon turned and looked at the window. "So?"

"What if we needed to get out of here really fast and we couldn't use the front door."

Sharon sat down on the cot next to him. "Are you alright James?"

James sighed and looked away. "Yes . . . I . . . I'm just tired I guess."

"And worried about your mother?"

"Yes, and my dad, and I don't know . . ."

She took the piece of metal out of his hand but stopped abruptly, looking at him. "It won't fry my brain or anything will it?"

James smiled. "No. It's done all it can do. At least, I think so."

Sharon held it up to the light and looked through the hole. "All of this because of a dirty little piece of metal. So weird."

She handed it back to James who put it back in his pocket.

"Do you trust Philip Harrington?" she said quietly.

James' head popped around to look at his friend. "Why do say that?" he asked, intently.

"I don't know. When he left this morning he was acting odd. At least, that's what it seemed to me. Not letting Nathan contact anyone at home that might be able to help us. Why not if it would help in finding your father."

The same thought had occurred to James but he didn't say so. "He's worked with my father for a while now. If something were wrong with him my dad would know."

"I guess you're . . ." Sharon didn't finish because there was an odd sound from the outer room and both of them stopped and turned to listen.

"What was that?" asked Sharon.

They heard Nathan push back his chair and then . . . chaos.

The door to the anti-chamber was smashed in and the sound of rushing feet came into the outer room. They heard Nathan cursing and the sounds of a struggle. There was a gunshot and then another.

Sharon leaped from the cot and ran to the door with James close behind her. He hardly saw anything before Sharon slammed the door, pressing her body against its dirty surface. "RUN!" She screamed the word so loud Larry jumped and tried to sit up on the cot.

James froze, staring at her. "RUN, JAMES! RUN!"

James jumped onto the cot where Larry was half reclining with wide eyes, stepping on Larry's side as he leaped at the small window and scrambled to pull his body halfway through its opening. He heard Sharon scream as she was bodily thrown onto the floor, heard the sound of feet rushing into the room, men yelling at him to stop.

Then he felt Larry's hands on his legs and feet helping him through the window. There was a cry of pain as Larry was backhanded across the mouth, falling onto the floor behind him. The intruders grabbed for James' legs but grabbed too late. He fell headlong into a small back street, his hands splayed out in front of him breaking his fall. He felt a sharp, stabbing pain in his wrists as his hands came down onto the rough stones of the roadway.

He didn't hesitate as a man's head and arm thrust through the small opening. He pointed his pistol and called for James to stop but James ran as hard as he could down the street. There were a series of sharp pops as the gun was discharged repeatedly. James heard the bullets flying past him but never paused or looked back.

He turned a corner and the shooting stopped. He could hear the man cursing behind him until that too ceased. He ran on blindly up and down small streets, past people who stared after him until he thought his lungs would burst.

Finally, he could go no further and collapsed against a dirty building as the sun dipped behind the buildings, casting purple shadows around him.

He was alone.

CHAPTER 18

His heart pounding in his chest, James closed his eyes, counted to ten, scrambled to his feet, and began to run once more.

He had to get away.

Almost immediately he heard the running footsteps behind him. He glanced back and saw two men round the corner at the end of the street. One of them yelled something in Arabic and there was another shot fired. The bullet hit the back windshield of a car sitting by the sidewalk, shattering it into a thousand pieces, little shards of glass raining onto James as he ran past.

He darted down another street as people began to run away from him and into doorways trying to escape the bullets that were being discharged.

His eyes darted from side to side. He had to find a place to hide, had to anticipate his next move – and the moves of his pursuers. Almost against his will, he glanced back once more.

And that was the reason he didn't see it coming.

The physical force of the blow that hit him propelled him stumbling across the road and down onto the pavement of the street crushing his arm underneath him and ripping his shirt half off. He cried out in pain and confusion, his arm in an agony that coursed up into his chest.

Two men, one on either side, grabbed him and hauled him quickly back across the street into the shadows of an alley and through an arch littered with garbage. He was smashed into a dark corner almost knocking the wind out of him. A hand was clamped down on his mouth so hard his teeth bite into the inside of his lips.

He could barely breathe. The man's eyes looked into James' own and he spoke with a foul, hot breathe. "One sound and you *die*! I swear to god you die."

The other man left them and ran back to the entrance of the ally. After an instant, he darted back into the shadows where they stood and spoke to the man holding James. "They're coming!"

"How many?"

"Three."

Before the word was out of his mouth the men chasing James ran past the entrance of the ally. All their eyes turned to look into the street.

"Wait . . . wait . . . NOW!" hissed the man holding James.

The first man ran back without pause directly into the middle of the road. He began to wave his arms. "HERE," he screamed. He's here! This way!"

James felt his whole body tense with fear and panic. He struggled to pull free. But his captor was bigger and stronger and he held him firmly in his grasp, crushing his head into the jagged surface of the wall behind him. The sound of running feet began to return coming closer and closer, louder and louder. James could hear them swearing. He went limp for an instant and then brought his knee up hard into the man's groan. His captor gritted his teeth and grunted in pain: his grip loosening – but only for a second. It clamped back down with a vengeance. He removed his hand from James' mouth and began to slap him across his face until blood was pouring out of James' mouth and he was sagging against the wall behind him: his face stinging from the assault and his eyes feeling like they were coming out of his skull.

James heard the footsteps run past him and fade away in the distance. He was aware of his own labored breathing and the pain in his arm and his face. The man suddenly dropped him where he stood and he sank down onto the dirty ground holding his arm and trying to get his breath. The man walked calmly away and went to the entrance of the alley, once more scanning the street left and right. When he was satisfied the street was empty he returned and stood over James who looked up at him through blurry eyes.

"Why he wants you alive is beyond my comprehension," he said. "If it were up to me you would have been dead ten times over."

James didn't respond. He felt himself slipping into darkness and he heard no more as he slumped over and passed out.

The man made no effort to help him but stepped back and waited. Fifteen minutes later the man who had led the pursuers away returned and they both came and stood over James once more.

"Did you lose them?"

"Yes. What do we do now?"

"We have to get away from here and I'm not sure how we're going to do it without them, or someone who works with them, seeing us."

"Is he dead, Ari?"

"No, Yassim, he is not dead. But I wish he was."

"Did you take it from him."

"No. That's not my place."

"But you're a priest."

"As are you. You want it, you take it!"

"No! I won't be touching their foul work," he replied as he cut his eyes to the ceiling.

"Nor will I. That's a job for the high priest."

Ari knelt down and pulled James up into a sitting position. James moaned and turned his bloody head to the side.

"God, Ari," said Yassim.

"He kneed me," Ari said shortly, looking back at Yassim. "Do you blame me?"

"Well, no," Yassim admitted.

Ari let James go and he slid back onto the floor. Ari stood up and stepped to the arch, leaning against its side.

"I can't believe this is happening," said Yassim.

"None of us can. I always thought the stories were made up or were so changed over time that they made no sense."

"We all did. We were wrong."

"Do you think it's safe to call anyone?"

"No. We can't do that right now. We have to keep him out of sight, and safe, until one of us can get back and transfer the information face to face. Their network is larger than I imagined."

"Yes," Ari agreed.

James moaned again. Ari stepped back, sat him upright, and turned his face to the fading light. His left eye and his lips were beginning to swell. Ari took a dirty handkerchief out of his pocket and wiped some of the blood off of his face and then stood back up.

"Do you think he needs a doctor," said Yassim.

"If he does there's nothing we can do about right now," replied Ari. "Do you know this place?" he continued, walking back to the arch. "Have you ever been here before?"

"Once, a long time ago. We came to visit an aunt of my father's."

"Do you think any of your family is still around here? Could we hide him there just for tonight?"

"That was a long time ago. She's probably dead by now."

"What about other family? Did she have other family?"

"Yes. But I haven't seen them in years. They wouldn't even recognize me."

"We're going to have to try. I can't think of any other way to handle this. We can't stay here all night and we have to get him cleaned up. A hotel is out of the question. Somebody would see us."

Yassim agreed. "Okay. I'll try to find them. I'll be back as soon as I can," he said and turned to disappear into the twilight.

Two hours went by before Ari heard footsteps come into the ally. James had been coming in and out of consciousness all this time. Ari tensed as he stood waiting to see if it was Yassim or not."

"Ari?" whispered Yassim.

Ari relaxed. "Yeeesss!" he said coming forward. "It took you long enough."

"As I said it was a long time ago. But I finally found them: one of my cousins and his wife and son. They were very surprised to see me. They didn't believe it was me at first."

"I'm sure. Will they take us in? Do you think we can trust them?"

"Yes and I believe so. Nadir works in construction. His wife stays home with the boy. I don't think they're involved."

"Okay. You're going to have to help me. He's still out of it. How far do we have to go?"

"Well, pretty far. I would guess it's about a mile."

"Damn."

"Can't he walk at all?"

"I haven't gotten him up since you left. He's going to have to try though. I'm not going to carry his ass for a mile."

James groaned as they pulled him to his feet. "James!" Ari snapped in his ear. "Can you hear me? James!"

"Yes." came the reply through clenched teeth and swollen lips.

"We're going to walk now. We need you to walk now! Understand?"

"Yes." And they placed their arms around his waist and helped him move to the edge of the street where they paused, looking up and down. There were a few street lamps here and there but their light was dim. The road seemed empty and deserted. Everyone was now indoors at their dinners except a few men they could see walking in the distance behind them.

"We'll have to be careful of the light," said Ari.

They began to hobble forward until they came to a street corner and another and another, always stopping to get an idea of who was about. With their nerves on edge, everything seemed unnaturally quiet but they went on without mishap until they were almost at their destination.

Yassim came up short and whispered, "Someone's coming!"

"Damn!"

They quickly looked around for a place to get out of sight. They didn't have much to choose from except a narrow side street with several garbage dumpsters sitting around. They hauled James to the first one and all of them sank down in the shadows behind it.

It provided minimal camouflage. If anyone walked into the street where they sat they would be exposed with nowhere to run. They waited, ears straining. Momentarily men's voices could be heard as they came to the corner of the street and paused.

"He got away," one said.

"He can't have gotten away. We have to find him!"

"It's dark! We have to wait until morning."

"By that time, the little shit will be long gone."

"Gone where? God, he's alone. We have all the others. We'll find him when it's light."

There was a pause. "Alright!" The first man said sarcastically, "You call Mohammed and tell him the boy was in our grasp and we let him get away!"

"We'll find him! Just not now. We could be running up and down these streets all night!"

"Have you looked down this one?"

Ari and Yassim knew from the sound that the man was indicating the street they were in. They both held their breath, waiting for the inevitable.

"Yes! I've been up and down it twice."

"What about the ones across the street?"

"No."

"Come on!" was the terse reply and the voices faded into the night.

"Damn it! They're everywhere!" said Yassim.

"That's why we have to get off the streets. That was close. Let's go."

They helped James to his feet once more and moved cautiously out into the main street again. No one was around and they quickly moved forward. Ten minutes later they came to a doorway that, once opened, lead into a small room with apartments on two sides and a staircase leading up into the second floor.

"Let me guess, they're upstairs."

Yassim gave his partner a wry smile. "Of course."

James was coming back into consciousness but they still had to assist him up the stairs where they stopped at the first door they came to.

Yassim knocked quietly and said, "Nadir, it's Yassim," he said. The door was slowly opened by a man who looked very similar to his cousin.

"Yassim," the man said.

"Yes. We're here."

They quickly moved inside. The apartment was small and sparsely furnished with an old coach, a television on a stand, some tables and chairs and a prayer rug on the wall. The floor was bare but very clean. A woman with long black hair and big eyes stood to one side, her dark blue robe studded with little glass beads that sparkled in the light from the lamp that hung from the ceiling. A small boy stood behind her peering out at the visitors. His eyes got big when he saw James and his bloodied face.

"My name is Ari. Thank you for letting us come here. He's had an accident," he said, indicating James.

"This is my wife Nadia," said Nadir.

"He needs to go to hospital," said Nadia, staring at James.

"No, we can't take him to a hospital right now. We need to stay here for the night. We'll be gone by first light."

Nadir looked at his frightened wife who returned his gaze with a slight shaking of her head. Ari turned to her.

"It's not what you think. We're not criminals. We just need to keep the boy here until morning when it's light. Nothing will happen. I promise you, nothing will happen."

Yassim looked at his cousin. "Please if you could just help us out."

Nadir paused and then nodded his head. "Alright," he said glancing back at his wife.

They helped James into the living area and sat him, half reclining, down on the sofa. Nadir told his wife to get some medicine from the bathroom. She turned without a word, returned with the supplies and gave them to Nadir. Then she took the little boy and went into the bedroom and closed the door without another word.

"I'm sorry, Nadir. There was no other place to go," said Yassim.

"It's alright. Let's see if we can help him."

Nadir took some medicine out of the case along with bandages and began to expertly see to James' swollen lips and face."

"Where did you learn to do this?" asked Yassim.

"Construction sites. There are always accidents," he replied.

Nadir took a tube, squeezed some white ointment on his fingertips and dabbed it on James' face. As soon as Nadir placed it on James' lip he came fully awake and lurched up into a sitting position. He cried out in pain but the sound died in his throat, his hand going up to touch the wounds.

"No, no," said Nadir. "You mustn't touch. The medicine will help you."

James pulled away from him, crawling down the couch, his eyes darting between the three men. "Who are you?" The words came out like a croak.

"You don't want to know," said Ari.

CHAPTER 19

For the first time since they had left home, Sharon was truly afraid. She sat, tied up and blindfolded, next to Larry in the back of a van that was moving rapidly through the back streets of Cairo. Every turn or sudden change in speed sent them lurching from side to side fighting to keep their balance. Philip sat across from them also bound.

She felt bruised and sore from being knocked down and she knew from his ragged breathing that Larry was in pain. When the masked man had struck him, sending him off the cot and onto the floor he had tried to get up only to be hit again: his head glancing off the second cot where she and James had been sitting only a moment before. The metal frame had cut a deep gash in his forehead.

It had all happened so fast she still found it hard to believe. At least five men had forced their way into the safe house. Nathan, caught completely off guard, had tried to stop them but was quickly overwhelmed and subdued. They had then gone after James and, but for quick thinking on all of their parts, James would be sitting with them now instead of free and out of their captor's grasp. That was the one great consolation. But the thought of him alone and scared in a strange city, with no one to turn to, was hard to take.

Once James had escaped the men had turned their attention to Sharon and Larry. They had pulled them up together and roughly forced them out into the front room. The tables were empty: the computers and all the papers they had worked on were gone. But Sharon and Larry hardly noticed. Nathan was lying on the floor, his face turned from them. There was no indication if he was dead or alive.

"Stop! Please! Stop! Please let us help him. Please!"

The men ignored her as they were pushed through the outermost storage room and into the street. Philip was already there and they were tying his hands behind his back. He looked to be wounded. Sharon and Larry were also tied up and they were all forced into the back of a black van.

Larry whispered, "Sharon?"

"Yeah?"

"Are you alright?"

"I think that's a question for you," she said. "Your poor head. Does it hurt really badly?"

"Yes," he replied honestly. "Where do you think they're taking us?"

She tried not to let her imagination run away with her. "I have no idea?"

"Do you think Nathan is still alive?"

"I don't know."

"Do you think James got away?"

"Yes. I think he got away, thanks to you."

"And you."

"Yes."

"Sharon?"

"What?"

"Do you think they're going to kill us, too."

Sharon paused. "Don't be stupid. Of course, they're not going to kill us. If they were going to do that they would have already done it." She didn't exactly believe what she was saying but she had heard it in a movie once and it seemed, at the moment, a good reply. "Besides, we don't know if Nathan is dead or alive."

They fell silent as the van continued to rattle through the streets. Philip had made no comment. Had he heard them? If so, he had made no attempt to join the conversation.

The journey lasted only an hour. But to Sharon and Larry, it seemed like forever before the van lurched to a stop and they heard the driver and passenger doors open and then bang shut again. The back doors of the van were wrenched open and hands reached in, pulling them out into the street and into the warm night. They were marched forward until a door was opened in front of them and they were forced inside a building. They went through several rooms before being pulled to a stop where their blindfolds were removed and their hands untied. There was a door directly in front of them which one of the men opened. The man made a stabbing motion with the rifle in his hand indicating they were to go inside. Philip went first and when they were all inside, the door slammed shut behind them.

Sharon gasped. "Mrs. Adams!"

"Sharon! Oh my god. Larry!" They ran into her arms where they stood for a moment, trembling and so relieved to see her they couldn't speak.

Marie held them until they had calmed down and then asked the question she feared. "Where's James?"

Sharon looked at her. "He escaped," she said simply.

"He's alone? Out there?"

"Yes. I'm so sorry. He escaped when they came and took us."

Marie nodded her head, her face contorted in pain. She looked at both of them. "You're both safe at least. I had no idea what happened. But why are you here? How are you involved with this?"

"We came back with James. He came back for his father. James knew something was wrong. Don't blame him. He was scared for his Dad. He would have told you but he thought you would try and stop him."

"I would have," she said. "Or I would have tried."

Philip finally spoke. "Mrs. Adams? If you remember I was the one who brought James home."

"Yes, I remember Philip. Are you alright?"

"I'm fine. A bullet just nicked my arm."

"There was nothing we could do, Mrs. Adam," said Philip. "They came on us so suddenly. It was a miracle James got away."

Before he could say more there was a sound from outside and Eric and Professor Stevens were escorted inside. Eric came up short, stunned at seeing Sharon and Larry. "What's this?"

"Dr. Adams," said Sharon.

"Oh, honey," said Eric to her. "What are you doing here? Where's James?" he looked around the room as if James was there.

"He's not here, Eric," Marie said. "He escaped. He's out there alone."

Eric ran his hand across his mouth. "God!" he said. "What happened, Philip? How did they find you?"

"I don't know," said Philip. "It may have been the cell phone."

"What do you mean?"

"Dr. Mohammed called my cell phone while we were in the safe house. I don't know how he got the number. Their people are everywhere, watching us. They may have hacked into the call and found our location."

"What did Mohammed want?"

"He asked for a meeting and I went thinking he might know something about you: where you might be, how to find you."

"Was that the reason?"

"Yes. He said he believed he knew what had happened to you, who had taken you."

"And who would that be?"

"Some kind of cult. He was very concerned for your safety and said he believed you had been kidnapped by some kind of religious sect: people trying to stop what we, what you, were doing in the dig. He said he would help us find you if he could. He said he would contact the authorities."

Eric nodded, "Yes. Dr. Mohammed will help us if he can. What about the other man who was with you? Nathan?" Eric asked.

"He's dead. At least I think he is."

"I see." Eric shook his head.

"Why didn't they kill you?" asked Sharon, abruptly.

Everyone turned around to look at her.

"What do you mean?" said Philip.

"Why didn't they kill *you*?"

Philip's gaze was steady as he answered her. "They tried, as you can see," and he held his arm. "I dodged their gunfire."

"It would have been point blank range."

"There was a struggle," he said turning to Eric. "I did all I could do."

"I'm sure you did," said Eric.

Sharon cut her eyes around to look at Larry.

"Eric?" Professor Stevens said softly, "could you introduce me to everyone."

"Of course, I'm sorry. This is Dr. Stevens, my archeology teacher from university. He is the foremost expert on Ancient Egypt and, I'm proud to say, a dear friend. You've already met Marie. This is Philip. He's been working with me for some time now. He's with the CIA."

Marie's mouth fell open. "I couldn't tell you," Eric said to her and she closed her eyes and nodded.

"And this is Sharon and Larry. They are James' best friends who I wish with all my heart were not standing here in front of me but safely back home in Virginia."

"It's a pleasure to meet you all," said the Professor. "And I wouldn't wish that they were safe back home, Eric. Fate may have brought them here, like the rest of us. We don't know what will happen in the end and I'm assuming they came for their friend which is a noble, loyal thing to do."

"Yes," Eric had to agree.

"He didn't want us to come, Dr. Adams," said Larry. "He tried to stop us but he was determined to come back to try and find you and we couldn't let him come back by himself."

"I know," Eric said. "I told him I would be home and obviously, I failed."

"That's right," said Sharon. "When you didn't come or call he knew something was wrong."

"Everyone pray he'll be alright. As Philip says, these people are everywhere."

"What happens now?" said Philip. "What is this place?"

"It's a hidden facility where they are working to decode the information on the wall."

"Is it working? Are they close?"

"Yes. Not everything, thank god, but they're close. It could be a month or two," he said wearily. "Or it could be tomorrow."

"What's going on?" said Sharon. "Can you tell us what's really going on? James said it was . . . it might be . . . alien technology."

Eric looked at her, his face lined with anxiety. "It *is* alien technology. The Egyptian government was doing construction in the desert south of here. They found what they, at first, believed was an ancient tomb. They called me in to help with the work. But it wasn't a tomb. I knew almost from the start that it wasn't a tomb. But I didn't really know what it was. I had never seen anything like it. It's something completely unique: a repository of information, alien in origin, coded into a wall carving.

The information is in their language. Hieroglyphic symbols on the wall match the alien language like the Rosetta Stone: two forms of writing, side by side, saying the same thing. If you can read the hieroglyphics you can read the alien code, more or less. All the translations up until now have been based solely on the hieroglyphics."

"My god. How can this be? All that in the wall we were working on?" said Philip.

"I know it sounds insane. But it's all true. And there's more. There's another key. The information is also embedded in a disc, a disc that has power. How much power? Who knows? It carries the final solution to the puzzle, the final interpretation. It can also be used as a weapon. But it is in three parts. These people, the people who are holding us here, the same people who are searching for James, have two of them."

"James!" said Sharon. "James has the final piece, doesn't he? It's that piece of metal he showed me."

"Yes. If all of them are joined, sooner or later, these people will know everything and have the technology at their disposal."

"*Alien technology?*"

"Yes."

"*To do what?*"

"To send a signal to the alien world that created the wall, and the disc, and tell them where we are – the location of Earth – so they can invade us. Enslave us. Destroy the world."

Sharon felt fear run across her skin. Her face was frozen in disbelief. "Can they do that?" she gasped. "Can they really do that? Can they send a signal like that?"

"Yes. If everything goes according to their plan."

"Why . . . why would they want to do that?" Sharon could barely get the words out of her mouth. "Why would they want creatures like that to come to us?"

"Because they came once before, many centuries ago, by accident. It's a very long story. Their attempt to destroy civilization –

destroy mankind – was stopped then. It may be too late to stop it now."

CHAPTER 20

Marie touched Eric's arm. "How close are they to making it work?"

"As far as sending the signal goes they are very close. They've broken the code to a point. They believe they have the general coordinates in Orion. They're going to use our own technology, our own satellites. If the plan works, they will be able to send a signal to a star in that constellation. And if the alien race is still there the odds are they will receive the signal and respond."

"It's all my fault," Larry said suddenly. Everyone turned to him.

"The binary code. If I hadn't mentioned the binary code none of this would have happened."

"What about the binary code?" said Eric.

"I told James I thought the symbols were a binary code, ones, and zeros. And it was. We translated a tiny fragment."

Professor Stevens turned aside with a tiny gasp.

"It's not your fault," Eric said. "They already had most of the information they needed. They would have discovered the rest of it sooner or later. It's not your fault."

"But if I hadn't said anything it would have made it harder. It would have taken them longer."

"Perhaps. But they have been working on this apparently for years, even before the wall was discovered. They are much further ahead with their plans then any of us thought. Plus . . . they have pulled so much information out of the Professor and myself they could still attempt it even without the information you provided."

"But they still need all the pieces of the disc to make it work. Isn't that right?" said Marie. "They still need what James is carrying," she said hopefully.

"Not for the signal to be sent. As I said they are much further along than I thought."

"But they'll leave him alone for now? If they don't need the other piece they'll leave him alone, give him time to escape."

"No," Eric said. "They will continue to hunt him. They don't need the completed disc to send the signal but they need it for what comes next. Once the disc is joined they will have all the knowledge it possesses, all the power it possesses, at their disposal."

"Is there anything we can do to stop it?" asked Philip. "Anything at all?"

"At this point, I don't see how," Eric replied. "If we could get a message to Dr. Mohammed, let him know what's happening, he might be able to stop it."

"So you don't think he's involved in this?" said Philip, easily.

"No, I don't. I believe Raza's behind it."

"The assistant?"

"Yes."

"Why do you say that?"

"Think about it. He's the obvious choice."

At that everyone dispersed around the room, silently trying to come to terms with what they had just heard.

Philip watched as Professor Stevens pulled Eric aside to whisper to him. "Eric. Some people believe the symbol of *nefer* is the Egyptian zero."

"*Nefer*? What do you mean? *Nefer* means beautiful."

"Some people say it has another meaning; that it means 'perfect.'"

When the Egyptians would build a structure, a pyramid as an example, they would lay the first course of stones. That first course would have to be perfect: perfectly flat, perfectly formed. Otherwise, every course of stone after that would be off because *nefer* had been laid less than perfect. The course of stone after that, according to the records, and even inscribed on some of the structures that remain today, was called '1' the first course of stone after *nefer*. So *nefer* is their zero."

"That is mentioned nowhere I have ever seen."

"But I have seen it. The sources are obscure but I have seen them. What if it's true? The panel directly about the figures on the wall, directly below the star chart, is obviously a code. If the boy is right and it is a binary code using ones and zeros then it is *the* binary code. They're looking right at it. The alien code would not need to be translated; the translation is in the hieroglyphics themselves. They are looking at the translation! They are looking at the coordinates of the other world."

"Do you know what you're saying? It's crazy."

"Maybe not as crazy as you think. The Egyptians used all of our base numbers. No other civilization used them before the Old Kingdom in Egypt. Where did they get them? Did they actually think them up by themselves, an ignorant race of people? Or were they given to them by another race of beings; beings much further advanced than they were themselves."

"They were building pyramids before the 'aliens' came. How did they do that?"

"No, they weren't. Not true pyramids. They were stacking mud bricks or blocks of stone on top of each other. No math was involved. All of the pyramids before the Great Pyramid were either mastabas, stair-stepped piles of stone like at Sequarra, or pyramids that were flawed. The Great Pyramid was the first mathematically true structure; the first one to use geometry. You can't have geometry without the numbers."

Before Eric could answer there were sounds coming from the hallway outside and a man in military garb entered the room. Two guards accompanied him.

"The boy and the girl first," he said pointing at Larry and Sharon.

"NO!" Eric stepped between them and the man. "They've told you everything they know."

"Don't worry, Dr. Adams," he replied with a smirk, "you're all coming along." He stood to one side and jerked his head toward the door.

They were all taken out of the room, down a hallway and into the room that contained the computers and the servers. The first night Eric had seen this room was the night he had been brought into the building with Professor Stevens. It had been active then but nothing like it was now. All of the computer stations were occupied, each man intently studying the screen in front of him. There was a large monitor on one wall with codes strings moving rapidly across its surface. Raza was standing in front of it watching the codes moving past, along with several other men. They were in deep conversation but he turned when he heard them approaching and waited, stone-faced, until they stopped in front of him.

He looked at Larry and Sharon. "I have to thank you both. You've been more than helpful," he said. "We would not be this far along without your insights and, of course, James' contributions as well." And he looked at Marie and gave a twisted little smile. "Don't worry, Madam, your son will be with you shortly."

"You should be very proud of yourselves," he continued, looking at Sharon and Larry. You did something even all our brilliant minds put together could not do," he said looking around the room. "You broke the code. What is that saying, Eric? Out of the mouths of *babes*." His voice hung on the last word with disdain and the smile, this time, showed his pointed teeth.

"What do you want, Raza?" said Eric.

"*Well*, first of all," he said, his tone solicitous. "I'm very curious. Is there more? Have you told us everything?" he said and he leaned down until he was on Larry's level and looking directly into his eyes.

Larry nodded his head in jerky little motions and pulled away from Raza's face.

Sharon did not pull away at all. "*He's told you everything!*" she spat. "*So have I. Go to Hell!*"

This time, Raza smiled broadly, his face a mask of madness and evil. "The one with spirit. I've heard a lot about you." He stood back up as the smile vanished. "We'll see how far your spirit takes you in the end."

"Leave them alone!" Eric snapped. "They've given you all they can."

"Ahhh, Eric," he said turning to the archeologist. "Always the champion of the weak . . . and the weak-minded," and he shot a glance at Professor Stevens.

"What do you want now?" said Eric again.

"Clarification," was the short reply. "If you can offer clarification, that is. Your translations to this point have been, well, less than satisfactory." He turned and walked to the white board hanging a few feet away. It was covered with various printouts. The computers had drawn the Orion nebula in astonishing detail: detail like had never been seen on the Earth before. Only advanced knowledge could have provided such knowledge. "As you can see the computers have done their job with the information we have obtained. However, there is confusion, and disagreement, about an important coordinate in the star map. I'll let Professor Amil explain."

Eric recognized Amil from his first interrogation in the building in the desert where he had been taken to after his kidnapping. As before, he was neatly and overly dressed as if he was going out to an expensive restaurant for dinner. Amil avoided Eric's gaze and gave no indication they had ever met before. He gave no greeting but business like, picked up a marker and pointing to the drawings, began.

"The computer translations, based on the new codes, indicates the home world is this star, this sun," and he pointed to Bellatrix.

He turned to stare at Eric, waiting for a response.

Eric looked from him to Raza. "So?" Eric said. "I've already said . . ."

"I told you he would not be cooperative," Raza interjected so hastily and loudly that Eric blinked. "You know as well as I do, Dr. Adams, that the ancients worshiped Sirius. Why, the earliest Egyptian calendar was based on its rising after it had disappeared from view for many months. Its reappearance signaled the annual flooding of the Nile. It's no wonder they considered it a god. They knew even then it was the home world . . . our world. The computers have misread the codes or the codes are so obscure the computers are working from flawed data. The names that are used are in "their" tongue. Those names mean nothing to us; there is no way to understand their naming of the stars. Sirius is the home world," Raza said emphatically. "I'm sure of it!"

"I don't see how that is possible," Amil said flatly. "Computers don't lie."

"They can easily lie if the wrong data is fed into them," Raza continued. "We control that data. Plus, and this is the most obvious reason, there is human error." He looked at Professor Stevens again. "The old man and the boy transcribed the symbols in their heads incorrectly. So we are thrown back onto the symbols, the hieroglyphs – their interpretation is all we have."

Amil looked at him as if he were insane. "We *do* control the data: the data that matters. The code is broken. It's Bellatrix!" The neatly dress man turned to Eric. "Is that not so?" he asked sharply.

Raza angrily stepped between Amil and Eric. His back was to everyone as he looked directly into Eric's face. "Over many days, as I was interrogating you, you told me repeatedly that the star we seek is Sirius – the Dog Star – that is the star we seek. That is what I have read in the hieroglyphics. That is what you have repeatedly said. This is vital. We must know the star of our origin. NOW! Tell me the truth. Is it Bellatrix or Sirius?" The word "Sirius" was spoken with a strong emphasis.

Raza's words were angry, but there was a change in his features. His face had taken on an ashen cast and his eyes, moments before full of disdain and dismissal, were now almost pleading as they looked into Eric's own. He seemed suddenly smaller as if he was straining under a great weight. "Speak the truth!" he snapped, "Or by the eye of Horus you will be sorry!"

The phrase sounded odd and out of place: Horus, the protector of mankind, suddenly a threatening force?

What was going on? Something had changed.

Eric looked from Raza to the other men and to Marie who was standing with Sharon and Larry behind her. Professor Stevens' face looked questioning. Everyone was silently staring at him, waiting for his response.

Eric turned back to Raza. Raza's eyes looked up at Eric's under heavy lids and he was biting his lower lip.

Eric heard himself speak and was surprised as everyone when the words came out. "Raza is correct," he said. "The star you seek is Sirius."

"How can we trust *him*?" was Amil's acerbic inquiry.

Raza suddenly snapped back into his former, dismissive self. "We can't! He lies! They all lie! But in this case, he is correct: his translation and my own are the same. The star is Sirius."

"Then why is Bellatrix depicted so large, so out of proportion to the other stars in the constellation? It's even larger than Rigel, the largest star."

"It was a long time ago. The stars change, shift their positions, grow," Raza said, echoing Eric's earlier words.

Amil looked at the other men with consternation. "That makes no sense whatsoever. Yes, the stars change and shift their positions but this was 5,000 years ago, a mere second in time compared to the age of these stars and . . . you forget the other possibility."

Raza turned on the man. "What other possibility?" he snapped.

"That the Fathers were telling us by its larger size that it is the origin!"

"Possibly. But you cannot discount the hieroglyphs! We know more from them than any other source except the united disc itself and we, at the moment, don't have that source available to us."

Amil crossed his arms over his chest, looked at Raza and calmly said. "What you say is very true, my dear Raza. The hieroglyphics do not lie."

"So you believe the computers have misread the information," said Raza.

"It's certainly possible, but improbable. The first transmission is tomorrow night! The computers, EVERYTHING, points to Bellatrix. That first transmission may be the only one that gets through in this cycle. The next chance for this could be DAYS away. If your information is wrong, if this decision is wrong, and the message goes astray who will take responsibility? It won't be me!" Amil's face was calm and without concern as he looked into Raza's own.

"*I* will take responsibility! The decision is made!" Raza said emphatically.

Amil stepped back, shaking his head with disbelief as he looked around at the other men.

Eric spoke. "Tomorrow night? You can't be serious! How?"

Raza whipped around to look at him. "How is not your concern and we're done here! Take them away!" he said to the guards who quickly rounded everyone up and marched them back to their room.

Once they were alone the Professor came to Eric. "*What* just happened?"

Eric shook his head. "I have no idea. We told him it was Bellatrix. The symbols say that is the star."

"Who cares what just happened. It worked. You agreed with him and threw them off the trail. It worked." said Philip. "The signal will go astray. That's very, very good, right?"

"Yes," said the Professor. "That's very good. But whose side is Raza on? What game is he playing now? Did we even mention Sirius?"

"Who cares," said Philip, again, "as long as this can be delayed as long as possible."

"He seems so evil, so much a part of this. I can never understand his mind," said Eric.

"Understanding a mind that is that twisted is impossible, my boy. There's no reason to even try."

"But this *is* good," said Sharon. "If the signal is sent to the wrong place it won't work. We're safe."

"For the moment, it won't work. For the moment we're safe," Eric replied. "Did you see those charts? Where did they get those charts? Whatever is going on they will continue to try until it does work. It will only be a matter of time before they discover the coordinates are wrong."

"Then there will be Hell to pay," said Philip.

Sharon was the only one who noticed that his face, looking at Eric, showed no concern at all.

CHAPTER 21

The plan to take James and leave the apartment as soon as it was light turned out to be a failure.

Ari had gone out, just as the first glow of dawn appeared in the sky, to scout the area and see if their pursuers had given up the chase or had moved on to search other areas of the city.

He returned shortly to say that many of them were still on the streets and it was unsafe to venture out.

At 9:00 Nadir, already late and much to his wife's consternation, left for work. Ari, Yassim, and James had heard them arguing in the bedroom and when Nadir had come out Ari had apologized repeatedly to him, telling him they would be gone as soon as it was safe.

"We will leave as soon as we can," Yassim had assured his cousin, as well. "Please tell your wife we will be gone as soon as we possibly can."

Nadir had conveyed this message to his wife and had said goodbye before leaving for work. But she remained in the bedroom with their son, only venturing out to get him something to eat for his breakfast and again for his lunch.

Around 1:00 the attempt to leave was made again with the same result. Yassim had returned with the same report: the men who were pursuing them were still searching the streets.

"We can't stay here forever, Ari," Yassim said.

"We may have to stay until nightfall," Ari replied. "We can't risk being seen or being caught."

"We can't stay here till then."

"Then what do you suggest?" Ari asked. "Obviously, they have called in reinforcements. Five men went into the safe house: three came out with the hostages and two were in pursuit of the boy. There are many more of them now. We can slip around five men but not any more than that. We'll be seen."

"Let me call. If we can get through we can have reinforcements of our own. They can throw them off the scent."

"What if the call is intercepted? They'll know where we are."

"They can't intercept every call, Ari."

"Why don't you let me go," said James. "That would solve all your problems."

"It might solve our problems for the moment but it won't help you at all. You think you've had it rough up until now?" said Ari. "Just let them get their hands on you. Then you'll know what rough means."

"Who are *they*? Who are *you*?" James said.

"We're your *protectors*," he said, "or haven't you noticed?"

"You're not protecting anybody. You want what I've got, that's all. Just take it and let me go. I don't care. I just want to find my father and my friends!" He reached into his jeans but Ari stopped him.

"Don't!" he said emphatically. "I don't even want to look at the cursed thing."

"Please let me go," James entreated.

"You wouldn't last a minute out there," said Yassim, quietly. "Trust me."

"I'll take my chances."

Ari laughed and looked at Yassim. "Not only naive but stupid as well."

James looked away from them. "I'm hungry," he said. He had been sitting on the sofa all morning without a word except to ask for water. He expected another sarcastic reply but instead received a calm acknowledgment from Ari. "So am I." Ari walked to the refrigerator and yanked open the door.

"We're not going to eat their *food*?" said Yassim.

"Again, what do you suggest? Running out and getting something down at the local café."

Yassim looked at the bedroom door, shook his head, took the bowl of berries Ari handed him, and gave them to James.

It was good that the food was small: James' lips were still painful and swollen and his left eye was black and blue.

Yassim put his fingers under James' chin and lifted his face so he could look at the wounds.

"He's *alright*," Ari snapped. "Eat! We may not get another chance all day."

Ari set what food he could find on the table and they all ate in silence. When they were done, Yassim and Ari cleaned up the mess and James retreated back to the sofa.

"Should we get them some food," asked Yassim indicating the bedroom door.

"They'll come out when they get hungry enough," was Ari's reply.

But by 4:00 in the afternoon the woman and boy had still not ventured into the living room. Every time one of them had to go to the bathroom they had knocked on the bedroom door and entered to find the woman sitting on the bed and the boy playing with some blocks on the floor: neither of them looking up or acknowledging their presence.

"I'll go out again," said Yassim, "and see if anything has changed."

"It's so close to nightfall we may as well wait until dark. Your friend will be . . ."

He didn't have a chance to finish his sentence. There was a sudden, sharp rapping on the front door. Everyone froze.

"Maybe it's Nadir," Yassim whispered.

"No. He left late. He wouldn't come home this early." Ari looked around the space. "Is there another way out of here?"

"Not that I can see," said Yassim.

"Get the woman," said Ari.

The rapping was repeated again only louder.

Yassim went to the bedroom door but it was opened before he could knock. "There's someone at the door," he said. "You need to answer it. Don't let on we are here. Do you understand?"

Her eyes darted to Ari and back to Yassim but she made no response. She pulled her son out of the bedroom and together they walked to the door.

Ari got James up and pushed him toward Yassim. They went into the bedroom but didn't close the door. "Ask who it is," instructed Ari as he pressed himself against the wall.

She spoke then directly into the panels of the door. "Who is there," she said.

A man's voice answered, "The police."

She looked at Ari. "Ask him what he wants," he whispered.

"What do you want?"

There was a pause before he spoke again. "There are some men in the neighborhood. We believe they have kidnapped a young American boy. They're very dangerous. Have you seen anyone like that around here?"

She looked at Ari who shook his head. She hesitated with her mouth open to speak. Ari jerked his head toward the door. "No," she finally said.

"Are you sure? I thought I heard men's voice when I came to the door. Can you open the door and just let me make sure you are alright and then I'll go."

She didn't look at Ari but instead said, "Yes."

Ari grimaced and felt his anger rise into his throat. He gritted his teeth and pressed himself further against the wall as Nadia slowly opened the door.

Ari could see the man through the frame of the door. He recognized him immediately. This was no policeman. The question was, was he alone. Ari listened to try and ascertain if there was someone else standing on the landing of the stairs. From his position, there was no way to know.

The man peered into the apartment behind Nadia. "Are you sure you're all right?" said the man.

"Yes. I am fine," she answered but too quickly and cut her eyes toward Ari standing in the shadow of the door.

"I see." The man's eyes followed her glance and he strained to see through the crack if someone was hiding behind the open door.

"Is this your son?"

"Yes," she said.

Ari watched as the man squatted down.

"Have you seen any men today," he said to the boy.

Ari knew this was the moment to act and their only chance to get away. He prayed the man was alone as he yanked the door back, pushing the woman and boy aside, and charged headfirst at the man on the stairs. Thrown off balance and unable to stand he fell backward, cursing Ari as they rolled down the flight of stairs onto the floor below.

Yassim yelled for James to follow him and they rushed out of the apartment as Nadia and the boy huddled by the sofa.

Yassim rushed to Ari's defense but he didn't have to bother. Ari had the man up against a wall pummeling him in the stomach and sending blow after blow of his clenched fist into the man's bloody face. He slumped down, limp and unconscious, onto the floor.

Ari stood over him, his breath harsh and labored, as Yassim searched the prostrate body at their feet. He quickly found what he was looking for – the pistol in the holster around his waist.

"We've got to get out of here."

"Yes. Bring the boy."

Yassim turned to James but he didn't have to say anything to him. James followed his lead and they quickly made their way down a side hall as Ari brought up the rear, checking behind him to see if anyone else appeared. They pushed through a side door and were out on the streets again.

"We need to move as fast as we can," Yassim said.

They darted down the street they were on but quickly picked another one at random and moved down that and then another and another.

"I know where we are now," said Ari. "This way!"

They kept up this pace until the sun had set when finally stopped to rest. They had seen no one nor could they detect that they were being followed.

"We're getting closer to the bazaar," Yassim said. "What now?"

"We blend in, get through it, and make our way to the others."

"How will we do that? We can't take a taxi."

"No. But we can walk."

"Walk! We'll never make it. We'll be seen."

"Nobody's seen us yet. Maybe our luck will hold," Ari said.

"Yes. And maybe it won't."

Ten minutes later they slowed their pace and walked past the first of the shops. At the corner they turned onto one of the main streets and walked along, stopping occasionally to talk and look around, giving the impression they were just killing time before going home for the night.

They were almost out of the bazaar and ready to head deeper into the city when Yassim froze and quickly turned around. "Stop! Look to your left."

"Akhem!" Ari breathed the name with relief as they watched a man walk into a store across the street. "Stay here. I'll get him. Don't draw any attention to yourselves!"

Yassim pulled James to the side and into the shadows as Ari walked across the road and into the shop in front of them.

"Who is Akhem?" asked James.

"One of us," was the short reply.

Momentarily the two men reappeared and moved carefully to where Yassim and James waited. Akhem was short and slight with a small mustache and black hair pulled back from a prominent forehead. James could see in the light that his face was pockmarked. He looked James up and down and said, almost in awe, "The boy."

"Yes. It's him."

"They are looking for you," he said. "Everywhere."

"Yes, we know. We barely made it here," said Yassim. "We have to get him away and hidden. Can you help us? Do you have any kind of transportation?"

"Yes," Akhem pulled his eyes from James as he said the word. "A car. But Ari, they're at the Pyramid."

Ari looked at him blankly. "So. They've been at the Pyramid for months?"

"You don't understand. They're at the Pyramid. It's tonight."

Ari shook his head. "What do you mean?"

"He means they're ready," said Yassim. "They're ready to send the signal!"

Ari grabbed Akhem's arm. "They can't be ready. Nothing is ready! They don't have all the information. They don't have the completed disc."

"They have everything they need at least for now. They broke through the codes. The other boy showed them how. They know where to send the signal. The satellite will be overhead at 10:00 tonight."

"I don't believe it! How? These kids don't know anything. How did they do it?"

"I don't know. I don't know how it was done. The computers figured it out with the information from the other boy. All I know for sure is they are there and the first attempt is tonight."

"What signal?" asked James. "What are they doing? Is my father with them? Is my father there?" He reached out and grabbed Akhem.

"Stop it," hissed Ari and he pushed James back against the wall.

"I don't know everyone who is there. I only know the first attempt is tonight."

Ari turned to Akhem. "Is Raza there? Is he at the Pyramid?"

"Yes. He will personally send the signal. They told me he wanted to be the first to attempt it."

"This may be why we haven't been followed since we left the apartment. They've all been called to watch it, the first transmission," said Yassim. "What can we do?"

"We have to get out there!" said Ari.

"And do what?" asked Yassim. "We'll be outnumbered?"

"We have to try." He turned to Akhem. "You say you have a car?"

"Yes. Just down the street."

"Go get it and we'll meet on the corner."

They watched as he walked away and disappeared down the street.

"Please tell me what's happening," said James. "Please tell me."

Ari didn't look at him but said, "Maybe the end of the world."

CHAPTER 22

As soon as the two vans had come to a stop the doors were opened and they were roughly pulled from their seats and into the night, guns pointed at their chests.

The full moon had risen, its light casting the deserted ruins of the Giza plateau in high relief. All the tourists had gone home hours before; the soda cans and food wrappers scattered on the ground were the only evidence that they had been there at all.

But for that touch of the modern world blowing around their feet, and the twinkling lights of the village in the distance, the group of people standing a few yards from the Nile could have easily fancied themselves in another time, another place, trapped in the ancient past. The Great Pyramid rose up in the distance. Even without its casing stones, it appeared ghostly and surreal, making them pause and hold their breath.

"Remember when we first got here and I said I wanted to see the Great Pyramid?" Larry whispered to Sharon.

"Yes," she replied.

"I don't want to see it anymore."

"Neither do I."

Eric and Professor Stevens were standing at the rear of the group. They felt rifle barrels urging them forward. Eric spoke to the others and they began to move en mass. Shortly they climbed onto a broad walkway, several feet wide, and paved with smooth stones.

"The causeway," Professor Stone said matter-of-factly as if he was giving a lecture in a classroom. "The path they used to drag the great stones to the building site."

They continued silently down this path for several minutes until the guards ordered them to halt. An officer in the front called to a man in the back and the man moved around them, walked to where the officer stood, and spoke to him, the words whispered and inaudible.

The man jogged away and quickly disappeared from view. The officer motioned for them to sit down. Larry and Sharon sank down where they stood while Eric and Marie sat down on the raised sides of the causeway, Professor Stevens facing them on the opposite side.

"Why have they brought us here?" asked Sharon.

"This is where the transmission will be sent unless I'm mistaken," Eric replied.

"How? Using what?"

"The Pyramid has been closed for many months. I'm sure once inside we'll discover it's full of the technology they need to send the signal. They closed it so they could prepare it to fulfill the actual purpose; the reason it was built. The pyramid is a transmission station. They want us to watch when they send the signal."

Marie looked at Eric. "It's not a tomb?"

"No. It was never a tomb. The wall speaks of it; reveals what it was meant to do. It's the only pyramid they ever built that has actual rooms inside of it; rooms laid out to facilitate the installation of the alien technology. All the other pyramids have rooms cut into the bedrock with the blocks sitting on top of them. Inside the king's chamber there is a stone box everyone believes is the place where the pharaoh was buried. It never contained a body; only a part of their machinery."

"What are we going to do?" whispered Marie.

"There's nothing we can do," Eric replied. "We're trapped."

"What will happen to James?"

"Hopefully, he will escape. Go home. Live."

"He'll never do that," Sharon said. "He will stay until he finds out what happened to you, what happened to us. He will never give up. He'll die trying to find you."

Marie leaned against Eric and began to cry.

"He'll be alright," Eric said. "He'll find a way."

At that moment, the guard who had disappeared down the causeway returned and spoke to the officer who had remained some distance in front of them. The officer turned and motioned for everyone to move forward.

Eric and the others rose silently and turned toward the pyramid.

Eric stopped suddenly and began to look quickly around them. "Where's Philip?"

They all stopped and looked at each other. "He was with us when we left the facility," said Professor Stevens. "He was with me in the van coming here."

"What have you done with him?" Eric yelled at the guard closest to him. The only answer he received was the butt of a rifle stabbing into his shoulder. He gasped in pain and pulled back.

"MOVE!" the soldier snapped and Eric was forcibly turned around and pushed forward.

They walked in silence until they had come to the base of the pyramid. There were more men here milling around and staring at them silently as they approached.

At the urging of their captors, they began to climb up the courses of stones, helping each other climb until they had mounted seven rows and stood by a gaping hole that had seemingly been forced into the blocks, its irregular shape showing only darkness within.

"The Robber's Gate," said Eric without further explanation.

One by one they were pushed inside to discover a low tunnel that had been forced through the blocks in antiquity, the roof held up by iron bracing. Illuminated by dim lights some distance inside, it would appear to be empty and deserted by anyone standing on the desert floor below.

Bent down they stumbled over the uneven floor, climbing slowly upward until they came out into a large space, its ceiling lost in the darkness above them. It was brighter here, the lights stronger so they could see more of their surrounding. Large cables snaked along the sides of the space from unseen rooms below; rooms housing the generators that would power the computers needed for the signal to work. Men moved rapidly back and forth on either side of them. The air was hot and stuffy and they could feel the weight of the great stones bearing down on them.

"The Grand Gallery," said Professor Stevens. "We will be to our destination very shortly."

They walked up the inclining floor and within minutes stepped into the Kings Chamber.

When they were all inside, they stopped and waited. Huge banks of arc lamps on tall stands illuminated the room with glaring light, making the already warm air even hotter. But no one seemed to notice their entrance. All the men in the room stood around numerous computer stations, their eyes locked onto the glowing monitors. Large screens to their left showed tracking software, another showed the earth and the path of the satellite that would shortly be in place. A part of the Orion constellation was showing on the last one.

Between them, a large computerized array had been built tight against the wall, more cables running from it to the computers where the men worked.

"They're using the star shaft for the transmission," Professor Stevens said. "I thought it was blocked.

"Not anymore," Eric replied.

Raza stood across the space from them, checking various components on the array. His back was to them but momentarily he turned and saw them. A slightly startled look came over his face that quickly disappeared. His jaw clenched and he turned away, back to his work.

A voice spoke behind them and Eric turned around at the sound of his name.

"Dr. Mohammed!"

"Yes, Dr. Adams. It's so good of you to join us."

Eric closed his eyes and hung his head as the full realization of what was happening came over him.

Dr. Mohammed went on. "I see you're disappointed. I'm sorry. I know you were trying to find a way to get in touch with me so I could help you escape. But you must understand how momentous, how earth shattering this event is going to be: living history. I couldn't have missed out on this," he said sarcastically.

Eric raised his eyes. "No. I imagine not."

"But cheer up. You, your family, and all your friends . . ." He paused in mid-sentence and called to Raza across the space, waving to him to come and join them, "will be witness to the most amazing event in the history of mankind: the actual moment when we reconnect to our creators."

Raza stared across the space between them and hesitated before handing a readout he was holding to a coworker. He slowly walked across to where they stood.

"Raza," said Mohammed, "my boy." He placed a hand on Raza's shoulder and looked at him with a smile. "None of it would have been possible but for this man," he said to everyone around them. "He is the reason we are all standing here now. It was his dedication, his unceasing hard work, his deep knowledge of the past that he loves so much, that has brought us here. I couldn't be prouder," he said as he turned to Eric, "or more disappointed in his betrayal."

Eric's face snapped around to look at Raza. Raza caught his breath and looked at Mohammed as the older man turned back to his disciple.

"Betrayal?" Raza mouthed the word as his face lost its color.

"Yes. And the word barely does you justice. Did you think you could actually pull it off right in front of me?" His voice began to rise and his body began to tense for the strike that was about to come. "Betray me, betray your brothers, and no one would see, no one would know!" He yelled the words as spit flew out of his mouth.

The back of his hand snapped across Raza's face so hard it split his lips, blood squirting from his mouth, hitting the men standing beside him.

Eric watched as some of the men moved to intervene, but others grabbed them and held them back, shaking their heads as they did so. Raza staggered, almost collapsing on the floor. He regained his footing and stood back up, his black eyes, under heavy brows, full of hatred and disdain, staring at his former mentor. His breath was labored, his body tense, ready to spring.

"I wouldn't do anything if I were you," said Mohammed, calm once more. "You would be dead in an instant." And he waved his hand around the space at the other men who were standing there staring at the altercation. Mohammed removed a clean white handkerchief from his pocket and wiped the hand that had struck Raza as if it had touched an unclean thing. When he was through he folded the handkerchief neatly and put it back in his pocket. When he was done he looked at Raza and said: "What's amazing is you almost got away with it. And the scene where you pretended the computers had misled us to the final coordinates was genius. Your acting skills are to be commended. It would have fooled almost anyone. And you can't help but laugh at what tripped you up."

Raza starred at the man without comment.

"Well, since you won't ask, I'll tell you. The alien symbols. Did you not see the symbols above the figures? The boy," he said glancing at Larry, "showed us the way. *Nefer* did the rest. It was there all along. We simply fed the symbols into the computers and they gave us the coordinates. All my years of searching and trying to understand and it's handed to me as simple as that. And not just rough coordinates mind you. Precise coordinates. Coordinates that we sent in a matter of minutes. But, I have to say you played your cards well, Raza. Who would have believed *you* would betray us all? Not I. Luckily, other eyes were watching you. Eyes that I can trust without question."

It was only then that Eric noticed the man standing several feet behind Mohammed, half hidden by the men standing in front of him.

"Philip," he said, incredulously. You did this?"

"Yes, your assistant, Dr. Adams," said Mohammed. "An interesting turn of events don't you think. The men we trusted the most betrays us both. But my betrayal will not go unpunished."

Raza smiled through bloody lips. "Of course not. I would expect nothing less from you. Tell me, how do you picture yourself in the new world order, Mohammed? The god of destruction, Set? How appropriate for you!"

Mohammed smiled at him like a parent dealing with an unruly, obstinate child. But the smile faded as soon as it appeared. "You silly man," he said. "Don't you understand? We are their *children*. What do parents do when they find their lost children?"

"Their children," Raza's voice was full of disdain. "They won't see their lost children. They'll see an opportunity just like they did before."

"You could have had it all," said Mohammed calmly.

"Had what? The life of a slave? Death?"

Mohammed laughed, the sound compressed below the tons of stone above their heads. He came and stood inches from Raza's face. "You're so intelligent Raza to be such a complete fool. You forget your heritage; your standing in the priesthood. You would have been revered, elevated."

"You *are* insane," Raza spat back.

Mohammed smiled. "I'm sure the irony of the present situation does not escape you."

"Oh, I appreciate the irony, I assure you. But I'll go to my death knowing I followed the ONE, honored his actions, his sacrifice, until my last, living breath. I never betrayed him and I never will betray him! I kept my faith!"

"You kept nothing! Your faith is twisted. Your beliefs empty and dead as you and your friends will soon be. You're blind. You don't defy the gods and escape their wrath!"

"The *gods*? The *monsters* you mean!" Raza glanced at Eric beside him.

Mohammed turned to Eric and smiled again. "You've had more of an influence on my apprentice than I thought, Dr. Adams."

He stepped to where Eric waited with the others. "You and the Professor. Who could have foreseen the part two naïve, ignorant Americans could play in this drama? Only the gods could have put you in our hands to use to their greater purpose: pawns to guide us to the final solution. They work in ways we cannot understand."

It was Eric's turn to laugh now. "Yes, they do. You never know what the gods will do next: never know whom they will use to get what they want."

Mohammed came so close Eric could smell Mohammed's foul breathe.

"Oooh, you're thinking of *James*, aren't you? Don't worry. He's safe; safe within the walls of this pyramid. Or he soon will be. He should be arriving any minute now."

Eric's face fell as Marie moved close to him.

"That right. He'll be joining us very soon and then everything will be in place. Tie them up!"

CHAPTER 23

"What's taking him so long?"

"I don't know," replied Ari. "But we can't wait much longer for him to come back."

They had driven to the end of the street in the village that bordered the plateau, parked the car and got out with the intention of going forward on foot. They had sent Akhem ahead of them to see how much activity there was around the pyramid and, once he knew, to return to them. But it had been over forty-five minutes since he had left them and time was running out.

"What do we do?" asked Yassim.

"Go on without him."

"No, I mean how do we approach this."

"We go to the pyramid and try to get word inside that we have the boy."

"There will be men all around. How do we get past the guards? We can't just walk up and go inside."

"The guards won't stop *us*. Besides, they will be on the north side by the entrance. There won't be anyone on the south side of the pyramid."

"How do you know?"

"I don't. But we have no other choice that I can see. We can go, climb up onto the pyramid, slowly make our way to the front, and see how many of them are guarding the gate. After that, we will need to make a decision on how to proceed. Come on."

They walked off of the pavement where the street ended and began to trek across the desert sand. Ten minutes later, Yassim came up short and raised his hand in the air. Everyone stopped. "Someone's coming," he said.

At this position, there was nowhere to hide so they stood still and waited. Momentarily they saw a figure in the moonlight approaching where they stood.

"Is it Akhem?" Ari asked.

Yassim relaxed. "Yes," he said, as Akhem walked up to them. "What the hell took you so long?"

"I had to take my time," Akhem retorted. "What did you want me to do? Run up and yell that we're here."

"What's happening?" said Ari.

"Most of them are inside the pyramid. The satellite is coming into range. It won't be long now."

"How many men outside and are they only on the entrance side. Is anyone at the Robber's Gate or inside the tunnel?"

"Ten or twelve men outside. No guard at the gate and no one inside the tunnel, at least when I went through." He paused. "They know about Raza."

Ari looked at Akhem. "Shit. How do you know?"

"I saw Mohammed confront him. Mohammed slapped him down and called him a traitor."

"Where is he now?"

"Tied up with the others."

"What others?"

"The Americans."

James gasped. "My father? Is my father there, my friends?"

"Yes. I think so. There are Americans. That's all I know."

James suddenly bolted past them and began to run. But he didn't get far. Yassim took off after him followed closely by Ari. They tackled him and he came down hitting the sand hard. "Let me go! Let me go! I want to see my father. I want my father!"

"Stop it you little fool! Do you want to see your father dead? Huh? Do you want him dead; because that's what he's going to be if you keep on acting like this. They will kill him and the others on the spot if we rush in there."

James began to cry but Ari had no sympathy whatsoever. He grabbed him by the collar and pulled him to his feet. Ari turned to Akhem. "How did you make your approach?"

"From the back of the pyramid."

"Then that's what we will do. Don't you try anything else!" he snapped at James as he pushed him toward Yassim and turned to lead them rapidly forward.

They didn't stop or speak until they had come to the southern side of the pyramid where they halted. Ari turned to James.

"The blocks are covered with a layer of sand. You will slip, your feet will come out from under you and you'll fall. We have to move fast but we have to move carefully. Do you understand?"

James nodded in the shadowy light. "I understand."

"How far do we go up?" said Akhem.

"How far up did you go?" he turned to Yassim.

He hesitated slightly. "Seven rows."

"The gate is on the seventh row. They didn't see you?"

"No. They weren't looking up. They were talking to each other below."

Ari made an exasperated sound in the darkness. "We're not going directly around. We'll go up twelve rows, see what's happening, and then go down to the gate."

No one questioned this directive but followed Ari as he started to climb. James went right after Ari. The others followed them but to the left and right. Ari had been right. The sand underfoot was slippery. James held onto the next stone above him to keep his balance. But it was slow going. Eventually, they came to the twelfth tier and once there they halted.

"Make no sound and follow me," he said to James and without another word they made their way to the corner, inched around it and continued to the middle of the tier where Ari stopped them and told them to wait. He then went forward alone and peered around and down to the desert floor below. Akhem had been right. Ari counted twelve men. He was about turn back when he saw another man exit the Robber's Gate below him. Ari moved back into the shadows but made sure he could still see what was happening. The man climbed down to the other men who gathered around him and began to talk. No one looked up and when he peered around the corner again no one else came out of the gate. There was a good possibility someone was in the tunnel. Should he leave James and the others where they were and try to get inside alone? Instinct told him no. James would find a way to draw attention to them and all would be lost.

He quietly returned to where they stood. "One man came out but no one else. We're going to have to try and get inside."

"With the boy? They'll see him! He needs to stay here."

"No. I don't want to leave him alone out here."

"As if they're not going to see him inside."

"Akhem said they were all in the Kings Chamber. No one will be below in the Queens chamber. We can leave him there with both of you and I can go forward and try to get to Raza."

"We're going to get caught."

"Then we'll have to deal with it when it happens."

He turned and they began to inch their way forward. Ari silently turned the corner looking down at the men below. James followed and when he looked down he gave a gasp. "Philip!"

Ari grabbed James by the throat. "I told you to be silent. You're going to get us killed!"

"But it's Philip."

"I don't care who it is! You be quiet, do you understand or I'll throw you down to them. Do you understand?"

James nodded and they continued. No one seemed disturbed or was looking around. They all remained huddled together talking. It occurred to Ari to wonder why, if this man worked with Dr. Adams, he was down, talking to the guards who were watching the entrance. But there was no time to question anything. The satellite might be now swinging into position.

He motioned to them to move down on the same level as the gate and they silently did so until they stood on the seventh tier. They inched their way forward until they came to the entrance and one by one slipped inside with Yassim, the last of the party to enter. They picked their way forward always looking and listening for movement behind them or in front. But no one appeared and they came to the Grand Gallery without incident. Everything was deserted. Once everyone was inside the gallery Ari moved to the left until they came to another gateway that ran down into darkness.

"Do we go all the way down?" asked Yassim.

"No. Go just inside and wait. If anyone appears, kill them. I'll be back as soon as I can."

They did as they were told, stepping silently into the shadows and watched as Ari disappeared up the ramp.

When he had come to the Kings Chamber he found exactly what Akhem had said he would. Everyone stood frozen in place, silently watching the computer screens in front of them. Ari stared at the tracking monitor and saw the satellite moving slowly into position. The countdown showed less than twenty-five minutes for everything to be in place. He slowly stepped inside the space and glanced around. Not everyone was watching the nightmare play out, however. Two men stood in the very back. They saw Ari the minute he stepped inside the room. He began to make his way slowly to them but the one closest to him held up his hand telling him to stop.

The man bent down, picking up a sack on the floor and they then began to move toward the entrance where Ari stood. When they had come to him the man holding the bag stopped and nodded his head toward the front. The other man pulled away from the wall and slowly made his way into the rows of people in front of him. Ari followed him at his side until they stood directly behind Raza.

Raza sat on the floor along with Eric and the others with full sight of what was happening.

Ari gently placed his hands on Raza's back and Raza slowly turned to him. Ari mouthed the words, "We have the boy."

Raza closed his eyes and sighed with relief.

Ari knelt down as the man who had come with him blocked everyone else's view of what he was doing. He untied Raza's hands and Raza slowly rose until he was standing. Eric turned but Raza shook his head telling him to be silent. Raza stepped back and his companion slowly sank to the floor taking Raza's place by Eric's side. They had one chance and they couldn't give anything away. If anyone noticed Raza was missing all would be lost.

Raza and Ari backed away but not before other eyes saw them go. Each of the men watching them made no sound but moved forward also blocking the sight of their movements until Raza and Ari stood at the back of the group unnoticed.

The man waiting for them handed them the sack he was carrying and then went back to his original position. Ari glanced at the countdown as he and Raza melted away into the Grand Gallery.

18:42 and counting.

CHAPTER 24

James leaned against the wall and slowly sank down to sit on the floor. On edge and tense for days, his body felt sore and exhausted. He looked to his right into the tunnel that ran down into the center of the pyramid and the Queen's Chamber. But there was nothing to be seen in the dim light except the cables running along the floor. Yassim stood with his back to him on the left a few feet from the Robber's Tunnel, looking out into the Grand Gallery, waiting for any sign of Ari's return.

Akhem stood across from him, his back to the wall, and his hands hidden behind his back, looking past Yassim into the Grand Gallery as well.

Not a single sound broke the silence. James had never experienced silence so profound before in his life. There had always been some kind of noise but not here. The lack of sound was oppressive and somehow made the heat more intense. He leaned his head back against the stone and closed his eyes.

When he opened them a moment later something had changed.

Yassim still stood waiting by the entrance. Akhem still stood across from him against the opposite wall.

But James felt himself tense and press himself harder against the stones at his back. He looked up at Akhem. The man wasn't looking away from him now but was staring down at him, his face blank; his eyes without emotion.

A second more and his hand came out from his around his back, a knife flashing dully in the half-light and he lunged at James.

James cried out and scrambled to his right, the blade barely missing him as it hit the sandstone wall glancing off its surface with a spark of fire.

Yassim twisted around with a cry and grabbed Akhem as James scrambled away. They fell struggled back into the Grand Gallery and down onto the floor. "Damn you," Yassim cried. "You're one of *them!*"

"We must have the disk. We need to be one with the gods!"

"I'm going to send you to the gods, you bastard." But Yassim lost his hold and fell with Akhem suddenly on top of him. The knife came down and Yassim cried out in pain as the blade sliced into his shoulder.

Like that moment in the safe house with Sharon, the words came: "RUN, JAMES, RUN!" Yassim yelled. Their bodies were blocking the entrance into the Grand Gallery. There was only one way James could go.

He stumbled into the robber's tunnel and began to work his way back outside falling repeatedly onto the uneven floor. He never felt any pain. Only one thought was in his mind. He had to get to Philip. Philip would help him find his father.

At that instant, Raza and Ari came into the Grand Gallery and rushed forward to where the men were struggling on the floor. Akhem's arm went up to strike the mortal blow but it was seized by a grip so strong he cursed in pain.

"He's one of them!" Yassim gasped.

Raza lifted Akhem up, swung him around, and flung him against the wall. He yanked the knife out of his hand and it flashed repeatedly as it entered his body over and over again until all life had left him. Raza flung the corpse to the side where it landed on the floor, the wall covered with blood."

"NOT ANYMORE!" Raza snapped. "Where is the boy?"

"Outside!"

"Stay with him!" Raza said to Ari as he scrambled into the tunnel calling James' name.

James heard his name but he didn't stop. He could see the moonlight ahead of him, could see the way out. Raza called his name once more and James glanced to the side, stumbled, and fell face down onto the stones with a cry. He instantly got back up, pain shooting up through his leg and into his hip. But he made it to the entrance just in time before Raza caught up to him.

Raza grabbed for him but only grabbed empty space.

James had been moving so fast the forward momentum almost flung him head first into thin air and down to his death on the stones below. But he caught himself and scrambled to his right. He began to inch his way along the seventh course of stones, looking back from where he had come.

Raza came out of the tunnel a second later and began to move toward him.

"Stop, James, stop!"

The men on the desert floor froze at the sound and, as one, twisted around with their eyes looking up, searching the face of the pyramid.

"Damn you!" Philip cried out. "Get him!" James heard Philip shout.

Was he talking about Raza or James?

Six of the men lunged for the base of the pyramid and began to scramble up onto the first course of stone. But the other six attacked them from behind pulling them away and back where they began to struggle and fight like animals.

"*What are you doing?*" Philip cried out. He ran to the base and began to climb up, calling James' name over and over. "I'm coming James, I'm coming. Stay where you are!"

"Don't listen, James. Don't listen!" Raza said as he moved closer to where James was standing, frozen in place.

"Don't come near me. Don't come any closer," James said to Raza as he began to move further away.

"Leave him alone, you devil," Philip called out. "If you hurt him I'll kill you!"

"Don't listen, James. He's a traitor."

"No! He helps my father. He helped me!"

"He betrayed your father, James! He betrayed us all."

"No! No! He wants to help me!"

"Then why? Why is he out here James, instead of inside the pyramid tied up with your father and mother and your friends!"

"My mother? My mother's not here! My mother's at home! She's at home!"

"They kidnapped her and brought her here! Against her will so they could use her to get to you."

"No . . . no! That's a lie!"

"Don't listen, James!" Philip cried as he climbed onto the fifth tier. "Don't listen. We can find your father. I know where he is, James! I know! We can find him together."

"Why isn't he inside with the others James?" Raza asked again as he suddenly jumped down to the sixth tier of stones just as Philip climbed up onto it.

The two men rushed at each other but the sand, the ever-present sand, was Philip's undoing. He stumbled and Raza caught him in a mortal grasp. He spun him around and his hands grasped Philip's head twisting it rapidly to the side. There was a snap and Philip collapsed, his neck broken. Raza flung him out and off the pyramid, his body like a ball smashing into stones at its base until the corpse hit the sand below.

James looked on in horror. "No. No. Leave me alone. Don't . . ."

Raza was one row of stones below him. "Don't what, James? Kill you the way I just did him? I would never willing harm you."

Five men had climbed up onto the pyramid from the fight below. James glanced down at the bodies strewn across the sand.

One of the men indicated for two of the others to climb above James and trap him from the other side. But Raza held up his hand. "No. Don't try to get him. He might fall," Raza said as he stared up at James.

Raza slowly climbed up onto the row of stones where James was standing. He stood several feet away. His face was fully illuminated in the light of the moon.

"You can go, James. You can go. We won't try to stop you. But if you do your family and friends will die. *We* will die. Help me, please. Help me. Give me the part of the disc you carry. Help me end this."

James looked around. The course of stone where he was standing was empty all the way to the corner of the pyramid. The path was bright and shining in the moonlight. He could run. He could get away.

But he turned back and looked at Raza. Raza's face had not changed. The eyes that looked into James' own only held concern.

193

Everything became quite. The only sound was the desert wind blowing around them. James' hand slowly reached into the pocket of his jeans and he fished out the little piece of metal. He handed it to Raza who took it from his hand.

"Thank you," Raza said, "Stay with him and keep him safe," he continued as he turned away.

"NO!" James cried. "Take me with you, *please*. I want to see my family!"

Raza turned back and nodded his head. "Alright. But you must promise to stay behind me at all times and to be silent. Do you understand?"

"Yes."

Raza turned to the other men and said: "Stay and guard the entrance. Let no one escape that is not one of us."

The men nodded and Raza led James to the tunnel. They quickly made their way back to where Ari was waiting with Yassim who was sitting on the floor while Ari held a torn piece of cloth on the wound.

"Is he alright?"

"I'm fine," Yassim said.

"How long before the signal?"

"As far as I can tell, three minutes," said Ari.

"Quickly . . . Raza said. Ari reached into the sack and pulled out a strange device of corroded metal. He stood up and snapped it around Raza's forearm where it clicked shut. Raza took the piece of the disc James had given him and snapped it into place in a round housing on top of the casing. The other two pieces of the disc were already there and in place. Nothing happened at first. But then they watched as the disc began to emit a soft sound that slowly increased in volume as it began to spin inside the casing. Channels running from the disc culminated at an end point resting on, but extending beyond, the top of Raza's hand.

Ari looked at Raza and then took his hand, kissing it. Yassim leaned up and did the same. "May the ONE be with you, my brother," said Ari.

Raza nodded and turned to James. They moved quickly up the ramp to the King's Chamber and, without pause, stepped inside.

Like snapshots moving quickly by in a slideshow, James' mind recorded what he saw in a few seconds. The chamber full of men staring as if hypnotized at the monitors on the wall, the computers rapidly calculating the approach of a satellite, the words "satellite in range," splashing across one of the screens, the backs of his mother and father, Sharon and Larry: the clock counting down.

55 seconds.

50 seconds.

43 seconds.

James recognized Dr. Mohammed as he turned, almost in slow motion, and saw Raza standing there. Mohammed's eyes darted to James as his face contorted in anger, rage, and sudden understanding of what was happening. "Damn you to hell . . . ," he screamed and began to rush forward.

"You first!" Raza said, his face contorted. He held up his arm and clenched his fist.

James saw a vision of blue light arching wildly up into the staggered ceiling of the King's Chamber and then down to bounce off its walls. For all its massive bulk, the pyramid began to tremble as the dust and sand of thousands of years rained down on the people from the ancient stones above.

Many of the men, as if they were anticipating this event, fell flat to the floor out of range of the weapon. The others stood dumbfounded and frozen in place as their death flowed out of the device. Eric yelled for Marie, Sharon, Larry and Dr. Stevens to fall over where they sat to try and protect themselves.

But all the others were caught off guard as Raza quickly gained control of the device and focused its blinding energy with deadly force.

James watched as the computers melted before his eyes, evaporated by the blazing energy: the transmission to the distant alien world dying at the moment of its birth. The monitors exploded in smoke, sparks, and fire as the horrific tableau of men being blown apart, their limbs flying into the air and smashing into the stone walls of the room played out before his eyes. Mohammed's curse died on his lips as his body exploded spewing blood and flesh across the room.

There was a sharp cracking sound and Raza cried out in pain, the device breaking apart and falling to the floor.

The carnage, and the choking dust was too much and James could take no more. His senses reeling he sank to the floor and passed out.

CHAPTER 25

James felt himself coming slowly out of sleep. He was laying on something hard and his body was rocking softly from side to side. In the distance, seemingly far away and dreamlike, he thought he heard the sound of lapping water and the soft hum of a motor.

He dozed off again but came awake once more to discover it wasn't a dream at all. He pushed himself up off the deck, his head aching, and looked around. The boat, of which he was a passenger, was gliding smoothly through the water while a soft breeze blew across his face. The moon stared down illuminating the boards of the deck and the others who were lying down or sitting silently, their back against the boat's sides.

His father was on his right, sitting a few feet away from him, his back leaning against the side of the boat while he stared forward into the night. His mother was there, apparently asleep and leaning against his father who had his arm around her.

"Dad?"

Eric's head snapped around to look at son. "James." He gently lowered Marie down to the deck and came to where James was half lying. He knelt down and took James by the shoulders and hugged him hard. Then Eric turned James' his face to the moon. "Are you okay?"

"I . . . I think so. I'm so sore and my head aches."

"It would, after all you've been through."

"Where are we?"

"On a boat heading up the Nile."

"Where are they taking us?"

"I don't know. At first, I thought we were going to Elephantine."

"The island?"

"Yes. But we passed it over an hour ago."

"Then where?" he said almost to himself. "And why?"

"There's no way to know."

James suddenly cried, "Larry! Sharon!"

"They're fine," his father said. "They're sleeping in the bow of the boat along with Professor Stevens."

"So they have us all."

"Yes. We all survived and they have us all."

They stood up and together they moved a distance from his mother so they could talk without disturbing her sleep. Their guards, faces hidden behind black pullover masks, rifles at ready, watched them silently but made no move to stop them. They sat down on the deck.

James continued: "Did the transmission get through?"

"I don't think so. It began but when the computers were destroyed it was all over."

"I can't understand what happened back there."

"I can't understand it completely, either."

Eric looked at James. "I was amazed to see you with Raza and I tried to get to you. But they grabbed us immediately, covered our faces, and took us out. We were some of the first taken away, I believe."

"Raza . . . he is not what I believed him to be but . . . he killed Philip."

"Yes. But that doesn't surprise me."

"So it's true. Philip was a traitor?"

"Yes."

"Who is Raza, Dad . . . what is he?"

"I'm not sure . . . It sounds insane, but I think he's some kind of alien."

James paused. "You're kidding, right?"

"No. He's like no one I've ever met, ever seen. Uncanny is the only word I would use to describe him."

"How? I mean how do you know he's an alien."

"I don't know. It's just a feeling. He's not one of us; not completely human."

198

"He killed a lot of people tonight. But somehow, now, he doesn't seem evil. He protected me when I was on the pyramid."

"I don't believe he's evil either. At least, I don't think he is: desperate to stop this, for sure, but not evil. Which is ironic to say. He's not evil but the Great Pyramid is full of corpses: corpses that will have vanished by morning."

At that moment, they turned to see Sharon walking slowly toward them. She watched the guards as she walked by and then sank down with Eric and James.

"Are you okay, honey?" said Eric.

"Yes sir. I think so. I'm a little cold, scared out of my wits, hungry and thirsty. But I think I'm okay?"

James laughed.

"The wind off the Nile can get cold. Here, take my jacket."

"Thank you, sir."

"I'll bet you wish you'd gone on home that night you came over to our house and got us all plane tickets," said James.

Sharon grinned. "Well, the thought had crossed my mind."

"I'm really glad you didn't."

"Me, too, actually. It's been quite an adventure."

"Yes," said James.

"And I'm afraid it's not over yet," said Eric.

As they sat there, they were joined by Professor Stevens, Larry, and finally Marie.

Marie came to James. "Oh, James. I'm so happy to see you," as she hugged him tightly. "I didn't know what to think. Are you okay?"

"I'm fine. I know you were worried. We tried to call after we got here but could never get through. I'm sorry, Mom. I'm sorry I lied to you."

"I understand. You had to find your father." She said, looking at Eric as she sat down between them.

"Would you like the jacket, Mrs. Adams?" asked Sharon.

"No, you keep it. I'm fine where I am."

James couldn't help but notice the look that passed between his father and mother.

"So, Larry," Eric said. "The next time I have any questions on computers, I'm coming to you. How are you doing?"

"I'm okay and no. Please don't ask me anything about computers unless it's about a video game!" Turning to James he said. "It's really good to see you."

"You too, Larry."

"Well, Professor," Eric turned to Professor Stevens. "What do you think?"

"I think I'm in a dream. And I think the dream is not over. Something is about to happen to us. I don't know what. But it's not over yet."

"What do you mean, Professor?" asked Sharon. "They saved us back there, right?"

"Yes," the Professor said. "But that doesn't mean we are out of the woods. These people . . ." and his voice trailed off.

Everyone looked at Eric. "What the Professor says is true," he said. "We're being taken somewhere unknown, somewhere hidden. For what I can't say."

"Why can't they just let us go?" said Larry.

"We've seen too much," said Eric. "We know too much. They will have to find a way to keep us quite . . . or make us disappear."

"How?" asked James.

"I have no idea."

Sharon felt a shiver of fear run across her skin. "Will they kill us?" she asked.

"Again unknown."

They all fell silent, listening to the wind and the water moving past.

"Dr. Adams," said Sharon. "When they took us from the safe house and brought us to you, you explained what they were trying to do. I asked you why they would try and do such a thing. You told me it was a long story. Can you tell it to us now? Did the wall tell you what happened?"

"Yes," said Eric. "Part of it at least. Enough that the men who took us believed their plans could work. The interpretations, even now, are sketchy and if there were several people trying to unravel the secrets of the wall they would probably each disagree on the actual details. I don't think we will ever understand everything. I can only give you the general idea. Part of what I will tell you is simply myself filling in the blanks. Raza would probably be able to tell you more. But who among us wants to talk to him?"

"Not me," said Larry.

"Me, either," said Sharon.

"Right. So I'll do the best I can," said Eric.

"Before recorded history here on Earth, a ship took off from a planet close to, behind or inside the constellation of Orion. Its destination was not Earth but somewhere beyond Earth. The name of that place bears no resemblance to any star or constellation we know. Whether their mission was military or exploratory is not explained. The wall also doesn't explain how they accomplished the feat of space travel on such a vast scale. Orion is well over 1,000 light years from us. But that is immaterial because they did it. They moved at the speed of light or found a shortcut that allowed them to cover the distance in a shorter period of time. What is certain is they traveled in a spaceship for lack of a better term.

As far as I can tell all of the passengers were male. They probably numbered around seventy or eighty with five of those in command positions. Whether it was before or after they entered our solar system, something happened to their ship and they realized they had to find a place to land or they were going to die. I can imagine them rapidly scanning the different planets orbiting our sun and coming to the conclusion that this planet would be the most hospitable to their species. It appeared hospitable, but that did not mean it was going to be a walk in the park.

The ship caught fire as it entered the atmosphere and crashed somewhere in the desert not far from the Nile. They were desperate to put out the fire and save themselves and what was left of their ship; it was the only way to get home and the only way to get a message back to their world of what had happened.

They finally managed to get things under control and they pulled back to assess their situation, trying to decide how to proceed. It must have been a gruesome scene: many of them would have been seriously hurt, dead, or dying. When the ship came down, the commander in charge was killed. The next one in command took control. In the hieroglyphic record, he is represented by the image of a serpent.

Their instruments must have told them that the ship was damaged beyond repair and, more seriously, their ability to communicate with their home world was now impossible. They had the various elements of communication but no way, without the ship, to make those elements work together; the power the various elements contained was too great. They had no method, at that time, to contain the level of energy and so they couldn't attempt any kind of communication.

They were stuck on an alien world and they knew it. They also knew they could not stay inside the ship forever. They had to venture out if they were to survive. This presented the next problem. The atmosphere would, I'm assuming, have been similar to their home world but not exactly the same. The main components of the air we breathe are nitrogen and oxygen. Perhaps the proportion of those two gasses was different or perhaps only one of them existed in the air they breathed on their planet. At any rate, as soon as they opened the airlock of their ship there was an immediate negative reaction. The wall speaks of their inability to breathe because the atmosphere was burning them. What followed were days and days of them being trapped inside the ship: basically inside an oven.

In the meantime, the humans, the early Egyptians, had discovered the location of the downed ship. They had seen it as it had streaked across the sky and had been afraid. But as the days went by and nothing happened they began to lose their fear and come closer.

The commander – the serpent – eventually made the decision to send out a scouting party to see if there was any way for them to survive. It was a suicide mission and all of them died except one – the youngest officer. We would call him a lieutenant today although the wall refers to him as 'the traitor.'" The point is, he somehow survived the ordeal of trying to breathe the alien air.

But he did not survive on his own. He had wandered from the ship in the direction of the Nile. Once inside the green belt that borders the river he collapsed. And it was there that he was found by some of the humans.

They took him, barely alive, to the river where they laid him in its waters. He revived but was still struggling to breathe so they carried him to where they lived and gave him food and water and tried to help him in any way they could. They expected him, I'm sure, to die as well. But somehow, perhaps because of his age, his struggle with breathing lessened over many days and eventually he came around. It was still hard but he could breathe enough to live.

There was a girl there, young like him, and she nursed him through the ordeal. His species must not have been that different physically from our own. As the days past and she continued to care for him, he began to experience feelings for her that were forbidden on his home world. On his world, all relationships were strictly controlled. But now he wasn't on his home planet anymore and they mated. When he finally left their dwelling he was unaware she was carrying his child.

He returned to his ship expecting all his shipmates to be dead. But when he arrived at the crash site it was not so. Some of them had survived as well, including the new commander. It is not explained how the others came to survive but probably by the help of the humans as well. They questioned him about where he had been, what he had been doing and he answered them honestly; he had been nursed back to health by the humans after almost dying by the river. He did not mention the woman. It would have been foolish to do so. But because he had returned in the manner in which he did there was an aura of suspicion around him and they began to watch him.

While he was away there had also been a change in the relationship of his species and the humans. They acted subservient to the commander and the other crewmembers. The lieutenant did not find this odd. After all, they were advanced and the humans were at the very beginning of their development.

The aliens commandeered the homes of the people, moving all of their belonging out of the disabled ship. They moved all of the technology out as well and over the course of the next several months, caused the people to build them more elaborate places to live, using designs from their home world. The people dared not resist because the aliens used some of their technology to show them "magic" and the people became afraid of them once more. Soon the relationship was one of master and slave. The commander was no fool. Their world was militaristic and they knew how to subdue a simple-minded population to their will.

The lieutenant had not forgotten the woman. He wanted to see her again, have her again. But he had to wait for the opportunity or he would be caught and then there would be hell to pay. He waited and finally he was sent out on some kind of mission and he took the opportunity to see her. She was overjoyed and they were in love and they came together again. It was then he discovered she was with child.

He had never had feelings like he was having then: wanting them with him, a need to protect them. But it could not be so. Not then. He would be caught. He went away but let her know that he would return again and they would be together always. He would never leave her, and the baby, again.

He went back and tried to carry on as before but it was impossible. He was changed forever by the relationship with the woman.

The commander, in the meantime, had not been idle. He had searched the area and had seen the vast resources available to them: the metals, the gems, vast quantities of stone, and unending quantities of slave labor.

He had an idea that would allow them to get in touch with their world. The ship was damaged beyond repair. It could not house the machinery that would allow them to send the signal but that did not mean they could not build another housing for the technology. He sent scouts out into the surrounding area. When they returned they told him of a place to the north. It was close to the river but was flat and of a stone so hard it could bear a massive weight. At night, there was nothing to obscure the sky and the stars from view."

"The Giza Plateau," Professor Stevens said.

"Yes," Eric replied. "The Giza Plateau. They would build a pyramid, the most stable geometric form known in the universe: a pyramid whose sheer bulk would have the capability to withstand repeated transmissions to the constellation of Orion, their world. The people would find nothing odd in this. They had already been trying to build these structures with more or less success. But the new pyramid would be nothing like the ones that had gone before: the first true pyramid, mathematically perfect in every way save for a slight variation.

The commander began to execute his plan. The first step was to indoctrinate the population. The aliens would become gods to them through fear and intimidation and once that was accomplished they would be completely under their control. The commander kept the details of this first part of the plan hidden from everyone except his tight inner circle: all of his officers, except the lieutenant. The commander was still suspicious of his youngest officer.

To enhance their god-like image they continued to show the people more 'magic' just to prove they were divine and to make sure there was no resistance. It was almost too easy to accomplish.

The lieutenant saw nothing amiss: they had crashed and the commander was doing all he could to make sure they could survive and get home. In the meantime his baby was born, a son. The mother named it for one of the sky birds because that was where his father had come from.

The people had been using a rudimentary method of communication where they would draw pictures to represent what they wanted to say. Their new overlords learned the language and began to meld it with their own. Now communication was not a barrier.

There were engineers among the crew. They took the human men who showed a talent for building and began to instruct them in the basics of mathematics. As they worked with the men they also introduced them to geometry and various construction techniques that would allow the quarrying, dressing, and transportation of the great stones that would be needed for the construction.

They went to Giza and laid out the base of the pyramid. Then they dug into the bedrock creating rooms below ground: rooms never meant to house mummies or treasures; just alien technology.

From there they laid the first course of stone and the pyramid began to slowly rise. The entire population of Egypt was forced into service, including the family of the lieutenant's woman. He would watch them as they labored in the quarries or doing the backbreaking work of moving the stones into place. He would question the methods being used against the people and was humored with meaningless answers from the commander and the other officers. They wanted him completely in the dark about their true motives – motives that had now changed. They knew he would not go along with their plans. As the commander and his men became more and more accustomed to Earth they realized it would be folly to simply send a distress signal home asking to be evacuated. There was too much to be gained in this world. The natural resources were vast and the inhabitants already bent to their will. The possibilities were limitless and the die was cast. They would send the signal home but not for evacuation. The request would be for an invasion and a total takeover of the planet.

The lieutenant suspected none of this. He spent his days among the laborers, helping them as much as he could. He was seen around the quarries, at the construction site, in the homes of the people. They grew to love him, and although they considered him a god, took him to their hearts like he was a son.

And he was not without friends among his shipmates. One of them took him aside and told him something he couldn't believe. The other officers had been careless with their talk and had been overheard in their plotting to take over the Earth and enslave its people.

Where before he had been accepting of his orders without question, now he began to look closer at what was happening and to listen for any sign that his friend was right. It didn't take long for the rumor to be proven correct.

Thus began a counter plot to foil the plans of the commander and his allies. The lieutenant gathered around him all the men that he knew he could trust. These men had been assimilated into the human population with families and children as he had himself. Like him, the officers did not know these members of the crew had been with the human females who were also carrying their children. The commander and officers raped what women they desired and when their babies were born they would be killed as the officers considered them mutants and not worthy of living.

The men who came to follow the lieutenant had no desire to enslave the people and probably had no desire to return to the strictures of the other world. They were content and would fight to protect their new life. They were small in number but they were counting on the people to follow them.

Twelve floods of the great river came and went – twelve years. His son, who looked like his mother, was now working in the construction. His father would see him every day unable to protect him from the labor, unable to comfort him. His anger grew to unbearable dimensions as the pyramid began to near its completion.

Another year passed and the workmen were now at the top of the pyramid and the final moment when the capstone would be dropped into place.

Already, much of the technology needed to send the transmission was inside the lower chambers. They had reworked the various elements, creating a device that when complete was akin to a powerful microcomputer: the disc. It contained not only the power to send a transmission into space, and across vast distances, but all of the schematics and data that had been used to build the device. It was also a weapon that could destroy anything in its path with laser-like precision. All that was needed now was for it to be implanted inside the technology that was now in place in the largest room in the pyramid – the Kings Chamber – aligned to its destination and activated. The King's Chamber in the pyramid, with its narrow star channel pointing directly to Orion, would direct the transmission as it leaped across the space between the two worlds.

But since everything had been embedded inside this one device it was vital that it not fall into the wrong hands. There had to be safeguards. Everything depended on it. So it was constructed in such a way that it could be broken into three components. Alone, each piece carried a certain amount of power and a certain of amount of information. Together it carried a power far greater. The commander retained one piece; two trusted officers each carried the other two.

But that wasn't enough. There had to be more protections in place to make sure their story, their technology, their way of life would live on in this new world.

While the pyramid was under construction they went into the desert, taking skilled artisans and builders that were already working on the pyramid. They built chambers under the sand, plain and unadorned but waiting for a future time to be finished. This would be the sanctuary, the ark, of their knowledge and their power. A secret place for them to congregate until the hordes of aliens arrived from the mother world.

One room and one room only had started to be finished; the main chamber with its homage to the all-powerful disk. And the wall mimicked the information on the disk itself. You had to have redundancy if you wanted to win in the end. The left side of the wall began to tell the story of what happened, why they were forced to come here. But that beginning was never finished. Something happened to interrupt it and that part of the wall was finished after what happened next.

The lieutenant made his move. He took the leaders of the people aside to a place where there was no chance they would be overheard. He told them of the plot and what it would mean to them if the signal ever got through.

By this time, the people despised their "gods." Years of hard labor, death, and disease had taught them to hate with a heat greater than the desert sun. They would follow the lieutenant into death if it meant their people could survive and rid themselves of their tormentors. They were given the plans of the attack and told that it would occur the minute the capstone of the pyramid was dropped into place because at that moment all of the aliens who followed the commander, and the commander himself, would be in attendance. There would be guards there who would be carrying weapons that would kill. The leaders didn't care. They went back and told the people the plan of attack and how it was to be carried out. And . . . they were sworn to secrecy.

The day arrived with everyone in attendance: the commander, his officers, all the workers and their families. The capstone was pulled slowly up the side of the structure and hoisted above its resting place. The lieutenant looked at the commander and waited for his signal to drop the stone into place. The lieutenant lifted his hand and sliced it down through the air. But the capstone never made it into position.

Instead hundreds of people with rocks and axes hidden in their robes turned and rushed their oppressors.

The people rose up. They turned on their 'gods' and began to tear them apart.

There was war. The aliens were caught completely off guard, but quickly recovered and began to fight back. They fought but because of overwhelming numbers they could not subdue the people. When they saw their doom was inevitable they took what they had created, the disk, and fought their way out.

The wall is obviously biased against the lieutenant and his adopted people so who knows what really happened at that point. Perhaps he was climbing down the pyramid to come and help the people attack their oppressors. Perhaps he was already down and fighting hand to hand. Perhaps he was yelling their names and telling them to fight with all their strength. The commander's suspicion was true. The young lieutenant was a traitor.

One of his enemies turned, saw him, and he was killed; blown apart with one of the alien weapons. When the people saw him die their rage grew a hundred fold. Because of his mercy to them, he was not only loved, he was adored and literally worshiped for the god they believed him to be. They had known from the beginning they were working side-by-side with his young son. Alien or not, god or not, because of his family, because of his love for the people, he was one of them.

The aliens, realizing that all was lost, ran for their lives, disappearing to be hunted down and destroyed.

But some of the officers escaped. They ran for the sanctuary, the ark, and it was there they realized the dream of communicating with the home planet was over, at least for the time being. They didn't have much time because the sanctuary was not safe. They quickly finished the wall so the ones who would come after them would know everything including the fact that they had been betrayed. One of them took the part of the disk he was carrying, wrapped it in papyrus and quickly hid it inside one of the empty rooms that had been constructed. The other two pieces went with them out of the ark. Their dream was that the disk would be reunited at some time in the future and all of the knowledge; all of the power would be theirs once more.

The stars were silent. The transmission never got through then, or at any time afterward. Slowly, over time, they were all killed off except the ones who had been assimilated into the culture. The commander's plan failed completely and the ark remained hidden; lost for millennia under the desert sands.

The battle was over at the pyramid but the people's pain was just beginning. They wept and mourned the loss of their "god," the one they worshiped and loved the most. They gathered the parts of his body, wrapped them in linen along with little pieces of gold and the blue lapis lazuli they loved so much, blessed them, and sank them into the Nile."

Eric stopped and everyone was silent.

"Did any of them have names? Real names?" asked James, quietly. "The aliens, I mean?"

"Yes, they all did," said his father.

"What was the lieutenant's name?"

Eric looked at his son. "In their language, it is a word that is completely unknown to me. A word I can't even pronounce. But the humans called him "Osiris."

CHAPTER 26

James' mouth dropped open. "The *god?*"

"Not a god. An alien who became a god: the god of the dead and the giver of life. He was buried in the river, and even though the river had flooded before, it was now Osiris who would cause the Nile to flood and bring life back to Egypt."

James suddenly understood. "The woman, the mother of his baby, was Isis."

"Yes."

"And the baby, named for the sky bird?"

"Horus, the god with the head of a hawk and the body of a man: the one who protects mankind. You picked up more archeology than I thought all these years," said Eric with a smile.

"And," said the Professor. "The evil commander became Set, the god of destruction, chaos, and darkness: always shown as a serpent."

"Yes," said Eric.

"Wow," said James, dumbfounded

"Wow, indeed," said his father. "And that's about the full extent of what Professor Stevens and I can piece together."

Eric turned to Sharon. "And to your question as to why would anyone try to contact an alien world that would come here and destroy us? I have no idea. That someone would attempt such a thing is the million-dollar question and one I simply can't answer unless they believed if they were reunited with their 'fathers,' they would be exalted by them and given the keys to the kingdom if you will."

Several of the guards had drawn close to them as they sat on the deck, listening to the story. They suddenly snapped to attention as their leader appeared from below deck. He spoke in Arabic and Eric translated what he said.

"They are going to separate and blindfold us. Don't resist anything," he said. "We have to let all of this play out and see what happens."

"They will kill us." said Larry.

"We don't know that," said Eric trying to reassure everyone's fears.

They took Marie and Sharon first, tied their hands behind their backs, blindfolded them and sat them at the front of the boat. Next it was Professor Stevens and James. They were marshaled to the back stern. Finally, Eric and Larry were bound, blindfolded and left in the middle of the boat where they were already sitting.

Time went on. Eric listened to the sound of the vessel cutting through the water and finally thought he heard a rooster crow somewhere on shore. He felt, more than knew, that dawn was approaching and whatever their fate would be it was now close at hand.

Shortly afterward the engine of the boat was cut and the only sound left was the sound of the water lapping against its sides.

Eric heard a man call out in Arabic and knew the boat was coming into dock. They waited listening to the sounds of the anchor being dropped and ropes being thrown to unseen hands on shore.

Soon after, they were all lifted from where they were sitting and brought back together in the middle of the boat. The leader of the guards spoke to Eric and told him to translate what he said to the others.

"Everyone listen, please," said Eric. "We're about to disembark. Do not try to remove your blindfold. Do not try to get away. If you attempt to do either you'll be shot on the spot. Does everyone understand?"

There was a chorus of "yes" all around. Eric explained to the guards that everyone knew what to do and would not cause any trouble. This seemed to placate the leader and without another word, each one of them began to be guided by a guard who took them by the shoulders and began to push them to what felt like a gangplank. When they would stumble, hands would be there to lift them up and set them straight again. Very quickly they were all on shore.

Eric noticed that as soon as he came ashore he stepped first into water and then onto solid ground. This was not some kind of dock. They had been taken off the boat directly onto land. They were standing on the shore of the Nile. If he were guessing he would say that there was nothing, no dwelling, no dock, nothing that anyone would recognize if they were sailing by. Where were they being taken?

Once they were all ashore they heard the boat's engine start up again and he knew it was leaving them behind. They were placed in single file and told to march forward. Dawn had definitely come as they felt the first rays of the sun begin to beat down on them.

None of their guards spoke as they trudged along. Neither did the prisoners. The path they walked seemed solid one minute and sandy the next so their feet and legs became tired as they tried to keep their balance. Just when they thought they could go no further one of the guards suddenly spoke and their march was halted. Unknown to the others, Sharon had fallen. The guards helped her back to her feet but they went no further for a moment. Instead, they were given water and allowed to rest if standing under the blaze of the early Egyptian sun could be called resting.

After a time, they were ordered forward again. This process continued until finally Eric spoke to the guards asking that they be allowed to rest out of the sun. The guard responded that the journey was nearly over and they had to continue. Shortly after, they were brought to a halt once more and told to wait.

They heard a scrapping sound like heavy stones being forced against one another. Once this sound ended they were pulled forward and for the first time felt the heat of the sun leave their skin. It was still hot but at least the rays of the sun were now blocked and they could catch their breath. They felt themselves inside some kind of enclosure but didn't have much time to try and figure out where they might be.

One of the guards spoke again in Arabic and Eric translated as before. "We're about to be taken down several flights of stairs. Let your guard help you."

Eric was taken down first. The going was very slow and seemed to go on forever before he was finally released at the bottom. Slowly everyone else was also guided down and stood huddled together waiting for what would happen next.

They heard a door open and were ushered into a room. Their hands were unbound and they heard the feet of the guards as they departed. The leader told Eric to have everyone remove their blindfolds.

For a moment, no one could see but slowly their vision returned and they looked around in amazement. They were in a small room, its walls, from floor to ceiling, was completely covered with wall carvings painted with faded but vivid colors. There were two small electric lamps burning on either side, powered by small generators. But the most amazing thing was a table in the middle of the floor covered with a clean white cloth, food, and drinks.

The remaining guard, without speaking another word, turned and left them there closing the door behind him.

"What is this place?" Sharon asked.

"The Mummy's Tomb!" said Larry very seriously. "They've given us enough food to last a day and then as one of us dies we'll have to resort to cannibalism to try and survive."

"Oh my god, Larry!" said Sharon. "It is not the mummy's tomb. Is it Dr. Adams?" she said turning the Eric half expecting him to say it was.

Eric couldn't help but smile. "No. It's not the mummy's tomb," he replied.

"Then what is it?" asked Marie.

But Professor Stevens answered her. "We're in some kind of antechamber. There is something beyond these doors and we are waiting here for something to happen. See here, Eric."

Eric joined the Professor where he stood examining the artwork on the two doors. "That's Osiris," said Eric to the others. "See his green face and the mummy wrappings around his legs. He was the ruler of the underworld. The Professor's right. We're underground. This must be a gateway to some kind of underworld."

"Gateway or not, I'm starving," said James as he picked up a piece of meat.

"What if it's poisoned," said Sharon.

"Now you sound like Larry," said James and he put it in his mouth.

"I don't think they would bring us this far just to poison us," said Eric. "If we're going to die it would be more dramatic I think. We may as well eat and drink. We may be here a while."

They gathered around the table and ate in silence. When they were done Marie spoke. "If we're underground, I'm assuming we are under the desert. So why is it so cool?"

"Well, it's *cooler* than the dessert but still hot. I don't know," said Eric. He got up and went to the door from which they had entered the room expecting it to be locked. But to his surprise, it opened when he pushed on it.

Beyond the room was a circular space with a stone staircase winding its way back up to the surface. He peered up the stairs but no one was around and everything was quite. "We may be under the desert but we could also be inside a cliff face."

"Like the tombs in the Valley of the Kings," said the Professor.

"Yes," Eric agreed. "It's cooled somehow. But who can tell?"

He walked back inside and approached the two ornate doors. "I wonder if these will open as well," he said and laid his hands on their surface pushing lightly. But the doors remained firmly shut.

He turned, his right hand still on the one of the doors. "Well, whatever this is I guess we'll have to wait to see what's on the other side."

At that precise moment, as if Eric's words were a magic spell, the doors began to slowly open. Eric quickly pulled himself back upright to keep from falling into the next room.

But the doors had not opened of their own accord. Two guards, powerfully built men with dark eyes and unsmiling faces, stood on either side. Their arms were tattooed and they were dressed like the men on the walls of the room Eric and the others were standing in: bare-chested, heads shaved, carrying spears and wearing linen skirts and leather sandals. Each of them also bore the unmistakable scar of some kind of branding on their shoulders.

They never spoke but stood waiting while everyone filed into the room. But "room" did not begin to describe what they were standing in. This was a temple like nothing either Eric or Professor Stevens had ever seen. Two large sphinx stood guard on either side of the steps they were walking down. The statues were facing two exact copies of themselves that stood across the floor. Between them, to the right, more steps led up to a throne sitting in front of a stunning mural whose top was lost in the shadows of the vaulted ceiling. The roof was supported by massive columns; each capped with the familiar lotus flower capitals. The spaces between them were covered with even more murals. Two gigantic braziers stood on either side of the throne. Unlike their companions in the anteroom, these were lit by fire, which was the only illumination. The shadows cast by the flames danced on the walls and floor making everything dreamlike and surreal.

They walked across the floor to the bottom of the steps that led up to the throne, the guards following close behind them. The anticipation of what was about to happen was so great that no one spoke. They waited, breathless, and just as Professor Stevens turned to one of the guards to ask why they had been brought to this place there was a sound behind the mural, which on closer examination, turned out to be a free-standing wall, like one of the pylons in the temples at Thebes.

Men began to emerge from the shadows at its back. All of them were dressed like the two guards who had opened the doors to the sanctuary. Some of the older men's shoulders were draped with animal skins and some wore gold armbands or gold bracelets. They ranged in age from what looked like twenty-year-olds to octogenarians. And many of them were recognizable from the events at the Great Pyramid.

Eric and the others felt like they had fallen through a door in time and had been thrust back into early history; back to the time of the pharaohs. And for all intents and purposes they had. It was impossible not to feel afraid. The men concluded their entrance and stood staring, emotionless, at the captives, the throne remaining empty.

But not for long.

A figure emerged through an unseen door hidden in the wall and came and silently sat on the throne. Perhaps they had stepped through a portal in time after all. He was wearing the white crown of the pharaohs; tall and shaped like a bowling pin. He carried a crook in one hand and a flail in the other. His chest was bare and covered with tattoos. The tattoos were hard to see because the heavy jeweled collar, that draped around his neck and covered his upper torso, obscured most of them.

James thought of King Tut and his death mask and the colored jewels and lapis lazuli that made up his collar. Like Tut, this god's jewels were all set in gold.

He was wearing a linen skirt like the others and fine sandals. But the two most amazing things about him were the green mask, like enamel, that covered his features and the large bandage covering his right hand.

If it was not Osiris it was someone so like him as to be indistinguishable.

He sat down.

One of their guards suddenly yelled at them to kneel. Everyone jumped, startled at his voice, and sank down on their knees.

Eric couldn't take his eyes off the bandaged hand and said, almost to himself:

"A god with a broken wing."

The words were barely out of his mouth when the guards rushed toward him forcing him back until he fell over, their spears pointed at his heart.

CHAPTER 27

"STOP!" the god screamed the word in panic as he rose halfway off of the throne. "Stop."

The guards heeded the command and immediately pulled back.

"Help him up!" was the next command and the guards obeyed.

When everyone was calm again, the figure on the throne told the man on this right to remove the mask that covered his face. When he did, everyone breathed the same word: "Raza." Only Eric seemed unsurprised.

"Hello, Raza," said Eric.

"Hello, Eric."

Eric looked down briefly and then back at the "god." "I meant no disrespect."

A smile played at the corner of Raza's mouth. "I know you didn't. By now I'm accustomed to your sarcasm . . . and your wit."

"How's your hand?"

"Badly burned and the ligaments of the arm are damaged, possibly beyond healing."

"I'm sorry. It was a terrible risk to take."

"Yes. But the only way I could think of to stop what was happening. I'm sure you would agree the alternative would have been much worse?"

"Yes." Eric glanced down again. "Yes, it would have been much worse. I have to say," he continued, "that I'm surprised you would bring us – anyone – to this place."

"It was not my first choice. No one besides the priests has ever been allowed to enter this temple since the beginning and certainly no women have been allowed inside," he said, looking at Marie and Sharon.

"We didn't ask to come here."

"I'm aware of that fact. But it would have been dangerous and rash to leave you at the pyramid."

"What are you going to do with us?"

"The punishment for entering the temple is death," he said calmly and without emotion.

"*What?* How can you . . ."

"No one must know we exist, *this* exists," he said indicating the cavernous space.

"Then why save us at all? Why not let us die back there instead of giving us hope?"

"Your silence for one. If one of you had escaped you would have exposed our secrets, exposed what has happened. We – I – couldn't take that chance. I brought you this far under my personal protection."

"And your personal protection ends here. Is that it?"

"I'm afraid so."

Eric glanced around at the other men. "And the other priests agree."

"Yes. Because you are here it is a sacrilege; it defiles the temple. They wish you to be sacrificed and your knowledge of our world to die with you."

Eric swallowed. He looked at the other men and saw no mercy in their faces, no understanding: just blank, cold stares.

Eric moved to the bottom step, Raza sitting above him. "We helped you."

"No, you got in the way and made things much worse than they could have been," Raza said coldly.

"Please. Don't hurt my family. Don't hurt my friends. If you need a blood sacrifice, then take me."

"Dad, *NO*," James cried out. "It's my fault all of this happened. Take me."

"If you destroy my family I don't want to live anymore," said Marie rushing to their side. She looked at Raza. "Can't you let the children go, swear them to secrecy, and let them go?"

220

"Stop!" said Professor Stevens. "I'm old with few years left," he said. "Spare the others and take me."

"To take one of you would not serve the purpose. The belief is once you are away from us you will betray us. While I am the high priest and have my opinion . . . I can't go against the will of my brothers."

"But who would believe it?" Eric argued. "Who could even conceive of something this fantastic? Please! Have mercy! Have mercy!" And he lay down at Raza's feet, his face to the floor. Everyone followed his example.

At the word mercy, the priests looked from one to the other. They began to whisper among themselves. Moments passed.

Finally, one came to Raza, who sat motionless, staring at the captives as they lay on the floor, and whispered something in his ear. "Is this everyone's will?" Raza replied. The man whispered something else and then moved back to stand where he had been.

"Rise," he said. Eric slowly rose, as did everyone else.

"My brothers have offered you what you ask. We will be merciful. But I warn you, it is mercy mixed with pain. Do you desire this path?"

"What is the pain?" said Eric, quietly, as he and the others rose to their knees.

"Do you desire this path?" Raza repeated as if he hadn't heard Eric's words.

Eric looked around at everyone, reading their faces. "There's nothing we can do," said Professor Stevens, "If we want to live."

Eric looked at Marie and Sharon. They both, wide-eyed with fear, nodded. He turned back to Raza. "Then yes, we choose mercy and pain."

"The men will swear their allegiance to Osiris, will swear on their lives not to divulge any knowledge of his world and will bear the mark of the god forever. This brand will mark you as his servant and on pain of death will you betray him. It will remind you to take your silence to the grave. You will go back into the world knowing that if you betray Osiris you will be hunted down and destroyed. Our brothers are everywhere on the Earth."

He continued. "The women will serve the goddess as her handmaidens and attendants at her alter. They too must bear the mark of the god. Do you still wish to continue?"

Eric looked at Marie and Sharon again. "They're going to brand us. Can you do it?"

Marie's face turned white. But she took Sharon's hand and looked at her. Sharon nodded. "We can do it," said Marie.

"So be it," said Raza, rising from the throne. "Prepare the ceremony."

As soon as the words were out of his mouth the other priests, except for four men, turned and began to silently file behind the throne and disappear through the hidden door.

When they had filed out, the guards made everyone rise from where they were kneeling. The priests took them to a small chamber containing a shallow pool of clear water. The women went first, bathed themselves and were given linen drapes to wear. The same pattern followed for the men who, when done, dressed themselves in the same linen skirts the priests wore. Then, bare to the waist, they joined Marie and Sharon.

The four priests lead them back to the throne room and through the hidden door.

The throne room had been stunning but the inner sanctuary made everyone turn around and stare in disbelief, making them almost forget their fears and what they were about to face.

The ceiling was covered with painted stars that almost seemed to twinkle against the deep blue of their background and the flickering shadows that moved across their surface. To their left, through an archway shaped like the great pylons of the temples at Karnak, was a smaller sanctuary dedicated to Horus. His statue was facing them; incense burning on his alter.

To their right was an identical space dedicated to Isis. Her alter also contained incense that was sending up a pale cloud of fragrant smoke. Flowers covered her alter. The floor they were standing on was polished inlaid stone and the walls were covered with the most beautiful, and untouched, ancient Egyptian paintings Eric or Professor Stevens had ever seen. Every surface was covered with images of the gods, incantations, and blessings.

But the most amazing feature stood directly before them. A colossal statue of Osiris rose from a large platform, his headdress almost touching the ceiling with other statues, bas-reliefs of his attendants, standing on either side of him. They were smaller but they completely covered the wall behind him and were almost hidden in shadow.

Osiris stood looking into space with the blank stare on his face that all Egyptian statues carry, one arm crossing his chest, the other rigid at his side, the hand holding an ank.

There was an overpowering sense of mystery, power, and fear that made the captives hold their breath waiting for the next event to unfold.

A large basin of fire, sitting on a low pedestal, stood before the statue's feet. A number of priests appeared carrying long thin pieces of metal like skewers with a metal tip on one end. They plunged the pieces of metal into the fire and stood back as the brands began to glow red-hot.

"What . . . what are they going to do?" asked Larry.

"We're going to be branded like the priests," replied Eric.

"Oh, god," Larry whispered, shrinking away. "I don't think I can do it?"

Professor Stevens smiled and looked at him. "You lived and fought through the events at the Great Pyramid, the greatest moment you will ever know in your life. You helped save the world from possible destruction. The momentary pain you are about to feel will be nothing compared to that. You can do this. We all can. I will help you."

Raza was standing behind the basin. When everyone was in place and there was complete silence, prayers and incantations began. This went on for several minutes and then abruptly ceased. He looked down at the initiates, the fire making his face look demonic. He nodded and a priest stepped forward and picked up a brand out of the glowing embers. He indicated James as the first to bear the mark. But Eric stepped forward. "No, please let me go first. Before the others so they can see it can be done."

All eyes turned to Raza who gave his blessing. Eric stepped forward and turned his left arm until it was facing the priest.

The priest did not hesitate but brought the glowing metal forward and touched it to Eric's arm. The smell of burning flesh suddenly filled the space, causing them to catch their breath and turn away. Eric did not cry out but he gritted his teeth and his face was contorted in pain. Then he breathed again and stepped aside. Next came James and Ari stepped forward and picked up a brand.

He leaned close to James and whispered in his ear. "A payback for the pain you have caused me," he said and smiled.

The brand instantly came down. James gasped but, like his father, did not cry out.

Larry came next assisted by Professor Stevens. Another priest stepped forward and the brand was applied. Larry tried but could not stop the soft cry of pain as the metal burned into his flesh. He swallowed hard and caught his breath and turned to Professor Stevens who took his place by the basin of fire. Larry stayed with the Professor while he went through the initiation. The Professor made so sound at all.

Marie then stepped forward.

She looked at Eric and James. Eric nodded his head as if to say you can do it.

The priest gently took her arm, and lightly touched the brand to her skin. She seemed to turn as if she was about to sink to the floor but Eric stepped forward and caught her, bringing her to his side.

Only Sharon remained. She stepped forward as a younger priest picked up the brand. She turned and looked at James. He immediately stepped forward with Larry. "We're in this together. We can't stop now. What would everybody think? You're weaker than a boy?" he said.

Sharon smiled slightly and closed her eyes, holding onto their hands as the brand came down. She cried out and they caught her as she fell, helping her down onto the floor.

The ceremony over, all of the priests, including Raza, silently filed out of the room as if they had been watching a play that had now ended.

Eric rushed over to Marie and Sharon. "Is she okay?" asked Marie.

"I'm okay," said Sharon weakly. "It hurts!"

"Yes," said Marie. "I've never felt anything like that before."

"Well, you've never been in a position to be branded before. You sure you're going to be okay," said Eric.

"Yes." He turned to everyone else. "Guys, are you going to make it? James, Larry?"

They were sitting a few feet away clutching their arms. Larry was crying from the pain. "We're going to be okay," said James.

"Professor Stevens?"

"I'm fine, my boy."

Guards appeared and took them back to the throne room where everyone sat down on the steps in pain.

"If we only had something to put on the burns: something to ease the pain. But there's nothing."

As if the words were his cue Raza reappeared and came and sat down on the steps with them.

"Leave us," he said and the guards walked across the floor, up the steps, and out the doors from which they had first entered the temple.

When they were gone, Raza turned to everyone and said: "Take this. It will ease the pain." He handed Marie a small alabaster dish, decorated with lotus flowers. It contained an ointment, that when placed on the burns, made the pain almost disappear.

Marie dabbed it on Sharon's arm. Sharon sighed and relaxed, closing her eyes as the horrible burning sensation from the brand receded from the wound.

They passed the dish around until everyone had received the medication.

"You're very brave," Raza said when they were done. "I've seen strong men collapse under the initiation of the Temple. I'm sorry, but it was the only way to get you to safety and keep you alive. I didn't know if it would work or not."

"They hate us that much?" Eric said.

"No. They are very grateful to all of you for the part you played in stopping this madness. You have to understand that our secrets are guarded with our lives. That is the oath we take and the oath you just swore. To defend the temple and its knowledge at all costs. I counted on the fact that when they saw you and heard you, you would change their minds and make them realize we have nothing to fear from you. We have come through a very dangerous test and you came through it with us. That carried a lot of weight with my brothers. That and the fact that you were willing to die for each other, like Osiris himself."

Raza paused and then continued. "I feel that I need to give you an explanation of the circumstances surrounding these events."

"You don't need to explain anything to us," Eric replied.

"I know I don't. But it is important to me that I do. That is, as long as you wish me to do so and as long as you are up to listening to the story after what you have been through."

"I don't speak for the others but I would greatly appreciate what you could tell me," said Professor Stevens.

"That does not surprise me," said Raza. "Your great desire to understand us and the history that created us is well known. We have been watching you for some time."

"We also would like to hear what you have to say," Eric said.

Raza nodded and began.

CHAPTER 28

"You already know much of what I could say. Many of my ancestors believed 'the visitors' had come here on purpose, executing a plan to colonize a new planet. But we now know this to be false. Earth just happened to be the closest, most habitable planet for them to land on in order to survive.

What they discovered when they were finally able to explore this world must have filled them with amazement: a human population one evolutionary step above the animals, with no discernable language and certainly no writing. What the *humans* saw were gods that came from the stars. What happened after that moment of contact became the fabric of legend: our only source of knowledge to help us understand these events." He paused, "Until now."

Their race was obviously advanced, more advanced than we are even today. How else can you explain their ability to travel over vast distances of space and merge human physiology with machines, as we have all seen with the power embedded in the disc and its ability to download information into the cerebral cortex; a stunning accomplishment for any race, even an alien one.

When the Egyptian government began construction of the solar array in the desert and the bulldozer fell through the sand into the outer chamber I was called in because of my work with the Ministry. When I arrived, it appeared to be just another tomb that had lain hidden for thousands of years. These things happen in Egypt on a pretty regular basis, and I, after seeing the sculpture on the cornice, surmised it to be an Old Kingdom site like others that had been robbed and pillaged over time. Therefore, I did not get excited or have any concern about what lay in the passageways beyond. But once inside, once I had seen the wall, I knew I was wrong.

The legends had come true. I was stunned and literally couldn't believe my own eyes. Legends are just that: legends. And like all legends, even the legends of my own religion, they live in the distant past and don't bother us in the modern world. But it could not be denied.

As I stood there on that first day I began to translate. My initial reaction was amazement for I soon discerned it was a record of the events that had occurred so long ago.

My second reaction was fear. As I moved across the panels I learned enough to know their desire to contact their home world and everything they would need to do it. But there was more, much more that was obscure to me. Some of the hieroglyphics were unique and to my knowledge unknown. Therefore, a clean translation was impossible. I could only go so far; could only translate so much. The rest was hidden from me. But I also knew from the first that the disc was at the center of it all. The disc ultimately held the key to everything: the power, the knowledge, the history, where to look in the night sky to find their origin. What the wall said was also on the disc. That is our belief. But the disc carried so much more knowledge and potential destruction. If it were ever reunited the repercussions could be deadly for everyone.

Over the next several weeks I translated all I could using my own knowledge and the corresponding hieroglyphic symbols that matched the alien code. Then I carefully brought in others of my cult, the brothers I could trust. They read what I read and like me were afraid. The legends had come true. Communication with the other world could be opened. Was it probable? No. Was it impossible? Again, no.

I cautioned everyone to stay calm. While it was, as you say, a long shot and *could* be done with modern technology, the idea that it *would* be attempted was another thing altogether. We also believed at that time that nothing could be done without the disc and the odds were it had been lost or destroyed thousands of years ago.

Several weeks went by and the ministry contacted you, Eric. I saw no reason to be concerned. Many of the people at the Ministry are not part of the priesthood. It was standard procedure. Let them bring in whoever they wanted. That person would never be able to translate the wall and make any sense of it whatsoever. Only we, the descendants, could translate and understand the markings. That was one of my first mistakes. I underestimated Eric's ability . . . and his tenacity.

I watched you as you began. At first, you seemed overcome with what you must have instinctively known was the greatest discovery not only in the past of Egypt but in the whole world: the absolute proof that beings from another world had come to Earth before the beginning of history and had influenced the development of the human race in amazing and frightening ways.

It was soon after this that Dr. Mohammed was informed of the discovery and he quickly returned. He had been out of the country on a lecture tour in Europe. He was one of my cult: a descendant like me of the star men. Not only a member of my cult but the high priest himself with a deep knowledge of the past. He had spent his whole life doing research, looking for every scrap of information that was known about our origins. I saw no reason not to tell him what had transpired or what I had translated to that point. His excitement was off the scale. I took his reaction as a normal reaction for the high priest. But it also struck me on a certain level as an overreaction. He canceled all of his appointments and quickly focused on the excavation and nothing else.

He began to call me to the ministry at night for private discussions. He questioned me on every aspect of the dig, the inscriptions on the wall and the people who were working there. He warned me about you, Eric, and told me to steal every scrape of your work I could in case it would shed light on what we already knew or give us insight into what we did not know. At the same time, paranoid of the possibility, however remote, that you would be able to make sense of what was happening, he instructed me to put up every roadblock to your research I could think of.

He compared his translations with my own. Then, together we would translate the same passage again, trying to look at every possible solution to make sure we were translating it right. His questions became pointed and he seemed upset that I could not tell him more.

I began to hedge my answers: giving just enough to be plausible without telling him everything I knew.

The truth was I had become afraid of him. At first, it was just a feeling of unease. But as time went on I began to fear him. He changed from the moment he was briefed about the excavation. He was searching for something and believed I could tell him the answer. His eyes betrayed him; I saw the beginnings of madness when he looked at me.

Late one night I was summoned once again to the Ministry. He always had people around him: personal bodyguards, assistants, and other priests. That night he dismissed them all and we were alone. He locked the door and began to talk, thanking me for all the information I had provided him, my dedication and hard work. He told me that of everyone, I was the one he trusted the most because he knew I was deeply conscious of my ancestry and revered my race, and my religion, above everything else. He also acknowledged my standing among the priests and spoke for the first time of an almost certain future outcome: I would be the high priest after he was gone.

I thanked him but my thanks sounded hollow in my ears. I simply could not shake the feeling he had become not only mad but evil as well. I wanted to leave but I knew he was about to reveal something to me, something vital, so I steeled myself to appear calm and relaxed. I waited.

It didn't take long. He told me he had something to show me. He rose from his desk and turned to the bookcase behind him. It was oddly constructed. It reached all the way to the ceiling. In the back of the middle shelves, once the books were moved aside, you could see a wide vertical piece of metal that ran from the top to the bottom. He reached underneath one of the shelves and I heard a little click. Then the piece of metal opened like the doors of an elevator and the shelves parted revealing a plain door behind them. He took a key from a chain around his neck, fitted it into the lock and opened the door. He reached in, turned on a light, and stepped inside.

I followed him but after one step into the chamber, I froze. The room was filled with every kind of art treasure you could imagine: sculptures, furniture, jewelry. There was so much gold it was blinding: priceless beyond calculation. The artwork of my people, stolen by the man entrusted to protect it. Stolen and sold off on the black market to finance his madness. In that first glance, I saw pieces from the Old, Middle, and New Kingdoms, artwork from the post-dynastic period, all the way through to the Ptolemys. I was horrified and angry at the same time.

He turned and saw my face but misread what he saw there. 'Amazing, Raza, isn't it? I've been building this collection my whole life,' he said. 'But this is nothing compared to what I want to show you now.' He walked to a low table and picked up a plain little box: no adornment, no inlay, no gold. Something you might buy as a tourist in the bazaar. He opened the lid and thrust out his hand to show me. Inside was one-third of a flat metal disc. I don't have to describe it.

I immediately recognized it from the wall. The room we were standing in was hot and stuffy but I felt myself grow cold. Against all odds, he had discovered a section of the of the disc from the other world. I forced myself to stay calm, to feign amazement, and to pump him for everything I could get out of him.

It didn't take very much effort for him give me what I needed to know. He was more than eager to share what he had found and how he had found it.

'You won't believe it, Raza. You won't believe what this is or what it can do. Do you recognize it?'

I indicated that I did.

'In my early years, right after university when I had just joined the staff of the Ministry I was part of a small expedition doing research at Armarna. You know how inaccessible it is and how difficult it is to work there. The city of Akhenaten, the Heretic, was becoming a new focus for excavation and we were one of many teams sent to the area for mapping and study. One day I became exhausted by the heat, and I left the people on my team to go and sit for a few minutes by one of the steles that mark the boundaries of the city. There was a bas-relief statue cut into the rock. You've seen it I'm sure. I was sitting there getting my breath and looking down at the sand, moving it around with my foot. I saw an edge of something metallic and when I reached down to pick it up, this is what I discovered.'

Had he actually discovered it at Armarna and in that way? On the surface, it seems absurd. You don't just sit thrusting your foot in the sand and come up with the most amazing discovery in the history of archeology. The odds are he stole it from a museum or found it at another dig. But who knows? In our history, it is known that Akhenaten, the heretical pharaoh who built Armarna, was a complete throwback to our ancestors. You can see it in his statues: a full-blooded alien. And the wall speaks of the three parts of the disk and what happened to them. A king was given one of the pieces, perhaps Horus himself. If so, it could have come down to the heretic in the royal line. Another thing we will never know for certain.'

Mohammed continued. 'I didn't have any time to spend studying my find: the leader of the dig called to me at that moment, telling me to return to the dig. I stuffed the object into my pocket and went back to work. I didn't tell anyone about what I had found; I wanted to study it first.

That night, back at my house, I picked it up, turning it over and over in my hands under the light of my desk lamp. It seemed at first to be just a piece of metal with odd markings on its surface. Then it happened!'

Mohammed moved closer to me and said: 'Take it!'

I knew better than to imply anything but excitement and I reached out, taking it into my palm. I expected something to happen but there was nothing. It lay there: a tarnished piece of metal.

He laughed at my expression.

'It's already given up its secrets,' he whispered to me. 'And they're all here,' he said, pointing to his head. 'And here,' he said pointing to his computer. 'Let me show you.'

He walked back to his desk and turned on the monitor. 'This was actually downloaded into my brain by this amulet." He pulled up a program I had never seen before and typed in a code. The alien symbols flashed across the screen. 'I believe we can use our own computers to talk to them!'

Talk to whom? I asked.

'The gods, our fathers,' he replied. 'And I believe the disc carries other powers as well. It is the ultimate solution to everything. After we put the first part of the plan in place we can unite the disc and have ultimate knowledge, ultimate power.'

What is the first part of the plan? I said slowly.

'To contact them; tell them where we are, where their descendants are located. The gods are trying to find us and have chosen this time to reveal the path we are to follow. You know what the wall says about the Great Pyramid. We have everything we need to make it work. Once we can break the code completely we can find a way to send the message, over and over.'

That would take decades! I said.

'No! It's already begun. It's already in place.'

What? How?

'My scientists have been working on it for years.'

Your scientists? I was stunned.

He went on to explain. He had gathered around him people versed in early languages, and computer hackers, to search through everything in the past, everything from the earliest recorded history to the present day to try and find a correlation, try to find any connection to the symbols and what they meant. The hackers were the ones who found you, Professor Stevens. They were as evil as he had become. But for years, they could find nothing. Then, like a miracle, the wall had come to light. Mohammed could translate as easily as I; the star chart was there, the roadmap was there. We just had to figure out how to read the symbols. The next group of men to be paid off and brought in to work, on the project, were scientists and astrophysicists.

He had closed the Great Pyramid months earlier for legitimate reasons: to test what effect so many people, tourists, streaming into it was having on the interior. That effort was stopped immediately and the focus turned to this new endeavor. He had started in the lower chambers of the Great Pyramid where he built the mainframe and worked up to the King's Chamber where the transmission would be sent. All he needed was the full translation of the wall, as many details as possible. He also needed the completed disc, but as he had said, not for the first stage of the plan. The transmission could go on without it. He would begin the transmissions and while that was progressing work on finding the other parts of the disc would continue.

His words were insane but my mind was racing.

How do you know what constellation to direct the transmission to? I said.

He seemed surprised at my questions. 'Isn't it obvious? The star chart on the wall; the star shaft in the pyramid also points the direction. That was the pathway for the transmission when our fathers made the first attempt. That shaft points directly to Orion. It's there in the carvings above the disc on the wall.'

It pointed to Orion in antiquity but the constellation has moved in relation to the pyramid, I said.

'We can still send the signal using microwaves and the satellites,' he replied.

I began to desperately try and stall him. But you only have one-third of the complete disc. How do you know what it says? How do you know what power, if any, it contains? We're grasping at straws.

He held up his hands pointing to the ceiling. 'The gods have smiled again. Very shortly we will have the second piece. There is an American, an old man, who has been talking for years about aliens. He has one of the pieces. He has been ranting for years but everyone thinks he's insane.'

Perhaps he is, I said.

'No, he has it. I'm sure of it.'

How could you possibly know?

'Dr. Adams.'

Eric? I said, surprised.

'Yes. We've been monitoring their correspondence.'

I took a breath. That still only gives you two, I said calmly.

'No. The other one is right under our noses. You perhaps have not gotten to that part of the translation of the wall. It's in the excavation itself! All we have to do is find it!'

That's where our meeting ended. He swore me to secrecy and I left him there. I didn't know what to do. I didn't know where to turn. The priests I had consulted in the beginning: were any of them in on this with him? I didn't know and I couldn't remember what I had said to them when we had looked together at the inscriptions.

Mohammed was right about one thing. I had not gotten to the translations about the third piece. He would not have lied to me about that. If the wall said it was there then it had to be there. A floor plan had already been created to show the various rooms inside the dig. I consulted it, pouring over it, trying to figure out where the piece could be hidden. The obvious choice would be in the room with the carvings. But somehow that seemed wrong. They would not do something that obvious. It must be hidden inside one of the unadorned rooms that branched out from the main corridor.

I began to search each chamber by myself. But I had to be very careful. Those areas had been blocked off for future study. If anyone found me there it might create suspicion and prompt questions I did not want to answer. I made a copy of the floor plan. I took a light and started at night to systematically search through room after room when everyone had gone. No sign of anything; each room looked just like the next: bare and unadorned. Had the builders done this on purpose? Undoubtedly. They wanted it to be hard to find.

In the meantime, James had arrived to visit his father. I thought nothing of it. The visit would not last long and what possible impact could a boy, with no knowledge, have on the proceedings. This was my second mistake. Again I underestimated someone who actually held a piece of the puzzle and would lead his father to a final understanding of what the wall was trying to tell him.

I met you both that first day after James arrived as Mohammed and I were leaving the excavation. But I didn't leave the area after you entered the site: I had business to attend to there. Shortly after you had gone in one my people, who were working inside, came to me and urgently informed me that James had provided an important insight and that now Dr. Adams was unlocking the secrets of the wall: translating the inscriptions as well as I could do myself.

Startled, I quickly made my way back inside. I came up quietly to the doorway and looked in. You were there, Eric, intently studying the carvings. My people were also there. But James was nowhere to be seen.

I slipped away and stopped in the darkened tunnel. He had not gone outside or I would have seen him or been informed that he had come out. There was only one place he could be: the rooms that had been blocked off.

I slipped under the tapes and cautiously worked my way inside. It was like night, completely black, but I dared not risk a light for fear of being seen. So I walked slowly on. Momentarily I saw a faint glow ahead of me that illuminated the doorway of the room, James, where you were standing. I crept closer and peered inside. You were standing by the wall facing away from me. There was a small hole in the wall in front of you and your head was bent down as if you were reading something.

Then you held up a part of the disk, turning it over in your hand and looking at its markings. At that moment I could have silently walked up behind you, strangled you, and taken the disc. So much was riding on it not falling into Mohammed's hands: possibly the fate of the world. I willed myself to do it but I hesitated. I thought of Osiris, his mercy, his love of his adopted people, and I was unable to carry out what I needed to do.

As I watched the metal began to glow and you froze as it downloaded its data. It only took seconds. Now I knew I had to act. But before I could move I heard movement in the passageway behind me. I could not be found there and I quickly melted away into one of the adjoining chambers. You had stuffed the medallion into your pocket and collapsed but your light still burned on the sand where you had dropped it. I knew they would find you and they did moments after I had slipped away.

What to do? Your father was now in possession of dangerous knowledge that could ruin us all. And you possessed one-third of the cursed medallion. I believed if Mohammed knew what you were carrying he would go to all lengths to take it from you and would show no mercy to you or anyone who was trying to help you.

I waited until they had gotten you to safety and everyone had gone and then I slipped out and set to work. I contacted as many people as I could that I trusted completely and I told them that we needed to find you as soon as possible: to find you and to hold you until I could get to you. We went to your father's rooms but no one was there. You had taken a hotel room in the city but before we could find it, you were gone, spirited away. Where? The obvious answer was you had been sent home, back to America. We contacted the airport and they found your flight but it was too late for us. You were already in the air.

That night I went back to the excavation and met Eric in the tunnel. I wanted to tell you everything, beg you to help us. But it was obvious you held me in low esteem and worse, distrusted me totally. I was also bound by our oath to keep the secrets of our religion hidden unto death from all outsiders.

We were on our own to try and stop the horror. I went inside and knelt in front of the wall, touching it and cursing the evil that it had brought to us, for evil it was.

While I was kneeling there you were outside being kidnapped by Mohammed's men. I came away and when I stepped outside the entire site was deserted. I knew at that moment everything was over and that Mohammed's plan was moving rapidly to its conclusion.

The next morning, Mohammed sent his men. They flooded into the dig and ripped it apart, looking for the missing talisman. They found the room where James had been, found the little hole in the wall where it had been hidden, found little pieces of parchment on the sand below and began to put the puzzle together. When they asked me what I thought I explained that the possibility was remote that James had found it and taken it away. They wouldn't listen: in their minds it was the only explanation. You had left in a suspicious way and so quickly that it could be the only answer to the missing piece.

I began to panic. As quickly as I could I organized a team to fly to Virginia to get you and bring you back. But again, we were too late. Mohammed had sent his own team as soon as it got into his head that James had taken the relic.

By the time my men arrived in America your home had been ransacked and they could find no trace of James or his mother. The police were everywhere so they came away and flew home, empty handed.

When they told me what had happened I feared the worst. They already had Professor Stevens and Eric. Now it seemed they had James and his mother as well. And with James, they would have the final piece.

What was I to do? What were *we* to do? I could not let Mohamed suspect that I was trying to stop his plans or I would be killed: and any of the other priests that he suspected were helping me. The only thing I could do was to play along and pray that somehow I could find a way to end the madness.

I doubled my devotion to the cause; became more of a zealot than even Mohammed himself. When it came time to interrogate you I asked to be the one to question you and break you. He was more than happy to let me do it. So I became what you, Eric, believed me to be: an evil alien who was out to destroy you and the whole world."

Raza paused and then continued. "But your instincts were correct. I *am* an alien as far as that goes. All of the priests are. We are descended from the **ONE**, or the others that followed him. But our blood is now so co-mingled with human life that almost none of **HIS** blood is left in us."

Raza paused once more thinking to himself. Eric spoke: "This causes you great pain."

"Yes. But it is the culmination of what Osiris himself set in motion. To deny our humanness would be to deny him, to deny what he gave to us. It would be more than a sacrilege. He loved the human race so dearly."

Raza continued his story. "It was shortly after you were moved to the main facility where they were trying to break the code that I discovered we had been given a break. James had not been found. Only his mother had been taken. I could barely contain my relief at the news. There was still hope. But . . . we had to find the last part of the disc. It was the second phase of the scheme for Mohammad and the men following him. To us, it was our only hope for we believed it was also a weapon of great power.

There were artifacts in our possession that had been kept in this temple from the beginning. I began to wonder about them, one in particular. It was an armband of a strange metal that could be snapped around your forearm with a circular housing on top: a housing that, to my eyes, was the same size as the completed disc. I could only guess and the only way to truly know was to find the pieces of the disc, reconnect them and see. It was a long shot but all we had. Mohammed had forgotten the artifacts. Our only hope was to try and find James and the final piece and then to attempt it.

I needed a way to divert them, to give them false information that could be fed into the computers and throw them off.

Everything, and everyone was being watched. I had to find a way to let you, Eric, know that we were on the same side. So I gave you the Eye of Horus, praying you would understand. But I feared you would not understand. You were being attacked at every turn. You backed up my story of which constellation was the correct one. But it didn't help. The rest of the story you know."

James spoke. "I don't understand how Philip was converted. He was an American. Why would he do such a thing?"

"Did you ever look at him closely: black hair, deep complexion, eyes so dark as to be black. His grandfather was an Egyptian, not of our line, but fed on stories at *his* grandfather's knee about the glories of Ancient Egypt and the unfairness of its subsequent decline. He passed all of this on to Philip along with other legends about our cult. Philip volunteered to work with your father at the dig because of his background and once in the land of his ancestors, and with connections provided by his grandfather, he fell in with men who slowly brought him around. He became a confidant of Mohammed while I was kept in the dark about him. In fact, I hardly noticed him until he took you home. Mohammed enjoyed playing people against one another."

"But if Philip was in on the plan, why didn't he just take my part of the disc when he took me home to Virginia?"

"Their plan was moving rapidly and at first, he wasn't absolutely sure what you were carrying. Eric had filled him in to a point but he wasn't sure. He probably found a way to test you to see if what he was feeling was true. There was no reason for you to doubt his loyalty to your father. So on the plane going home, you may have revealed that it was true; you had the final piece of the disk.

He could have taken what you had but probably calculated it was the wrong time to do it. The plan was at a delicate stage. He reported everything back to Mohammed and Mohammed agreed to leave you alone until you were needed. They didn't want to draw any attention to themselves. If something had happened to you your father or mother would have immediately called for help. There would have been a flood of agents coming down on the dig, on us, on everything with a great possibility that what they were doing would have been exposed. They were so close they didn't want to risk anything. Plus, it never occurred to them that you would, on your own, return to Egypt to find your father.

They always viewed Americans with disdain believing you to be stupid, easily manipulated, and afraid of your own shadows. In their minds, you were being held in a perfect place, your own home, where you would sit unaware of the danger you were in. When the time was ripe you would have been grabbed and returned here for them to do with you what they would – after you had surrendered your part of the relic."

Raza paused and then continued. "It was a race against time but a race we have won, thanks be to Osiris."

"What will happen to us now," said Eric.

"You will stay in the temple tonight and tomorrow you will leave us. You will be taken back up the Nile and left in a place that will allow you to find your way back to Cairo. You will disappear from our world forever."

CHAPTER 29

Larry was the last one off the boat. They had left the sanctuary as the first light of dawn began to tint the sky with color and the stars began to fade. Blindfolded as before they were lead back onboard and the boat began their return journey up the Nile. Eventually, their blindfolds were removed and they watched the shore moving past until the boat pulled to the side and let them off in an area that showed no sign of any human habitation.

Without any acknowledgment, the men had departed leaving them on the shore to find their way back to Cairo. Had it been a dream? If any of them thought so, the brand on their arms told them what they had seen, what they had experienced, was very real.

They were glad to be going back to civilization but sad to have left one of the party behind.

When they were preparing to leave the sanctuary, the priests had gathered before them once more. Eric had thanked them for showing them mercy and for allowing them to see wonders like no one had ever seen before. They had again, voluntarily, offered their oaths of silence, which seemed to please the priests.

At that moment Professor Stevens had stepped forward and asked for a special compensation: he wanted to remain within the temple and not return to his former life.

"Professor," Eric said. "No! Come with us. After all you've done, stay with us."

"Eric, my boy," he said. "I have nothing to return to. I have sworn an oath of silence and even if I hadn't I would still be ridiculed and laughed at. I have no family. No one to return to."

"You have us," Eric said, "always. You know that. You can stay with us if you like."

"That's very dear and I so appreciate you, all of you. But this has been my whole existence and it would be my honor to die here where everything began."

He turned back to Raza. "I've spent my entire life trying to understand your world. Receiving part of the disk, for good or ill, opened that world for me," and he pointed all around him. "I have no wish to return. But it's your decision if you will accept me as an attendant until my death. I swear complete loyalty and faith."

He stopped and Raza turned to the other priests. There was discussion amongst them and after a few minutes, they informed Raza of their decision which was to give their consent.

"Thank you." Professor Stevens said. He turned to Eric. "I knew you were special from the moment I met you. I'll never forget you or what you've done for me."

"Oh, Professor," and Eric embraced his old teacher. "I should be thanking you."

"Goodbye everyone," the Professor said. "Thank you for going on this journey with me."

He then walked down the steps and joined the priests in front of the throne.

Silently, Eric and the others turned to go, but at the doors of the sanctuary, Eric turned around for one last look. He lifted his open hand in a salute to Raza.

Raza smiled and returned the salute with his bandaged hand and said. "May HE be with you always." Then Eric and the others walked the door and were gone.

Now they were standing on the banks of the Nile as the sun rose in the East. They had to find their way back to Cairo, so their only option was to follow the river north until they could discover exactly where they were. The idea of spending the night in the desert with no food or water was not something any of them wanted to contemplate. As they walked along, James turned to his father.

"What will you say when we get back, Dad," James wanted to know. "What will you say to the authorities?"

"I'm not sure because I don't know what the situation is in Cairo. I don't know who knows what or if any evidence was left behind."

"Philip will be missing."

"Yes. I'm not sure how I will explain that. We can only wait and see."

"Will you lie if it comes to it?"

"Yes. I will lie with every breath I've got. I swore an oath and I will keep it no matter what happens."

"What about the rest of us?"

Eric came up short. "I didn't think about that." He turned to the others and they gathered around him. "In case all or any of us are questioned we will need to get our stories straight before we speak. I won't break my oath to Raza. Does everyone feel the same?"

Everyone nodded.

"Okay. I'm open to any suggestions as to how we proceed."

Marie spoke first. "Will anyone know that I'm even here? The men who took me are the only ones that knew and they're dead."

"That's right. We just need to keep you hidden so there will be no questions."

"What about James, Sharon, and Larry?"

"The only people who would know would be Mohammed's men and they're all dead."

"Nathan knew," said Larry.

"Yes, that is a question mark at the moment," said Eric.

"What about the scientists. Did any of them survive?" asked Sharon.

"I don't fear them. They participated in murder and everything else you can name. They will have run as far away as possible. And I'm sure they don't want anything to come to light that would incriminate them. But I had no idea Philip was working with anyone else. Again we will have to wait to find out if Nathan survived."

"He was in the safe house. Larry helped him decode the symbols," said James.

"He must have been a tech Philip brought in. Do you know if they contacted Washington with any kind of information?"

"No," said Larry. "Nathan wanted to but Philip told him it was too early. They needed to wait."

"That would make sense," said Eric. "Philip would not want to give anything away, which is a good thing for us. What happened to Nathan when the men came to the safe house and took you?"

"He was shot," said Larry

"Did he die then?"

"We couldn't tell," said Sharon. He was on the floor when we were taken out."

"If he's still alive we won't know how dangerous he is to us until he learns we have returned."

"Was anything left in the safe house?" Eric asked.

"No. They took everything: the computers, the papers, everything."

"Then that's also good. No trail of evidence."

"What did you say to Washington the last time you spoke to them?" asked Marie.

"I told them that the work was turning out to be something of interest. And I requested assistance. They sent me Philip. After that, I didn't contact them again. Philip was always the one who would be in communication. He certainly didn't tell them anything about what was really going on."

"So to them, at least at this point, there was nothing to raise an alarm or any reason for them to send more backup," said Marie.

"I believe so," said Eric.

"What about the excavation itself. How will you explain that?" asked James. "Or your disappearance?"

"I'm not sure about the excavation. As to my disappearance, no one that matters at the moment would know I had gone missing except this Nathan. At least, that's what I hope."

"It was a hoax," said Marie suddenly as she looked at Eric. "It's just that simple. The whole thing was a hoax. You were working in the excavation. It seemed real but you later discovered it was an elaborate hoax. You left the dig for several days testing that theory and discovered it was true. Everything was fake; the symbols, the artwork in the dig, everything.

You said yourself in the temple that nobody would believe it. And you're right. Aliens from outer space who started civilization on Earth? It's too fantastic for anyone to take seriously. Plus, Raza said the dig was torn apart. The priests have everything in their possession. As to Philip you are just as amazed as anyone that he has disappeared. You don't know where he is."

"But won't they wonder about the dig? Won't they want to see the excavation?" asked James.

"I don't know. We're just going to have to play the hand we've been dealt and see what happens. I just hope that this Nathan is nowhere to be found."

Two hours later they suddenly came over a small rise of land and saw the outskirts of a large town.

Eric stopped and shaded his eyes with his hand. "We're in Minya," said Eric.

"Minya?" said James.

"Yes. It's a small city about 150 miles south of Cairo. This is good. We can grab some food and something to drink and find transportation."

Two hours later they had eaten and hired a driver to take them north.

"The excavation is between Minya and Cairo. I don't know whether to stop or not," Eric said as they moved along.

"Maybe not," said Marie. "Let's drive by."

But an hour later when they came abreast of the site Eric looked and then quickly leaned forward to tell the driver to stop.

They all got out of the car and looked to see . . . nothing. The desert had returned to his former self. There was no sign of the dig at all. The excavation had been filled in and all indications that there had been any kind of archeological work going on in the area was not to be found.

"What happened?" asked James.

"It's been erased," said Eric. "They did away with this part of the evidence."

"Oh, I'm sort of sorry," said James, walking to the place where the steps had been that led down into the chamber

"No. It's a blessing," said Eric. "There will be no reason for them to come here now. Our luck is still holding. We'll see what awaits us in Cairo."

At 8:00 that evening they arrived back in the capital, rented rooms in a hotel and ate dinner. Then they went to their rooms, collapsed into bed and fell asleep.

CHAPTER 30

"I've told you everything I know," Eric said sharply. "Now unless there is anything else I would like to go. I have a flight to catch."

"You're lying. I was there. I saw his son and his friends and I know what I saw on the computer screen." Nathan, very much alive, turned to Chuck Armstrong, the agent that had been assigned to the case after Nathan had contacted the agency to tell them what had happened over the last several days."

"As I said, the whole thing was a hoax. An elaborate hoax I grant you, but a hoax none the less," said Eric.

Eric had gotten up that morning, had showered and gotten dressed at the hotel before calling the agency in Washington to explain that he had information they might want to have concerning the excavation. He had decided the best way to handle the situation was to call the agency directly instead of waiting to see if they would find him.

He had been surprised that an agent was already in Cairo, summoned there by Nathan after Philip had seemly disappeared. Now they were grilling Eric on the events that had occurred during the last days. James had asked to come to this debriefing but Eric had felt it best if he and the others leave Egypt as soon as possible. Now he was very glad his son had stayed away.

The good news was that Nathan had not been involved or had seen anything that had gone on at the Great Pyramid. He had been left for dead but had been found and taken to a hospital. As soon as he had been able he had left the hospital and called the authorities. Now, for the last two hours they had gone over everything that Eric knew. He didn't know where Philip was. They had not spoken for several days. He kept repeating that what had seemed real was a hoax.

"If all of this was a hoax explain the part of the disc that your son was carrying. Explain the symbols on the computer screen."

"I'm afraid I don't know what you're talking about," said Eric.

"Your son James showed us one-third of a disc. The computer would act up whenever it came close to it. Your son transcribed symbols that were in his head; symbols that allowed us to construct something with the aid of the computer – diagrams of alien technology."

"Symbols in his head?"

"YES, YES! The part of the complete disc he carried downloaded information into his head!"

Eric's eyebrows went up and his eyes got big. "You're saying that some kind of an alien device downloaded information into my son's head?" He turned to Chuck Armstrong, opened his hands and made a slight laugh under his breath. "I wasn't aware there was a technology that could do such a thing."

Chuck Armstrong scowled at Nathan. "Are you insane?"

"I'm telling you what I saw."

The agent turned to Eric. "Is there anyone that can verify where you went and the people you talked with to say this was a hoax?"

"I . . . well . . . I," Eric was suddenly at a loss.

There was knock on the door and Armstrong turned from Eric and said, "Come in."

The door opened and an assistant walked into the room. "The director of the Ministry of Antiquities is here, sir. He would like a word with you if you wouldn't mind."

"Good. Maybe he can shed some light on this."

Eric froze. The director of the ministry; had Mohammed somehow survived? Eric kept his gaze on the floor until Armstrong spoke. "Dr. Raza I believe? Thank you for coming."

Eric's head snapped around.

"I'm afraid I'm the interim director, Mr. Armstrong – just until a successor to Dr. Mohammed can be found. And it's just Raza."

Raza looked at Eric who returned his gaze.

"Of course, I was so sorry to hear of Dr. Mohammed's death. Such a tragic accident."

"Yes," said Raza. "He was a good man."

"I'm sorry to bother you, but I know you were involved in the dig south of Cairo and I wanted to ask you some questions," said Armstrong.

"He wants to know about the dig being a fake and a hoax," said Eric easily.

Raza's eyes locked onto Eric but he didn't miss a beat. "Yes," he said. "A terrible disappointment to us, as I'm sure you can imagine, Mr. Armstrong. We felt we had found the very origin of civilization. For it to turn out to be fake was beyond disappointing. Hopefully, the perpetrators will be found and brought to justice."

"So it was a hoax?"

"Oh yes. So elaborate it fooled even us."

"What were they after?" said Armstrong.

"I have no idea. Perhaps just the satisfaction of knowing they had pulled the wool over everyone's eyes. In this age of mass communication people will do just about anything to gain attention and notoriety on the web, on television, anywhere they can find an outlet."

"So you're saying that someone went into the dessert, dug a massive hole in the sand, built rooms, decorated them with carvings and then waited for someone to come along and discover it just to get on television," said Nathan.

Armstrong turned to Raza waiting for him to respond.

"I'm not sure of how it was done. I'm simply telling you that it was a fake. Like those complex crop circles in England that appear overnight with no one knowing how they are created."

"What evidence do you have that it was a fake?" asked Armstrong.

"The inscriptions. I'm sure Dr. Adams has told you what the inscriptions said."

"No," said Eric. "I haven't mentioned anything about them. But put simply, the hieroglyphics would go along saying things that I'm sure the people who created the site found in old translations in art history books. Things like 'Beloved of Ra' and 'Living image of Amun.' A lot of them were from the tomb of King Tut. Then there would be gibberish and suddenly you would run across one that basically said 'Hi, Mom.'"

Raza turned to Armstrong. "As you see, a complete fabrication." "What about the symbols? The alien symbols?" Nathan persisted.

"Those made no sense to anyone," said Eric.

Raza agreed. "We thought, at first, it was like the Rosetta Stone with the hieroglyphics saying the same thing as the symbols. But we could not make any sense of them. In the end, we simply came to the conclusion that they were made up as well."

"So if it is a fake you wouldn't mind if we went to the dig and saw for ourselves," said Nathan.

"I'm afraid that will be impossible," said Raza calmly. "The site has been filled in and is no longer accessible."

"Filled in? How convenient!" Nathan was getting angry.

"Nathan! Calm down," said Armstrong.

"They did it on purpose!" said Nathan.

"You are correct. It *was* filled in on purpose," said Raza. "I'm sure you can appreciate, Mr. Armstrong, how this would reflect not only on the Ministry of Antiquities but the government of Egypt as well; a breathtaking discovery from the beginning of time that turns out to be a complete fabrication. But only after the government and the ministry have told the world about the greatest discovery ever found and the manpower and resources that had been expended to bring it to light. We would have been a laughing stock all over the world."

"Yes, I can certainly understand that," said Armstrong.

"What about the Great Pyramid. Everything centered on the Great Pyramid. I went over there this morning. The interior is damaged. Something was in there. You can see the damage."

"Another unfortunate occurrence," said Raza. "Dr. Mohammed had closed the structure for repair. But vandals got inside and did a lot of damage. We are in the process of restoration now."

"Okay. What do you know about the disc?" said Nathan.

"The disc?" said Raza. "I'm not aware of a disc. Was something found in the excavation I should be aware of, Dr. Adams," he said turning to Eric.

"We found nothing like he is describing," said Eric. "I have no idea."

"But your son does. How do you explain him and his friends?"

Eric looked confused. "My son? My son was here visiting me while I was working. He went home for a time but was so excited about what I was doing he asked if he could bring some of his friends over to see the sights. That's all."

"So James can come in and explain just that."

"We're all about to catch our flight home," Eric lied. "But if it's important."

"That won't be necessary Dr. Adams," said Armstrong. "You've done enough. Thank you and I appreciate you coming in Raza. I know you're a busy man."

"Stop! There are two things I don't understand," Nathan said. "If it was a hoax why did they shoot me, almost kill me, there in the safe house?"

Raza looked at the young man. "It was a hoax but one perpetrated by very dangerous men. I don't know what you mean by a safe house."

Nathan's face was red when he spoke. "Okay, then where is Philip Harrington?"

Everyone looked at him.

"Philip Harrington?"

"Philip?" said Eric. "Is something wrong with Philip?"

"He's disappeared," said Nathan. "I haven't seen him in days."

"Nor have I." Eric looked thoughtful. "I just assumed he was here. Have you tried to locate him?"

"Yes. Numerous times. He disappeared that night. The night your son was taken."

"My son hasn't been taken anywhere," Eric said, turning to Armstrong.

"I'm sure we will locate him," said Armstrong, looking at Nathan. "There's no need for you to trouble yourself any longer, Dr. Adams."

"Well, if you're sure it's okay."

"Absolutely."

"Then I'll be going. Thank you."

Nathan shook his head as Armstrong showed them out.

When they were on the street, Eric turned to Raza. "So you save me again. How did you know I would get into trouble?"

"I didn't. But I had a feeling you would. After you left the temple I suddenly realized that, although we could cover all of our tracks, you were going to be exposed and would need backup. Who better to collaborate your story but the interim director of the Ministry of Antiquities?"

Eric laughed. "You were very quick in there to pick up where I was going."

"Well, to treat these events as a hoax was brilliant."

"I can't take any credit for that. It was my wife's idea."

"A wise woman. I thought you were divorced."

"Not for long I hope."

Raza smiled. "Well, this is the final goodbye, Eric. And thank you."

"You're welcome. But someday I may be returning to the Egypt. We may meet again."

"With this land everything is possible. I will look forward to it."

"Please take care of Professor Stevens and yourself."

"You have my word. Thank you."

And Raza turned and walked away.

CHAPTER 31

They had been back in Virginia for two weeks and had settled back into their usual routine with school and other activities. Sharon and Larry had to dance around the true facts of what had actually happened to them but had finally convinced their parents that the trip to Egypt had been a crazy, sophomoric stunt they had all cooked up together and nothing more. It took some convincing, but Eric had played the part of a shocked and disappointed parent who couldn't believe they had tried such a dangerous thing. He had called both sets of parents, and the police before he had left Egypt to explain the story.

"What were they thinking?" he had demanded with feigned anger when he had talked to Larry's mother. "I've never heard of anything so crazy. They could have been killed! And for what? Some kind of joy ride half way around the world." He had gone on to say that he and Marie, who had flown to Egypt suddenly once she had discovered what they had done, had brought them home as soon as they could find them and got a flight out. They would have called sooner but could never get through. Also, unfortunately, their house had been robbed in the meantime. But it was okay; nothing of value had been taken. As for James, "He'll be an old man before he leaves his room again!"

"You know, this is soooo cool," Larry said as he turned his left deltoid back and forth in front of the mirror in James' bathroom admiring his brand.

Sharon looked at Larry. "You didn't think so when it was happening. I know *I* sure didn't." She was sitting on a chair next to

James who was lying across his bed. "What did you tell your mother when she saw it?"

Larry walked back into the room. "That I fell down on a stick."

Sharon and James laughed out loud. "And she bought it?"

"I guess. She didn't say anything else, just mumbled under her breath and walked away."

"Well, I agree with Larry. I didn't think it was cool when it was happening," James said. "But he's right. It's pretty cool now."

Sharon rolled her eyes. "Boys. The more tattoos and scars the better; as if they're not ugly enough to begin with."

James looked at her and smiled. She blushed and looked away.

"So," Sharon said, "I'm hearing rumors about your parents."

James looked down and smiled to himself, "Yes. They're getting married again."

"Are you happy?"

"I don't think I've ever been this happy. It's like a dream."

"All of it is like a dream to me," said Sharon.

At that moment, Mrs. Adams called up the stairs. "James? Ask Sharon and Larry if they would like to stay for dinner."

Sharon held up her hand at James, stood up, and walked to the door. "We would love to stay Mrs. Adams," she called out. "Thank you very much."

"It'll be ready in a few minutes."

"Okay. Thanks. We'll be down."

"You know you don't have to stay if Dad's stories bore you."

"Are you kidding?" said Sharon. "I could listen to your father's stories forever."

Sharon and Larry headed for the door but James held back. "Guys?"

They stopped and turned around.

"I never thanked you. For going with me, I mean."

"I wouldn't have missed it for the world," said Sharon.

"Me, neither, said Larry. "Now let's go to dinner before I starve."

THE END

CLASSIFIED INFORMATION: DO NOT DECODE.

01011001 01100101 01100001 01110010 00100000
00110010 00110000 00110010 00110001 00101110 00100000
01010100 01110010 01100001 01101110 01110011 01101101
01101001 01110011 01110011 01101001 01101111 01101110
00100000 01110011 01110101 01100011 01100011 01100101
01110011 01110011 01100110 01110101 01101100 00101110
00100000 01001001 01101110 01110110 01100001 01110011
01101001 01101111 01101110 00100000 01101001 01101101
01101101 01101001 01101110 01100101 01101110 01110100
00101110

Printed in Poland
by Amazon Fulfillment
Poland Sp. z o.o., Wrocław